SAINT BLAISE

SAINT BLAISE

A NOVEL

ROBERT DEWAR

Copyright © 2025 Robert Dewar

The moral right of the author has been asserted.

Apart from any fair dealing for the purposes of research or private study, or criticism or review, as permitted under the Copyright, Designs and Patents Act 1988, this publication may only be reproduced, stored or transmitted, in any form or by any means, with the prior permission in writing of the publishers, or in the case of reprographic reproduction in accordance with the terms of licences issued by the Copyright Licensing Agency. Enquiries concerning reproduction outside those terms should be sent to the publishers.

The manufacturer's authorised representative in the EU for product safety is Authorised Rep Compliance Ltd, 71 Lower Baggot Street, Dublin D02 P593 Ireland
(www.arccompliance.com)

This is a work of fiction. Names, characters, businesses, places, events and incidents are either the products of the author's imagination or used in a fictitious manner. Any resemblance to actual persons, living or dead, or actual events is purely coincidental.

Troubador Publishing Ltd
Unit E2 Airfield Business Park,
Harrison Road, Market Harborough,
Leicestershire LE16 7UL
Tel: 0116 279 2299
Email: books@troubador.co.uk
Web: www.troubador.co.uk

ISBN 978 1836281 450

British Library Cataloguing in Publication Data.
A catalogue record for this book is available from the British Library.

Printed and bound in Great Britain by CMP UK
Typeset in 11.5pt Adobe Garamond Pro by Troubador Publishing Ltd, Leicester, UK

I wish to thank Fr. Russell Pollitt SJ, Fr. David Harold-Barry SJ, and Fr. Thomas Plastow SJ, who helped me in my research for this story. Any factual errors, however, are entirely my own.

Ad Majorem Dei Gloriam

Chapter One

Blaise Cressingham, all of thirteen years old in June 1968, was torn between two equally compelling choices. A vacancy had arisen among the altar servers in the school chapel (Danny Doran had been removed as an altar server, due to an unspecified act of gross indiscretion witnessed – unbeknownst to him at the time – by Brother Bernard Riley), and Father Gerard Howard thought that Blaise's angelic features would more than adequately grace his sanctuary during the twice weekly Mass that the body of the school attended. Blaise had always loved the Church's rituals, in particular the Liturgy of the Mass, and the thought of becoming a school altar server had long exerted an appeal for him. Except that Blaise was already a chorister, a member of the school choir, his as yet unbroken voice rising in an exceptionally pure and powerful treble, and he could not properly fulfil his commitment to the choir if he had to absent himself from it twice a week.

When Blaise raised his voice in praise of God during a liturgical service, he experienced something very near bliss. The school's Choirmaster, an Englishman named Brother Luke Carter, had attended the prestigious Westminster Abbey

Choir School in London, and, following his conversion to Catholicism as a young man, he had become a member of the Catholic Westminster Cathedral Choir, before following a calling to join the teaching order which ran so many Catholic schools around the World. After taking his vows, he had expressed a wish to teach music in South Africa, and now here he was, Choirmaster at the Order's school in Cape Town; a man for whom God was found in music. And of all the school choristers, Blaise was perhaps nearest to him in sharing this same understanding.

It was not that the altar servers wore scarlet cassocks with lace at the collars and cuffs, and white surplices over them, for the school choristers wore identical garments (and anyway, Blaise was similarly dressed at least one Sunday a month, when he would serve at the altar at Saint Mark's Church in Newlands, the Catholic church at which his family worshipped); no, it was the visual, oral and (although as yet largely unconscious of this) the spiritual beauty of the Mass, that drew Blaise, and which made him consider asking Brother Luke whether he could be excused choir service twice a week for the rest of the year. Being an altar server was, as he already knew, the next best thing to being a deacon, or a priest, and altar servers developed an especially close relationship with the Mass celebrant, a relationship which was not experienced to the same degree by the boys making up the body of the congregation at the school Mass.

'Rather you than me,' said Blaise's best friend, Gregory Dillon (who was neither a chorister nor an altar server). 'I'm quite happy not to stand out. Anyway, you've told me that you feel something special when you sing.'

'Yeah – I do. I don't know; I just think I would enjoy it.'

Gregory threw his arm around Blaise's shoulders. Blaise flinched momentarily, before settling himself. He was not very keen on physical contact. Soon, Gregory would struggle to place his arm around his friend's shoulders, as Blaise was rapidly overshooting him in height. Along with a large number of boys identically dressed in the school uniform, they were making their way between the school and the Brothers' quarters, along an avenue of ancient, wintry oak trees, their leafless branches a complex tracery. Above the trees, no very great distance away, loomed the impressive bulk of Devil's Peak, the top of which was lost in heavy grey cloud. A cold front had settled over Cape Town a few days earlier, and it had been raining when Blaise had left home for school early this morning.

'Well, if it's what you want, go for it!' Gregory said, releasing Blaise.

On the 6th June the annual feast day of the Order's founder was celebrated, and the boys were heading for the refectory for a proper sit-down lunch. The lunch would be (the boys anticipated) rather special. Usually, the boys (all of whom were day boys) would eat the lunches they had brought from home, but on high days and feast days, they joined the Brothers and other academic staff in the refectory for a sit-down lunch. These occasions were eagerly anticipated by the boys: a welcome change from the egg, or cheese, or (if they were fortunate) ham and mustard sandwiches that their families' maids* at home had prepared for them, which were so often (along with an apple, and sometimes a five cent bar

---

* The term "Maid" in South Africa was applied to a female house servant.

of chocolate as a special treat) all that most of the boys had to eat during the midday lunch break.

Father Justin Hurley, the Father Guardian, recited at some speed the blessing in Latin: *"Benedic, Domine, nos et haec tua dona quae de tua largitate sumus sumpturi, per Christum Dominum nostrum. Amen."** Tomato soup was served, followed by roast chicken with peas and carrots, accompanied by heaps of golden baked potatoes. The boys, most of whom were always hungry, helped themselves eagerly to the tender chicken and the baked potatoes, over the top of which they poured warm gravy from the gravy jugs.

And there was boiled baby for desert! Oh, how Blaise enjoyed boiled baby! He poured lavish amount of syrup over the dumpling, and tucked in greedily. He had a pronounced sweet tooth.

The lunch break, at forty-five minutes in length, was just long enough to do full justice to the meal, before the refectory began emptying of boys. Several of the Brothers remained at their seats, enjoying a second cup of coffee, and perhaps a cigarette also. Blaise and Gregory had a History class to attend. For Blaise, this would be an unalloyed pleasure: he enjoyed History and always did well at History exams. For his friend Gregory, History class was a mixed blessing. Far from keenly interested in History, his boredom expressed itself in daydreaming (and little wonder, perhaps, that he did nowhere near as well as Blaise in the end of year History exam). Gregory however excelled at Maths, which

---

* Bless us, oh Lord, and these Thy gifts which we are about to receive from Thy bounty, through Christ, our Lord. Amen.

Blaise found a challenging subject, and one in which he failed to achieve much more than a pass mark.

It is often said that opposites attract, and perhaps there is much truth in this adage, for not only were the two boys' academic preferences markedly different, but they were complete opposites in appearance. Blaise, at thirteen, was tall for his age, and as pared down as a peeled willow withy, with a shock of flaxen hair. He had a sensitive, creative temperament. Gregory however was short, with a sturdy build and dark, unruly hair, and the practical, down-to-earth, somewhat blunt character of the engineer he was to become. Despite – or perhaps because of – their differences in appearance, academic leanings and characters, the two friends were very close. Their homes were situated not far apart: both lived in the sought after suburb of Bishopscourt, located on the eastern slopes of Table Mountain, just below the world-renowned Kirstenbosch National Botanical Garden, and they had known each other since beginning school together in January 1961. They might never have known each other otherwise, despite living in the same Cape Town suburb: the residential plots in Bishopscourt were each of at least an acre in extent; the houses were large, and screened from their neighbours not only by distance, but by well-established hedges and trees. You did not live in Bishopscourt if you sought cosy neighbourhood community; privacy was what Bishopscourt offered – yet the suburb was within easy reach of all the usual conveniences of urban life.

Blaise and Gregory were both in Standard Six, sitting in the same class, in their first year of high school. Brother Edward Daley, their History master, was explaining what had prompted the Great Trek – that iconic expansion of European exploration and settlement into the southern African hinterland. During the next school term, they would be looking at the establishment of the various Boer republics which arose from this significant movement inland of Dutch speaking settlers from the Cape Colony. Blaise was fascinated. He had of course already read the History text book for the entire academic year from cover to cover. Gregory however was dreaming about rugby, Brother Edward's words just a distant drone, and in his imagination he was scoring try after try against those heretics from Bishops (the Anglican school located not far from them, their foremost opponents in both rugby and cricket).

How very different the two boys were! Blaise could not abide rugby, that supreme contact sport, but during the two winter terms he played soccer. (Participation in either rugby or soccer was obligatory during the winter terms, so Blaise chose soccer, for which he had little fondness, but it was better than rugby, and you were not expected to fling yourself at a member of the opposing team and wrestle him to the ground). He also ran cross country, which he enjoyed tremendously. The boys began their run in Newlands Forest, on the lower slopes of the mountain (being transported the few miles which separated the school from the mountain slopes in one of the school's mini-buses), ascending to the Contour Path which ran along the side of the mountain, and descending again via Skeleton Gorge above Kirstenbosch Botanical Garden, and so back to Newlands Forest. Blaise was conscious, without analysing his feelings too much, that the sylvan and rugged mountain setting the cross country route took the runners through, was very beautiful. The seeds of Blaise's future passion for, and love of, the natural world were already being sown.

During the summer months, Blaise played tennis at school, which he did not mind at all, for he was a competent tennis player. However, he showed much promise in one sport in particular: in the person of Brother Anthony Tobin, the school's PT teacher, there existed also an excellent fencing master. Brother Anthony, who was still in his twenties, conducted a fencing class once a week. He had been educated at one of the well known secular private schools in South Africa, a school where he had been taught how to fence in both foil and sabre. He took great delight in coaching boys who showed keenness in either of these weapons, and in Blaise, he had a student who showed some promise in sabre.

'Use your reach!' he would shout at Blaise, and, 'If you cannot out-think them, batter them down!' he would instruct the stocky Gregory. Both boys fenced sabre; their fencing styles were very different, but both of them tended to win their bouts more often than not.

So, these two unlikely friends had the sport of fencing in common. What else (aside from their homes being not at all far from each other, and aside from attending the same school, and from sitting in the same classes together) explained their friendship? It was quite simple: each admired in the other the very qualities which so differentiated the pair. Blaise admired Gregory's sturdy build and practical, no nonsense character; Gregory admired, indeed, envied, Blaise's height, and his skill with words. He also appreciated (without necessarily admiring) his friend's sensitive spirit. Of course, neither boy had ever articulated to the other what he admired in his friend: that was not the way of boys. Brother Bernard Riley, their form master, sustained a classroom joke when he sometimes referred to Blaise as "David," and Gregory as "Jonathan."

That afternoon, the rain just holding off, but the air already growing chill (it grew cold in Cape Town during the winter, and those with fireplaces in their homes would light a fire in the evening), Gregory had rugby practice to attend, but Blaise was excused soccer practice, as it clashed with choir practice. (As a result of this weekly clash, Blaise only had to attend one of the two soccer practices a week that would otherwise have been expected of him. This did not upset him in the least). After choir practice, Blaise spoke to Brother Luke about his wish to become (if only for the next two terms) an altar server.

'Oh no, Blaise!' Brother Luke exclaimed. 'It would be all wrong! God has given you a singular gift: a superb voice. To reject such a gift would be almost blasphemous.'

Brother Luke, who had heard many truly excellent voices over the years, considered Blaise's voice – its purity and power – to be exceptional. The idea of Blaise absenting himself from the school choir, even twice a week, appalled him. He had plans to make Blaise his star in the ambitious production he intended mounting for the Christmas pageant. This was to be Allegri's *Miserere Mei, Deus*, arguably the most beautiful choral music – based on Psalm 51 – ever composed. It remained to be seen whether this was too ambitious a goal for a school choir, no matter how good, to achieve. But if Brother Luke was to succeed in his aim, it was essential that Blaise remain fully committed to the choir.

In fact, Blaise had been feeling more than a little guilty at his willingness up to now to sacrifice his choir practice for altar service, and so he understood Brother Luke very well. Understood, and in truth, agreed with him. How could any joy hope to compare with giving his voice free rein to soar into the upper reaches – almost (it seemed to him sometimes), to Heaven itself?

The school choir comprised half a dozen of the Brothers, three of whom were tenors, one of whom was a baritone, and two of whom were basses, and a dozen or so boys, the majority of whom were still trebles (but some of whom possessed youthful versions of their later adult tenor and baritone voices). Blaise's wondrous treble, however, stood out from all the other voices in the choir. So Blaise considered Brother Luke's words, and he came to a sudden decision: the lure of altar service was a temptation sent him that he must resist. Brother Luke patted him on the shoulder when Blaise told him of his decision.

'You have made the right choice, Blaise,' Brother Luke said.

Father Gerard Howard was disappointed, but not greatly so, when Blaise told him that he would not be accepting the offer of altar service. 'The choir is too important to me, Father,' he explained.

'Right-O, Blaise. Thanks for telling me. I'll find someone else.'

And so, Blaise was able to resist the first great temptation sent him in his young life. Rejecting vain pomp and glory, he remained true to the gift that God had given him. Blaise did not know it, but he was setting foot on the path that he would follow for the rest of his life: *"Enter in at the narrow gate, for wide is the gate and broad is the way that leads to destruction, and many are they who go in by that way. Because narrow is the gate and narrow the way which leads into life, and few there are who find it."* (Matthew 7:13-14)[*]

---

[*] Biblical quotations in this novel are taken from the Jerusalem and New Jerusalem Bibles.

Chapter Two

Blaise's father, Guy Cressingham, sat in his study, which was veneered in glowing, golden bird's eye maple. One wall was given over to bookshelves crammed with books – most of them non-fiction – ranging from Caesar's *Gallic Wars* in the original Latin (these volumes remained unread, for now, although Blaise, who was studying both Latin and French at school, would dip into them in a few years' time), through to *Das Kapital* by Karl Marx (which latter, in English translation, Guy had bought – the better to know the enemy. He had made a start on reading it, but after ten pages or so he had abandoned it. It was too heavy, far too dense, for his taste. Blaise however had begun reading it during the Easter holidays).

Guy ran his eye down the columns of figures his general manager, who was based in Grahamstown in the Eastern Cape, had forwarded to him. With his practiced eye, Guy could assess the individual health of each of the stores he owned, and of the business as a whole. He felt some small concern, heard just the faintest of alarm bells ringing: income was still disappointing at the new stores, and he had a large bank loan to service. (He had late last year acquired another half a dozen trading stores, taking out a bank loan to do so). He would certainly go ahead with the spring tour of his retail outlets in late September; it would ginger up the store managers and staff. But that was still three months away.

A black and white photograph in a silver frame stood on his desk: his three sons sitting on a bench in the garden, aged about six, nine and eleven at the time, with little Lawrence looking out solemnly, and Hugh (the next youngest) and Blaise smiling cheerily at the camera. If there was one small irritant in the otherwise generally smooth running machinery of Guy Cressingham's world, it was Blaise. Of course he loved the boy! Indeed, Blaise was a loveable child. But Blaise's father wished that his firstborn showed more interest in the practical things of life. Hugh was far more like his father than Blaise was. There was too much of his mother, thought Guy, in Blaise. A sensitive, otherworldly, artistic spirit was all very well in a woman – but in his eldest son? (As for Lawrence, the youngest of the three Cressingham brothers: he was, at only eight years old, still too young for his father to make a firm judgement on his character – although he was, his father thought, already showing signs of a rather acquisitive nature, and he might grow up to be good with figures and business. Time would tell).

Guy Cressingham, who was forty-two years old, shuffled together the papers he had been perusing, and pushed his chair back. It was almost five o' clock. Blaise and Hugh would be home soon – what was it they stayed behind for on a Thursday? Oh yes – choir practice for Blaise. Hugh however would have been playing rugby this afternoon; a manly sport. Guy had played rugby at school. He turned to the two year old spayed Alsatian bitch lying on the rug nearby. 'Walkies, Heidi!' he said, and the dog leapt to her feet and followed him through to the hallway, gambolling at his feet before standing still while the lead was attached to her collar.

The house was situated some distance up the southern slope above Bishopscourt. Guy and the dog followed the road as it climbed gently towards Rhodes Drive and the top gates to Kirstenbosch Garden, passing large houses behind high walls, beyond which the tops of well established trees could be seen. Near the junction with Rhodes Drive, it began to rain, so Guy turned around and they retraced their route. Had the weather been more inviting, Guy would have taken Heidi for a much longer walk. But on their return, the rain began to ease off. Heidi had still to do her business, so, having removed the lead from her collar, Guy left the dog free to wander the garden for a while. Guy hung his coat inside the entrance hall, and crossed the hall to the sitting room, which was filled with the aromatic scent of burning pine logs from the fire in the wide fireplace. Anna, the young Cape Coloured Maid, had lighted a fire for the evening. Guy made for the drinks cabinet. Irene, his wife, was out – some committee meeting or other. (Probably, thought Guy, something to do with the theatre, or art. There was no harm in that: a rich woman ought not to be completely idle). He poured himself a large scotch, neat, and sat down near the fireplace, picking up that day's *Cape Argus*.

Blaise's father liked to preach the merits of hard work, but the truth was, he did not push himself very hard. There was no need to: he had an excellent general manager, and sound individual store managers. The fact was, Guy Cressingham, as Chairman of Cressingham Retail Holdings, had very little work to do, although he alone made all the strategic decisions for the business, which currently comprised about three dozen native trading stores in the Cape (none of them further north than the southern bounds of the Great Karoo, and the majority of them located in the Eastern Cape, in Ciskei and Transkei), and a small shopping centre in King William's Town. Blaise's grandfather, an English immigrant, had bought his first trading store in the Eastern Cape shortly before the start of the Second World War.

The Cressinghams had historically been prominent Catholic Recusants in Lancashire: the family (like a number of families from the north of England) had remained true to the old faith after the Reformation, despite the punitive laws which were periodically enforced against Catholic Recusants. Blaise's grandfather (who was still alive, although retired) had been a younger son, and he had emigrated to South Africa to seek his fortune. There, he did more than seek his fortune; he made it, and this explained why Guy Cressingham, his only son, and Guy's family, lived in a fine house on an acre of land in the select suburb of Bishopscourt.

Blaise knew that the present Baronet (back in Lancashire) was his cousin of some degree (he was in fact Blaise's first cousin once removed), although Blaise rarely gave any thought to the precise relationship. South Africa's society was an altogether more egalitarian one than that of

England. At school, perhaps as many as half of the student body (including Blaise's friend, Gregory) was of Irish Catholic origin, with the remainder being made up of the sons of Portuguese and Italian immigrants (with a few boys of Lebanese Maronite extraction, and even fewer from old English Catholic families).

But at the age of thirteen, Blaise was barely conscious of the ethnic origins of his fellows at school. Among white South Africans, the great divide was that between English and Afrikaans speakers; the greatest divide of all, however – utterly unbridgeable at that time – was that between blacks and whites. The colour divide was not as extreme in the Western Cape, that heartland of the Cape Coloured population, many of whom lived lives similar to those of working class whites, and who retained, within the Cape Province, the right to a qualified vote – for Coloured representatives – in Parliament. Of these political and constitutional complexities, Blaise was of course completely unaware.

And what of the Brothers themselves, the members of the religious order that ran the school? Almost all were of Irish Catholic extraction, a generation or two removed, with a relatively few among them being of English (or in one instance, West Highland Scottish), descent. In fact, the Catholic Church in South Africa was overwhelmingly Irish in its ethnic origins.

Mrs. Dillon, a tiny woman as delicate as a bird, completely dwarfed by her sturdy thirteen year old son, was collecting the boys – Gregory, Blaise, and his brother, Hugh – from school this week. (Irene Cressingham had earlier made a special trip to collect her youngest son, Lawrence, who was in Standard One, and who finished school earlier than his brothers, and had no extramural activities that afternoon). Mrs. Dillon and Irene Cressingham alternated, week and week about, taking the boys to school and collecting them in the afternoon. Gregory's mother dropped the two Cressingham boys off at the gates to their home shortly after five o' clock. It had begun to rain, a cold, penetrating rain.

'Thank you, Mrs. Dillon,' said Blaise. 'Cheers Greg – see you tomorrow.'

'*Ja* – see you, Blaise.'

Unlike Hugh, who was wearing his rugby togs, Blaise wore his school uniform. In winter, the boys wore long trousers of dark grey wool twill, and a pullover beneath their blazer. They wore a blazer, and a boater embellished with a ribbon in the school colours, right through the year. Hugh's socks were around his ankles, and his white shorts were muddy and grass-stained. He had a bad graze on one knee. He needed a wash as badly as his clothes needed a laundering. The boys ran down the gravelled driveway through the rain, and burst through the front door. (It was made of African mahogany, a very beautiful hardwood). Anna met them in the hall.

'*Ag*, look at you, Hugh!' Anna exclaimed. 'What a mess! Take off your boots. You must have a shower before dinner. Leave your dirty clothes in the bathroom.'

'OK, Anna,' Hugh responded. He sat on a replica Sheraton chair and removed his boots, which Anna picked up, then, jumping to his feet, he took the stairs two at a time, still brimming over with energy, and made for his bedroom, to fetch some clean clothes. Blaise went to find Tinker, the two year old neutered Siamese tom. The cat was sleeping in the den, and when Blaise bent and picked it up, it gave a raucous Siamese miaow of greeting and began to purr. Blaise was very fond of Tinker. (He was just as fond of Heidi, the Alsatian dog, but Tinker was his special pet). Putting Tinker down again after a while, Blaise too ascended the stairs, his school bag in one hand, but at a gentler pace than his brother. He intended getting the bulk of his homework done before dinner. In the summertime, the brothers would probably have made for the swimming pool in the garden, leaving their homework for after dinner, but at this time of year, at this time of day, the outdoors did not entice them.

Neither boy thought to find and greet their parents. Their father, they presumed, would be busy in his study (he was in fact taking Heidi for a walk), and had their mother been home, she would have greeted them. The boys knew that they would certainly be seeing their parents at dinnertime.

Irene Cressingham entered the dining room at half past seven, still wearing the dark green dress and matching jacket, in a fine wool suiting, that she had been wearing for her committee meeting in Rondebosch. She was, aged thirty-eight, a fine looking woman, with a slim but shapely build which gave no indication that she had borne three large boy-babies. Her hair was of the palest spun gold in colour. She wore it in a *chignon*, leaving her elegant neck bare. She was not naturally given to participation in group activities such as committee meetings, but she possessed a strong sense of duty, and she had been brought up to believe that women who were blessed with privilege and wealth were obliged to undertake some charitable and public service. She was of course an active member of the Catholic Women's League, and she currently occupied the post of treasurer at the local CWL Section. Irene (and in this, she was very like her eldest son) did not have a head for figures: she struggled to fulfil her duties as treasurer, and she looked forward to next January, when a new treasurer would be elected. It never occurred to her, however, to resign her post.

Blaise was already sitting at his place at the table. He stood as his mother entered the room. 'Hullo Mum.'

'Hullo Darling,' she responded. Blaise lowered his head and kissed his mother, who kissed him on the cheek. Already, Blaise was several inches taller than his mother. He would very soon begin to tower over her. 'How was your day?' Irene asked him.

'OK, Mum. Choir practice went well. Brother Luke was telling us that he plans a performance of Allegri's *Miserere Mei, Deus*, for the end of the year. That would be amazing, don't you think?' Blaise had an LP recording of Baroque choral music, which his parents had given him for his twelfth birthday. (His father had wanted to give him a leather football, but Irene's wishes in this matter had prevailed). The LP included this magnificent seventeenth century composition, based on Psalm 51, by Gregorio Allegri, which was how his mother knew of it, for Blaise played it frequently, sometimes on his own record player in his bedroom, sometimes on the record player in the den.

'That's very ambitious of him. Do you think the choir is up to it?'

'I hope so. I would love to give it a go.'

Blaise's mother smiled. 'Presuming your voice hasn't broken by then.'

'Brother Luke doesn't think my voice will break. He says it will just gradually merge into a tenor voice. But he thinks I'll probably be singing treble for another year.'

Hugh bounded into the dining room, with Heidi following him. Like Blaise, he was wearing corduroy trousers and a pullover. He had had a shower, which had turned his short, naturally honey-blonde hair very dark. It stood up *en brosse*. 'Hi Mum!' he greeted his mother and went to kiss her.

Irene Cressingham smiled at her middle son, accepting his kiss. 'Heidi shouldn't be in here, you know that.'

Hugh called the dog's name and pointed at the door. 'Outside!' he commanded her. The dog obediently left the room.

'Heidi listens to you,' Irene remarked. 'You're looking scrubbed and shiny, Hugh. Was rugby practice OK?'

'Yeah – Brother Anthony says we stand a good chance against the under-thirteens at Bishops at the end of term.'

'That's good ...' The boys' mother broke off and greeted her youngest son, Lawrence, who took his place at the dining table. 'Lorrie – have you been busy this afternoon?' Irene bent and kissed the top of his dark brown, curly hair. Lawrence was by a long way the darkest of the three brothers.

Lawrence nodded. He was a solemn child, who rarely smiled. 'Yeah. I was doing some homework. The teacher says we will begin learning "cursive" handwriting next term.'

The two older boys looked at their younger brother. 'Joined-up writing?' asked Hugh.

'We have to call it "cursive,"' responded Lawrence.

'Yes, that's right,' their mother interjected. 'Where's Dad?'

It was just after half past seven. In the sitting room, Guy, the newspaper open on his lap, was lost in a reverie. He had been pondering various moves to increase turnover at the under-performing stores he had bought not long ago. He was loath to admit to himself that perhaps they had not been a good investment, and that there had been a reason why they were for sale. It was important that his other stores continued to pull their weight, if he was not to find that the bank loan he had taken out to buy the six new stores left him dangerously overextended.

'Guy – it's dinner time. Are you coming?' His wife's voice, as she stood in the doorway, intruded on his thoughts.

'Oh – yes, of course.' He stood, and followed his wife into the hall and through the double doors leading to the dining room. Blaise would be several years older before he realised that he could rarely remember his parents ever using terms of endearment, such as "Darling," between themselves – or, in fact, having much to say to one another at all.

'Hullo boys,' Guy greeted his three sons.

'Hi Dad,' they chorused. When the family was seated, Irene rang a small silver hand bell at her end of the table. Anna appeared a few minutes later with the soup course, making two trips: she could not quite fit five bowls of lentil soup on one tray. Lawrence, as the youngest present, had to wait on her second trip for his soup. But when each of them had a bowl of soup in front of them, the boys sitting with their hands on their laps, Guy Cressingham, his elbows resting on the table, clasped his hands and bowed his head.

At this, the others bowed their heads also.

'Bless us, O Lord, and these, Thy gifts, which we are about to receive through Thy bounty. Through Christ, our Lord. Amen,' Guy intoned. His "Amen" was echoed by all present. Blaise and Hugh reached for a bread roll each, and while Blaise buttered his bread roll, Hugh broke his into small pieces which he dropped into his soup. Anna stood to one side of the room, the tray she had been carrying resting on the sideboard.

It being a Thursday, Magda, the Cook, had prepared one of her delicious curries. Both she and Anna made several trips in and out of the dining room, carrying the plates of roti and chapatti breads, and the bowls of fruit chutney, accha, grated coconut, chopped tomato, and diced banana, which accompanied two large china tureens, one of beef curry, and one of white rice (the latter cooked in the South African fashion, with butter). Magda's curries were popular with the entire family, and especially so on a cold, damp winter's evening.

'Thank you, Anna, Magda,' Irene told the two Coloured women.

Ja, dankie Magda – ons hou baaie van jou lekker curries,' said Blaise to the cook, smiling. Blaise could at times exhibit a singular charm, seemingly without even being conscious of doing so. He had a gift of making the person he was addressing (or listening to) feel as if they mattered more to him than anything or anyone else in that moment. This gift was to follow him right through the course of his life, and win him many devoted friends and supporters.

Magda, a large, cheerful, amply proportioned woman

in her early middle age, wearing a clean white apron (which she had probably put on just to enter the dining room) over a brown cotton twill dress (similar to that worn by Anna), with a light brown *doek*[*] on her head, returned Blaise's smile. *'Dis my plesier,* Master Blaise,*'* she responded.

Both the servants had only fairly recently begun addressing Blaise as "Master" when in public. Perhaps this had something to do with the fact that he had now passed from childhood to adolescence; perhaps it was simply that he was growing, suddenly, so much taller than any of the women.

Indeed, Blaise was no longer quite a child – but he was still a long way from becoming the adult he was destined to be.

After dinner (the desert had been Peach Melba – a favourite with the three boys, particularly after one of Magda's hot curries), Irene and her husband retreated to the sitting room, with its fire. It would be almost eight years before South Africa had a public nationwide television service, so Guy turned the wireless on. It was tuned to *Radio South Africa*, and some light music was playing. Guy Cressingham picked up the novel he was reading, *The Doomed Oasis*, by Hammond Innes, a writer whose thrillers neither challenged Guy's extremely conventional outlook on life, nor overextended his intellect. His wife, however, was reading *The Anti-Death League*, by Kingsley Amis, whose anarchic, dystopian plot and unbelievably larger than life characters she was at times rather surprised to find herself enjoying.

---

[*] *"Doek"* – Afrikaans – In this context, a headcloth.

The boys had made their way to the den (a much smaller room than the sitting room). Its walls were panelled for a third of their height in a warm, polished wood veneer, and there were built-in bookcases either side of the fireplace, crammed with books, many of which were children's books. There were framed family photographs in black and white on the walls, reaching back three or four generations, and the room was furnished with a comfortable sofa and three large, well-padded armchairs. A fire was burning in the fireplace. After Anna had taken coffee through to the sitting room for the boys' parents, she brought Blaise a coffee, which she placed on the low table in the middle of the room, which was cluttered with toys belonging to Lawrence, along with a number of ashtrays, a scattering of magazines, and several children's comics. (*The Beano,* and *Look and Learn* could be seen). Blaise had only just begun to drink coffee, and at first he had not enjoyed it, but he had persevered, and he had now acquired the taste.

Hugh turned the wireless on. It was tuned to the popular radio service, *Springbok Radio*, which the boys preferred to *Radio South Africa*.

'Let's play some checkers,' Hugh addressed Lawrence.

'Yeah, OK.'

Hugh reached for the checkers box, which was kept in one of the bookcases, opened the board and set up the pieces. He and his younger brother began to play. Blaise was reading the second book in the *Master of Grey* trilogy, by Nigel Tranter, the author of a number of historical novels set in Scotland, novels which were particularly suitable for young adults. Blaise could not get enough of Tranter right now. *Springbok Radio* was playing popular music, the fire was dancing and crackling, the dog was sprawled on the rug in front of it, and the brothers were content. Lawrence would be going up to bed at nine o' clock, Hugh at ten o' clock, and once he had turned thirteen, Blaise's bedtime had been extended to half past ten.

The family was at peace.

Chapter Three

By the time he was sixteen years old, Blaise's perception of the existence of a spiritual dimension, one in which he could commune directly with his Creator, and be open in turn to God's promptings, far outstripped that felt by almost all adults, and certainly left his peers behind entirely. He became aware that there were occasions (and not always only during the Mass) when he felt the presence of God so strongly, that his spirit was lifted high above his daily concerns, to a plane of existence where (as best he could explain it to himself) he experienced a blissful sense of near perfect union with the Divinity. This was not an impersonal and formless divinity, but a communion with God Himself – a person, a spiritual being all-embracing – through His Son, Jesus Christ. Blaise became certain that he had been chosen; for what, he did not yet know. He had as yet studied only a little formal theology, and that at a most basic level, so he lacked the intellectual tools to express clearly to himself a concept of which he was nonetheless conscious: it was, that he had been chosen since before Time, through the sacrifice of Our Lord Jesus Christ, as one of the Elect of God. Blaise was an unwitting Jansenist, although had he then heard that term, it would have meant nothing to him.

Blaise felt that he was privileged beyond measure, and that he would be called upon to serve God in some very specific manner. This certainty fed within him an enormous sense of gratitude, and a hunger for spiritual knowledge. He approached Father Gerard Howard, that extremely well educated and enormously well bred priest from England who celebrated the school Mass the boys attended twice a week. (Indeed, Father Gerard celebrated Mass seven mornings a week, a Mass which the teaching and other Brothers at the school attended before their official duties commenced, and he additionally acted as an occasional supply priest, celebrating the Mass at nearby parishes on a Sunday).

Father Gerard thought he saw in Blaise a singular boy, very likely someone with a genuine calling to the priesthood (if not in fact quite possibly to the Communion of Saints), whom he could help by providing him with some of the intellectual tools he needed to explore his calling, so, during a series of weekly one hour sessions after school (they could not meet more frequently, due to Blaise's other extramural activities), he taught Blaise a broader and deeper theology than he was taught during Religious Instruction classes, and he leant him some books to take away with him, in which the religious and spiritual life was explored. Blaise hungered for such knowledge; he read these books avidly, and returned to Father Gerard with further questions, which he was each time better equipped to frame.

Mass attendance became central to Blaise's life, for during the Mass he not infrequently experienced something which could well be the bliss that the saints had known. He spent at least half an hour on his knees in prayer every night, something he was able to do without being interrupted, for each of the three brothers had their own bedroom in the big house. He could hardly imagine a life without prayer: how empty such a life must feel! Blaise's family began to notice a difference in him. That otherworldly quality which had always, to some degree, clung to him, became far more pronounced. On a practical level, he became far more tolerant of Hugh's enthusiasms and over-exuberance, which had in the past often irritated him; now he regarded Hugh's antics with a seraphic smile, that same half smile he wore so often, an expression of which he was himself unconscious.

Yet in all other respects, Blaise was a fairly normal, healthy teenage boy. To be sure, most boys did not sing in the school choir (and, having given up altar service at Saint Mark's parish church one Sunday a month, he sang every Sunday in their church choir also). By the age of sixteen Blaise had acquired a clear, pure tenor voice, infused with the freshness of youth, and he was able to take a descant part too. Brother Luke had been right: there had been no traumatic and embarrassing breaking of his voice; he had graduated to tenor without any fuss. Choral worship still brought him much joy. As did (on the opposite extreme) his weekly fencing practice: Blaise was now an accomplished sabreur, his height and reach (aged sixteen, he already stood six feet tall in his socks) serving him well. But mere height and reach would have been of little advantage had he not also been very fast.

Blaise led a very full life, with one or another extramural activity five afternoons a week. During the winter, he still played soccer at school once a week, and he ran cross country too (with his long legged, light build, he was almost always among the first three home, not infrequently coming first); he sang every weekday morning in the school choir, and he attended choir practice at least once a week in the afternoon; he also attended a Saturday afternoon choir practice at Saint Mark's parish church, and sang there on Sunday mornings; and during the summer he played tennis at school once a week in place of soccer. On a Sunday afternoon, unless he and his family were visiting his grandparents far down the Peninsula, he was away up the mountain, setting off on foot from home, for it was only a few hundred yards up the road to the top entrance to Kirstenbosch Botanical Garden, with its access to Skeleton Gorge, which took the hiker directly to the Back Table. (Skeleton Gorge was also known as the Smuts Track, so named after the great South African wartime Prime Minister and statesman, Jan Smuts, who had ascended the mountain via this route well into his old age). Sometimes Gregory Dillon, his friend, would accompany Blaise, but often, he would hike alone, for in the mountains, surrounded by the beauty and tranquillity of Nature, he had found that solitude did not equate with loneliness. He grew to know the mountains very well indeed, their fauna and flora, and he was conscious that his love for this wild world reflected in some fashion his love for its Creator.

When Blaise was not busy with these pursuits, indoors and outdoors, there was homework to be done. At sixteen years old, he had reached Standard Nine, and in his penultimate year of school, he now had a fairly heavy load of homework.

At least once a fortnight after Sunday morning Mass, there were family outings to relations who lived further down the Peninsula. Blaise's paternal grandparents lived in a rambling single story house built of stone in the early twentieth century (it replaced a much smaller early nineteenth century farm house), with wide verandas almost overgrown by pink and purple bougainvillea on two sides of the house, and a roof of corrugated iron, painted green. The house was located on about one hundred acres of land, up against a rocky *krantz*[*] halfway between the tiny seaside village of Kommetjie, on the Atlantic Ocean, and the dormitory and resort town of Fish Hoek, on the False Bay shore. Blaise's paternal aunt, Fiona Denholm (his father's younger sister), and her husband, Jeremy, lived with his grandparents, as did his two young cousins, Margaret and Jessica.

Blaise loved the Farm, as the family called it. There were horses, a milk cow (and often, a calf), geese, ducks, chickens, cats and dogs. Corn – known locally as *mielies* – grew on about half an acre of ground, and there was a large kitchen garden. There were two male Cape Coloured labourers, who (one of them with his wife, who worked in the house as the maid) each lived in two-room cottages behind the farmhouse. Blaise's Aunt Fiona kept three horses, and Blaise frequently went riding with her, or with Margaret, the eldest of his two young cousins. Sometimes

---

[*] *"Krantz"* – Afrikaans – a steep ridge.

his grandmother would join them. They rode across the wild, unkempt tract of land – given over to low *fynbos* scrub, and dotted with *vleis*[*] – which lay between the town of Fish Hoek, and Kommetjie village, straddling the Peninsula at this, its narrowest and lowest lying point. (It was clear to any thoughtful observer that this sandy neck of land had once been submerged beneath the sea).

It seemed to Blaise that he had been able to ride since as far back as he could remember, and having long ago become perfectly at ease on horseback, he now rode with casual, long limbed confidence. Sometimes they rode as far as Long Beach (technically, it was named Noordhoek Beach, but the entire stretch of beach, composed of finely crushed and ground shell sand, was known locally as Long Beach), which ran for a distance of about four miles, from Kommetjie village in the south to the foot of Chapman's Peak in the north. Invariably, the beach, gleaming as white as any tropic strand under the sun, was empty of all signs of Humanity. If the conditions were right (ideally, an ebbing tide), they would touch their heels to their horses and break into a canter along the beach, the ubiquitous Kelp Gulls taking to the air with shrill shrieks ahead of them. Occasionally, their horses would pound through the retreating surf, and the glistening spray, flung high by their hooves, would soak their riders' legs. Blaise would whoop with excitement, joined by his Aunt Fiona's happy laughter. Blaise always rode Mars, a powerful seventeen hands grey gelding, and if he gave the horse its head, he could easily leave his aunt (who

---

[*] *"Vlei"* – Afrikaans – a stagnant body of water.

was riding a fifteen hands chestnut mare, her usual mount) behind him.

Once in a rare while, Fiona Denholm prevailed on her brother Guy to join them in a ride, but Blaise's father was not nearly as keen on riding as his son was. 'The trouble with a horse is it doesn't have a steering wheel, a footbrake or a gear lever!' Blaise's father had once announced disparagingly. And Blaise's brother, Hugh, had never acquired his older brother's complete ease and confidence with horses, and he only rarely rode. As for Lawrence, he showed not the least interest in riding, or in almost any other family group activity. As he grew older, Lawrence became ever more an occupant of a private world, ever more obsessed with his collections – be they collections of Corgi, Matchbox and Dinky die cast model cars, his stamp collection, or his scores of toy soldiers.

Now aged seventy, and fully retired from the family business, Blaise's grandfather was still an imposing figure: a big man, still broad shouldered, with a shock of white hair and dark, bushy eyebrows. He had been educated at Ampleforth College, a leading Catholic public school (as English private schools were known) in Yorkshire, and he still retained the well bred, upper-class accent of the English ruling class. Until three or four years earlier, Ambrose Cressingham had maintained an active interest in the family business, but he had since then handed over the reins completely to Guy, his only son, and he seemed happy to be able to spend more time now in his workshop (he had a beautifully appointed workshop in a large shed to one side of the farmhouse), and on maintaining and showing the 1938

Rolls-Royce Phantom III V-12 car he had restored. Blaise admired the car as an object of aesthetic beauty, but it was Hugh who shared with his grandfather the practical, hands-on skills necessary to maintain it in perfect condition, and Hugh and his grandfather spent many Sunday afternoons together in the workshop, machining some new part for the Rolls-Royce's engine.

Blaise was closer to his grandmother, Teresa Cressingham, who, aged sixty-six, was still a fit, active, and very attractive woman. It was from her, perhaps, that Blaise had inherited his charm, for she had a particularly sweet manner about her, and people were strongly drawn to her. Like Irene Cressingham, her daughter-in-law, she sat on a number of charitable committees, and she was active in local community affairs. Unlike her daughter-in-law, Teresa Cressingham was a sociable woman, a popular member of any group she belonged to. She shared in Blaise's enthusiasm for History, and she had a large library on the subject, from which Blaise had always been at liberty to borrow books.

In addition to his grandparents, and his aunt's and uncle's family, Blaise had other relations living nearby. Teresa's brother, Blaise's great-uncle William Crichton, and his wife, Josephine (known as Aunt Josie) had a house on the lower slopes of Elsie's Peak on the southern side of Fish Hoek, overlooking the town. Their two children (Blaise's father's first cousins, both girls) and their families lived in and around Cape Town. Both had married out of the Faith, although their children were being brought up as Catholics.

Blaise felt secure, safe, and loved within his extended family, and many would have been envious of his childhood, so rich in blessings it was.

Chapter Four

Two days before Christmas 1972 (Blaise was then seventeen years old), the school's Matric Ball took place. It was held in the school hall, on a Friday evening, with a number of the Brothers present to ensure that the boys behaved themselves, and volunteer duennas drawn from among the mothers to chaperone the girls. For those boys in this all-boys school who had no girl to ask to the Ball, candidates were put forward from within the Matric class at the girls' convent school not far away. Blaise however had asked Gregory's younger sister, aged sixteen, and then completing standard nine, to be his partner at the Ball.

Gregory had been visiting his friend at the Cressingham home late one afternoon during the final week of the Matric exam period, seeking Blaise's help with revision of English Grammar (the English exam would be held the next day), and he had stayed for dinner. After dinner, the two friends had walked to the Dillon home, which was not far away, and they had found Nicolette, Gregory's sister, along with her parents, in the Dillons' sitting room. Blaise had given the girl (an elfin blonde, not at all like her sturdy brother

Gregory in appearance) one of his charming smiles, but as she was more than halfway in love with him already, this was not really necessary. 'Nikki,' he said, 'if your parents will give their permission, I would be very pleased if you would be my partner at the Matric Ball.'

Nicolette Dillon blushed. 'I would be happy to. Thank you for asking me, Blaise.'

Mr. and Mrs. Dillon smiled benignly. They thought that Blaise was a fine young man.

'That's good,' said Blaise, smiling again. 'I'm pleased. I'll collect you at quarter to eight on Friday next week, OK?'

Adults frequently observed that Blaise showed a remarkable degree of self possession in one so young.

Irene Cressingham gave her son some lessons in the waltz, the foxtrot and the quickstep. With a life so full of outdoor, physical pursuits, Blaise was a quick learner, and he proved to be a graceful dancer. He would not be shaming Nikki at the Ball.

Nikki Dillon was excited to be asked to the Ball by Blaise. Not only would it be the first formal dance she had ever attended where her family was not present, but Blaise was so good looking! The other girls would be envious of her, she was sure. Oh gosh, she needed something to wear! She and her mother put their heads together, and they made a shopping trip into Cape Town. Blaise and his mother also made a special trip into Cape Town. Blaise already possessed a quiet, very dark grey suit of light wool he wore to church, but Irene wished her son to stand out at the dance. Accordingly, the two of them visited Cape Town's foremost gentlemen's outfitters together, where Irene prevailed upon her handsome son to choose an outfit with a white dinner jacket, a black bow tie (it was not a ready-made up bow tie; it had to be tied by hand; Guy Cressingham taught his son how to tie it), fairly narrow black trousers, and a couple of white dress shirts. It was time Blaise possessed a dinner jacket, his mother thought. (Although she doubted it would be much use to him for more than a year or two: although Blaise had reached what would prove to be his full height, of six feet and two inches, his shoulders and chest were still to gain in breadth). Blaise's mother also bought her son a pair of size eleven Italian-made dress shoes in fine leather.

A few days before the Ball, Blaise and the other Matric pupils were presented with their exam results. Blaise had done very well in History, English, and French; he had achieved acceptable passes in Biology, Latin, and Afrikaans, and (God be thanked) he had just managed to scrape a pass in Maths. On the whole, he was satisfied with his results. The University of Cape Town would place no barriers in the way of his registering for a Bachelor of Arts degree. Blaise was being urged by Father Gerard to enter his priesthood, but he was attracted by the idea of teaching – perhaps after taking a postgraduate degree. And yet, there was always in his mind the powerful conviction that God had a special plan for him; that God had something particular He wished him to do.

'How can I be sure whether I have a vocation to the priesthood, Father?' Blaise asked Father Gerard. 'I'm also drawn to the idea of teaching.'

'You can be both a teacher and a priest, you know,' Father Howard answered the young man.

'Perhaps,' suggested Blaise, 'I should study for a degree in History and English – and maybe French as well. They're all teaching subjects. If I want to become a teacher after my BA, I can follow that path. But if by then it has become clear to me that I have a calling to the priesthood, I can study Theology, and perhaps enter the Seminary at the same time.'

'That seems a sensible plan, Blaise,' Father Gerard had responded. 'You are very young; there's no great urgency to make up your mind. And while I have been convinced for some years that you have a vocation for the priesthood, I must not impose my wishes on you.'

'I do know there's some special task God has in mind for me,' Blaise said earnestly. 'Perhaps things will become clearer while I'm studying for a degree.'

Blaise commenced studying for his Bachelor of Arts degree in February the following year, 1973, while he was still only seventeen years old, too young in South Africa to drive a car, but nonetheless, university represented Blaise's first venture into adulthood. For much of Blaise's first term at university, it meant his mother alternating week by week with Mrs. Dillon to drive Blaise and Gregory to and from university. The University was located on the slopes of Devil's Peak, above the suburbs of Rondebosch and Rosebank, some miles nearer Cape Town proper. But before reaching the end of term, Blaise (now aged eighteen) had passed his driving test and he had obtained a driver's licence. Guy Cressingham then bought his son a car, a five year old Triumph Herald hardtop, a rather sporty little English saloon with a wood veneer dashboard and fairly advanced suspension. Blaise grew to love that car. It afforded him virtually limitless freedom. It seemed to put the seal on his having entered the adult world.

In return for a payment of one Rand fifty each time, Blaise could have got Henry, the Cressinghams' full time gardener and odd-job man, to wash the car once a week, but Blaise often washed, cleaned and polished the car himself. Hugh enjoyed working on the car's mechanics, and he tackled the car's monthly servicing – the oiling and greasing. When a part needed replacing, Hugh would attend to it. Blaise's monthly allowance (his father was not ungenerous) was spared the shock of motor mechanics' fees.

Guy, anxious that his eldest son might not be sowing sufficient wild oats at university, also gifted him at this time the guest suite at the Cressingham home. It could be accessed via the end of the bedroom corridor on the house's first floor, but it also had a private entrance up a flight of stairs next to the garages. This suite consisted of a bed-sitting room, a bathroom and lavatory, and even a tiny kitchenette. However, Blaise continued to eat with the family when he was at home in the evening.

Blaise knew at least half a dozen boys from school who were also registered for a BA course at UCT (which was the name popularly given to the University of Cape Town), and he sustained fairly close friendships with two or three of them, meeting them at the Students' Union cafeteria for lunch, and occasionally visiting their homes. Once he had a car of his own, he sometimes went out with them in the evenings. Gregory Dillon had, like Blaise, also begun university that year, opting as Blaise had for deferment of his military service. A university graduate would usually receive an officer's commission after basic training, and his life in the SADF (the South African Defence Force) as an officer, even a humble second lieutenant, would be very much more pleasant than it might have been as a mere *troopie*. Gregory was, however, studying engineering (as Hugh too would be doing the following year), and Blaise did not see very much of him on campus. Nonetheless, they met in the evenings sometimes, and they went to several movies together. Once in a while they hiked together in the mountains at the weekend. It was Gregory who introduced Blaise to the Pig and Whistle, the iconic student pub with a half timbered interior located in Rondebosch, where Blaise learned to down pints of ale, although he failed to take to alcohol with the eagerness shown by some of his peers. Here he also smoked his first cigarette. But it would be a couple of years before smoking was to become a habit.

'You look like you've fallen from Heaven,' a girl in one of Blaise's classes at university told him at the Pig and Whistle one evening, her words a little slurred, her gaze disconcertingly direct. She had already had a couple of Camparis with lemonade. Blaise smiled at her, not entirely unaccustomed to interest shown in him by girls. 'You're too perfect for this world,' she declared.

In later years the truth of this assertion was to become more broadly apparent, but all the young woman then saw was Blaise's height, his mop of flaxen hair, his dark eyebrows and his golden tan. Blaise possessed a beauty of feature and a grace of form which made him stand out in any group. Yet, although he took care of his straight hair, which he now wore in a floppy centre parting style, he felt little vanity, and he had no real appreciation of the impact his appearance made on others – on girls especially. He was still somewhat surprised when his looks were drawn to his attention. Sometimes the girls in his university classes almost threw themselves at Blaise. He found sex – obtaining it, indulging in it – the easiest thing in the world during his first two years at university. And he took full advantage of this fact, although each time he slept with a girl, he would experience remorse and self-loathing afterwards. "God forgive me," he would pray; "Oh Jesus, deliver me from lust."

But there was an unexpressed condition attached to this request for deliverance; it was the words, "Not yet." In this, Blaise was no different to that great saint and Church Father, Saint Augustine of Hippo, who had famously prayed for deliverance from lust – but not yet. Blaise's father, who had half feared during his son's last few years at school that he might be a pansy – there was Blaise's unearthly beauty; his dislike of contact sports; his membership of the school choir; and his extreme piety – was able in time to forget his fears for Blaise's sexual orientation, for once Blaise had begun university, Guy soon became aware that his son sometimes brought girls back to his flat above the garages (although never overnight).

Encouraged by his father to find a part-time job (Guy Cressingham felt that it would do the boy good to earn some money for himself), Blaise began working Saturday mornings at one of the two big department stores in Adderley Street in Cape Town. His father was right: it did feel good to be earning some money, rather than relying entirely on his allowance. The store's personnel manager, a short, stout, mincing little man, much taken by Blaise's striking appearance, placed him in Menswear. There, women shopping for their husbands would buy three or four dress shirts at a time, or two pairs of trousers, or a complete lounge suit, or half a dozen pairs of socks, simply for the pleasure of engaging with this beautiful young man. One Saturday morning Blaise was called upstairs to the personnel manager's office.

'We would like to offer you a full time position, Blaise,' the man told him, 'and enrolment in our in-house management training course.'

But Blaise knew that he was destined to be something more – much more – than a shopkeeper, so he turned the offer down.

'I'm happy just to continue working Saturday mornings, Mr. Carstairs,' he responded.

'Well – if ever you change your mind …'

In early December 1974, towards the end of Blaise's second year at UCT, Blaise's mother began to complain of a constant headache and periods of nausea. By February 1975, the Cressingham family had begun to notice inexplicable mood swings, forgetfulness, and periods of brooding ill humour from Irene.

"Irene is too young to be going through the change," her husband reasoned. He took her to see their family doctor, Dr. Gilmore. He in turn referred her for scans and X-rays at Groote Schuur, Cape Town's main hospital (which had become internationally famous since Christiaan Barnard's human-to-human heart transplant operation on 3rd December

1967, the world's first such procedure). Dr. Gilmore's worst fears were confirmed: Irene was diagnosed with an inoperable brain tumour. The specialist at Groote Schuur informed her that she had six months at the most to live.

'What do we tell the boys?' Irene asked her husband.

Guy's features were stricken. He held his head in his hands. He did not think he could cope with this.

'Blaise is old enough to be told – Hugh too – but Lawrence?' Irene continued. 'How can we tell him he is going to lose his mother?'

'I don't know. This is a nightmare. Oh, Irene!'

Guy felt a sudden welling up of pity and compassion for his wife. For a long time he had not felt much more than companionable familiarity for her. Nor had he embraced his wife for a long time, but he did so now. Irene returned his embrace.

'We have to be strong,' she said.

'Yes, we must be strong – for the boys' sake.'

The family assembled in the den that evening. On learning that their mother was going to die, Hugh burst into tears, and went and hugged his mother tightly. Blaise felt a shock so profound he thought his heart had stopped, then he too began to weep. Lawrence's face went white, but he did not cry.

'Oh, my boys,' Irene said, 'we must take refuge in our faith. We know that in Jesus Christ we never truly die; we are never truly lost to one another.'

Blaise knew that this was true, yet he could find no comfort in the knowledge. 'Is there nothing they can do?' he asked. 'Surely there's something they can do!'

'No, the tumour is inoperable, Blaise. There is nothing to be done,' his mother answered him.

'Mummy, how long have you got to live?' Lawrence asked.

Their father answered his youngest son. 'They told us that Mum has six months at the most.'

'Well, I shall pray for a miracle,' Blaise said, sniffing loudly. 'God works miracles sometimes. Perhaps He will work a miracle this time.'

'We must all pray, of course,' Irene responded. 'Nothing is impossible for God.'

But God worked no miracle for the Cressinghams. The brothers had to watch their mother's increasingly dreadful (and for Blaise, almost soul destroying) deterioration, and towards the end, she was partially paralysed down her left side, and she struggled to communicate coherently. She was taking large doses of morphine against the pain. Blaise felt his faith being torn from his soul and ground to dust, and when, in late April that year, about a month after the saddest Easter Blaise would ever know, his mother died, he felt, amidst an unbearable anguish, a terrible, guilt-stricken relief: relief that her suffering was over at last.

Hugh wept unashamedly at his mother's funeral, but in time his natural ebullience was to reassert itself. Lawrence however, who had only just turned fifteen, withdrew even further into himself, and his communications and smiles became even more rare.

Blaise was henceforward to cease to respond to the girls who pursued him so eagerly. He felt, without having articulated the idea to himself, that to indulge in any more casual sex would be grossly disrespectful of his mother's memory. His prayers – for deliverance from lust – had been answered in the most terrible fashion.

The Requiem Mass for his mother, held at Saint Mark's parish church in Newlands in early May, would be the last Mass that Blaise would attend for many months. In late May (almost midway through his final undergraduate year), he ceased attending lectures and tutorials at university. He found the call-up document the SADF had issued him during his Matric year, along with his deferment papers, and, quoting his call-up number, he informed the SADF that he was no longer a university student, and that he wished to undergo his military service.

Guy Cressingham thought that his son had taken leave of his senses. 'You were going to graduate at the end of the year,' he said. 'Have you any idea how tough it can be in the army as a *troopie*?* You could have obtained a commission.'

But Blaise felt that nothing mattered now: God had turned his face from him. How could he continue to believe in a loving God, when God had permitted his mother to die in such a fashion, and so young? Blaise was suffering a major crisis of faith. The very foundations of his belief in a loving God had crumbled. And so he did what many young men over the years have done when stricken by anguish at a love unrequited or betrayed: he joined the army.

---

* *"Troopie"* – Slang – a popular term for an SADF conscript soldier.

Chapter Five

At that time, all white male South African permanent residents were obliged to undergo military service for nine months on leaving school. (There were exceptions made in the case of foreign passport holders who indicated that they would not be applying for South African citizenship in the future). Blaise and Gregory, both of them South African citizens, had been granted deferments in order to study at university. Blaise would now be serving his time in the SADF, as part of the July intake, most likely in South West Africa, the League of Nations mandate territory (once a German colony) granted to the Union of South Africa after the First World War. Today, South Africa treated the territory in effect as a fifth province, and until April the previous year, it had been the responsibility of the South African Police to combat the armed wing of the South West Africa People's Organisation (SWAPO). SWAPO's armed wing, the People's Liberation Army of Namibia (PLAN), waged guerrilla war against the occupying South African forces. The use of landmines on roads, and periodic attacks on isolated police stations, were PLAN's favoured tactics. In April 1974, the SADF took over responsibility from the police for combating PLAN. By 1975 there were fifteen thousand SADF soldiers stationed in South West Africa.

However, with the collapse the previous year of Marcelo Caetano's right wing regime in Portugal, Portugal moved rapidly to divest itself of its African colonies, and Angola (then a Portuguese colony) had been promised independence by November 1975. Angola had rapidly descended into civil war, as rival black nationalist independence movements, each with its own ethnic base and ideological stance, fought each other for eventual rule in Angola, and SWAPO took advantage of this chaos to increase the number of its incursions into South West Africa from PLAN camps north of the Angolan border. South African forces were in due course to find themselves drawn into Angola's civil war, as they attempted to prevent these incursions.

Two of Angola's black nationalist movements – the FNLA in the north, and UNITA in the south – opposed the Soviet supplied Marxist movement, the MPLA, and it seemed imperative to the South African government that it support UNITA and the FNLA in their struggle against the MPLA's armed wing, FAPLA. In August 1975, SADF forces occupied Calueque hydroelectric dam (which supplied electricity to South West Africa), in the south of Angola. From late October 1975, South Africa began to commit SADF forces in support of UNITA (which portrayed itself as anti-Communist and pro-western), in the south of Angola. FAPLA was already being advised by Cuban personnel on the ground. South Africa feared that if the MPLA succeeded in seizing power, it would support PLAN militarily and lead to an unprecedented escalation of the fighting in South West Africa.

This then was the situation which was to develop soon after Blaise began his basic training in the SADF in July. But having failed to complete his university degree, he remained after basic training a humble, downtrodden *troopie*, and it was the especial delight of Afrikaner non-commissioned officers to torment educated English speaking conscripts. However, Blaise spoke Afrikaans tolerably well, and his innate charm (and despite his private grief, his cheerful willingness, his physical toughness and his ready smile), far from infuriating these hard bitten Afrikaner non-coms, won most of them over, sparing him the worst of their excesses. Indeed, Blaise found life in the army far from unpleasant. He had no time for morbid grief, and he took to the discipline and the routine with surprising ease. Nor did homesickness engulf him, as it did some of the very young conscripts. He had a private grief to cope with far deeper than mere prosaic homesickness.

He enjoyed in particular the warm camaraderie within his company, and he grew to value the friendship of another lad from Cape Town, a Bishops boy. Roderick, a year older than Blaise, was even taller and leaner than him, but he was dark where Blaise was blonde, and gangling where Blaise was graceful. He was a quiet young man, and educationally and intellectually a good match for Blaise. His mild, unassertive personality and his obvious lack of leadership qualities meant that despite possessing a university degree, he had not been offered a commission. Roderick was the only fellow conscript with whom Blaise shared his deepest thoughts. That Roderick loved Blaise with all his heart was his own private torment, for he dared not express such a love, and

Blaise was oblivious to it. That Roderick was not a Catholic was part of his appeal for Blaise. Blaise had (for the moment at least) turned his back on his faith. He felt bitter and angry with God. This alienation from his faith was, however, not to last: shock, trauma and horror were, later in the year, to force him to turn to God again.

But for now, army service seemed to be just what Blaise needed: his complete removal from a familiar environment – associated so strongly with the mother he had lost – and the presentation of completely novel challenges to distract his mind, helped him manage his grief. By the end of most days he was so exhausted, he had little energy left to brood, and (like his comrades) he welcomed lights out at ten o' clock in the evening.

In mid-October, Blaise and Roderick, along with the rest of their company, were posted to a motorised infantry battalion based at Rundu in northern South West Africa, on the Cubango River, which formed the border between South West Africa and Angola. The SADF base at Rundu (which in addition to serving ground forces, functioned as a major air force base) was expanding enormously, as the SADF built up its numbers on the Angolan border. Everyone there (it seemed) knew that they would soon be seeing action: against whom, precisely, many of the *troopies* themselves were not entirely clear; the *Terrs*, most likely, but there were even rumours that they would be fighting the Cubans. However, the prospect of imminent action excited almost all of them, Blaise and Roderick included – even if these two young men were both imaginative enough for their excitement to be cut with a dash of nervous anticipation.

In late October that year, the SADF launched its first major incursion within southern Angola. South Africa's strategic objective was to ensure that UNITA (in the south) and the FNLA (in the north) were able to defeat the MPLA, before Angola's formal independence date, which had been set for the 11th November. The motorised infantry battalion of which Blaise and Roderick were members, participated in this exercise, which was known as Operation Savannah.

Within a matter of mere days, the SADF had overrun considerable territory and captured several strategically important settlements. The advance of the South African troops was so rapid that it often succeeded in driving FAPLA out of two or three towns in a single day. South African casualties were minimal: this, thought Blaise, was the way war should be fought! But then, in late December, the SADF encountered regular Cuban forces, allies of FAPLA, and suddenly, this war wasn't much fun anymore. Engagements were always bloody, and hard fought. Their first encounter with Cuban regulars had been so shocking – the sheer severity of the exchange of gunfire, the refusal of the Cubans to immediately melt away into the bush (as had been the habit of the FAPLA forces), and above all, the casualties the South Africans were taking – that Blaise had been left near traumatised. Fear was now a constant companion; fear of a bloody death, or worse, a terrible, crippling injury. Blaise's embargo on God collapsed: he began to pray again. But he had not yet regained that intimate connection with the Divinity that he had felt in the past; his prayers were desperate pleas, one day at a time, that God keep him from harm.

For the first time in his life, in order to cope with the fear he now felt all the time, and the stress he was under, Blaise resorted to the use of liquor in the evenings as a palliative. Beers from the commissariat were in plentiful supply, spirits less so. (Whiskey and brandy tended to be reserved for the officers). He also began to smoke: army issue cigarettes cost next to nothing, and almost all his comrades now smoked.

One evening, sitting beneath the harsh glare of a pressure lantern hanging from the tent pole, a can of Castle lager in one hand, a cigarette in the other, Blaise said, 'This is the Legion of the Damned.'

'Yeah,' Roderick responded. 'Somehow I never imagined it was going to be like this.'

And then a few days after Christmas (a Christmas that had passed with little celebration) the horror became so focused, so extreme, that Blaise felt his sanity buckle. What made it worse was that it was a horror visited upon his senses not by the enemy, but by members of his own company; by his comrades. Their company had just occupied a small village; they would catch up with the main body of the battalion a few miles ahead, once they had ensured that the village posed no threat in their rear. The settlement was not much more than a collection of mud-walled single room huts, but there was a "cuca shop" in the middle of the village, a trading store built of brick and concrete, roofed with corrugated iron. They had met with no Cuban forces that day, and the Recces reported none in the immediate vicinity. There had been no resistance from within the village.

The troops, before pushing on to rejoin the battalion, were taking a breather in front of the store. Several of the men appeared from within the store, bottles of Coca-Cola, or cans of beer, in their hands. They sat down beneath a large, spreading umbrella thorn acacia in the clearing of beaten red earth that fronted the store, and lighted up cigarettes. Blaise had not participated in looting the store, but he joined his comrades in the clearing, and somebody passed him a bottle of Coca-Cola. Blaise and Roderick lay back against their heavy packs, their R1 rifles across their laps. Blaise felt himself nodding off: he seemed to want to sleep all the time now.

There was a sudden ripping clatter of automatic gunfire from across the clearing – all the more shocking for its being unexpected – and in front of his horrified gaze, two of the resting troopers near Blaise jerked, bloody blossoms erupting from their bodies, and lay still. Blaise and his comrades flung themselves flat on the ground and were bringing their weapons to bear on the apparent source of the noise. The gunfire appeared to have come from a hut across the clearing. Then their sergeant stood, drew back his right arm, and lobbed a grenade into the dark doorway of the hut. The explosion tore the structure apart in a cloud of smoke and dust. Then there was silence, but for loud groaning from one of the two SADF casualties.

'Medics!' the sergeant shouted. 'We need medics here!'

Two medics ran from the rear, where the troop transporters and the company field ambulance with its medics (or "tampax tiffies" as they were popularly known), had come to a halt on the edge of the village. One of the medics felt for a pulse from the silent soldier.

'Hierdie een is dood,' he declared.

There was a low growl from the men in the clearing. One of them, Hennie Van Tonder (who had a reputation as something of a troublemaker in the unit), walked up to the doorway of the trading store and fired a burst from his R1 automatic assault rifle. He then walked to the nearest hut and kicked the flimsy wooden door in, and after a moment, he let off another burst of gunfire. Several of the South Africans had followed his lead, and were fanning out and firing indiscriminately into neighbouring huts. Lieutenant Morris, an English speaking university graduate, called out 'Cease fire! *Ophou, manne*!' But the men ignored him, and both their sergeant and Captain Hendriks, the Company OC, remained silent. Blaise and Roderick looked on in horror.

By the time the massacre had ended, the men had killed more than a dozen people – almost all of them women, old men and children. One of the troopers owned a Kodak Instamatic camera, and he took several photographs of his grinning comrades striking poses behind black bodies that had been dragged from the huts. It was this – their total lack of shame or remorse; his comrades' pride in their terrible work – that Blaise found both inexplicable and insupportable. Similar occasions had occurred before, during their rapid advance through the bush, but the bodies in those scenes had been either Cuban troops, or FAPLA combatants. This – these helpless, ill dressed, obviously impoverished civilians – this was too terrible to bear. Something broke within Blaise. The wall he had built against God was breached, and the image of the crucified Christ was suddenly clear in his mind's eye. Blaise called out – not as an imprecation, but in desperate need – 'Oh Jesus!'

Chapter Six

Within a day or two it was known by many in the company that Blaise was *"bombevok,"* or shell-shocked. His gaze was that of someone staring into a deep chasm; he carried out his tasks as if unaware of their purpose; worst of all, he would weep silently, like a lost child, at odd moments. At times, his eyes shut, a low mumble would issue from between his moving lips. Was he praying? His comrades shunned him, embarrassed. Only Roderick – whose heart was breaking for his friend, but who dared not seek to comfort him as he wished, with an embrace – had time for him, and it was he who spoke to Lieutenant Morris, who then referred Blaise for a medical assessment at Battalion HQ, following which he was classified as G4K4: that is, he was recognised as a soldier with a serious medical problem, and he was shortly thereafter granted an immediate medical discharge. Just a few days into the new year, Blaise was flown out of the operational area, along with six seriously wounded personnel, in a Puma helicopter transporter. From Rundu Air Force Base he was flown to Ysterplaat Air Force Base at Cape Town on a standard run by a C-130 Hercules transporter aircraft.

The first that Guy Cressingham knew of his son's arrival was a telephone call made by some nameless Air Force lieutenant at Ysterplaat, who was moved in part by common humanity at Blaise's obviously damaged mental condition, and in part by the boy's Bishopscourt home address. Guy was on his way to the base within ten minutes of receiving the call. The sun was going down when he collected Blaise, whose gaze was unfocused and who had an absent look in his eye.

'Blaise! What have they done to you?' his father exclaimed, seizing hold of his son's hand. Guy turned to the nameless lieutenant. 'Do you know anything about this?' he asked.

'Nothing Sir, only that Private Blaise Cressingham has been discharged from the SADF on medical grounds.'

'But surely there must be a doctor – someone I can talk to!'

'Normally there would be, Sir, but your son seems to have travelled unaccompanied.'

'We're going home, Blaise,' Guy told his son. 'I'll get you to a doctor in the morning.'

The drive home, during which Blaise sat silently in the seat next to his father, took almost half an hour, the evening traffic quite heavy. Guy could get no response from his son when he questioned him. Guy – like almost every other South African civilian – was unaware that the SADF had been fighting a war in Angola. (Although rumours had begun to circulate, the newspapers had not been permitted to report them). The troopers' letters home had been heavily censored, with all references to their location or their active combatant status removed. But from February, when the South African government began to withdraw its forces from Angola, the fact and details of Operation Savannah (which had been a strategic failure, for all the SADF's initially rapid advance through southern Angola) became more widely known. Only then did Blaise's father begin to form some idea of what his son had been through.

Blaise however was finished with the army. He spent the rest of January and part of February at Valkenberg Psychiatric Hospital, in the suburb of Observatory, very near Cape Town proper. After a week had passed, safe and secure in a comfortable, detached, shared unit located with others in a cluster in the hospital's extensive grounds, Blaise had begun hesitantly to relate to others again. He became rapidly institutionalised, relishing the absence of any need to make any decisions whatsoever, and he was happy there. Hugh, about to begin his third year in engineering at UCT, and the proud owner of an almost new Mini Cooper, visited his brother every three or four days. The two brothers grew closer than they had been for quite a while, and Hugh acted as a far more useful therapist than the psychiatric staff themselves, for the two brothers had of course a shared childhood in common. Blaise was able to communicate disjointed memories of his time in Angola to his brother, who proved a good listener, though how much he actually understood, remained unclear.

Hugh told Gregory Dillon, Blaise's best friend from schooldays, where his brother was, but Gregory visited Blaise only once. The visit proved awkward: Blaise was not yet well enough to conduct a conversation at any length, and Gregory was embarrassed to have to visit his friend in a psychiatric hospital. Their lives had anyway been diverging since they had left school, and although they would remain friends, the closeness that had once united them, was gone. Gregory had yet to undergo military service. Back home, Gregory told his sister, Nicolette, that he had seen Blaise.

'I felt I hardly knew him,' he said. 'He wasn't the Blaise I remember.'

'Do you think it would be OK if I was to visit him?' asked Nicolette.

'I don't see why not.'

Roderick, now wearing the uniform of a two-stripe corporal, visited several times. (His three month tour of operational duty had ended in mid-January, and he had been posted to Youngsfield Military Base at Cape Town). The lanky young man showed himself to be a most faithful friend. On his first visit, he brought a carton of Peter Stuyvesant cigarettes with him. When he first saw Blaise, he said, shaking his friend's hand, 'I've missed you, Blaise.'

Blaise smiled, and gazed at Roderick almost as if he had not met him before. They were standing in the small common room attached to the unit, then Roderick suggested they sit down.

'Yes, of course.'

'How have you been, Blaise?' Roderick asked.

'Not so good at first, but I'm getting better now,' Blaise replied.

'I've brought you some smokes,' Roderick said. 'I wasn't sure whether you still smoked.'

Blaise, who had lighted one of his own cigarettes

immediately after sitting down, smiled again. 'I do, as you see. Thanks, Roddy.'

But Blaise had little to say during that first visit. However, Roderick elicited a response from his friend when he asked him, 'Do you ever think about those days up north?'

Blaise's mouth twitched, almost a grimace. But he answered, 'Not at first. More and more often now, though. At first I couldn't bear to remember.'

'Things went downhill fast, after you left, Blaise. We really were the Legion of the Damned. We had bitten off more than we could chew.'

For several minutes, the two friends sat in silence together, then Blaise said, 'Once I'm out of here, we must get up the mountain. That's what I've been missing the most: somewhere high and clean and unspoiled.'

'We'll do that. I'll look forward to it.'

Silence descended for another minute or two, and Blaise drew on his cigarette, then he said, 'You know, Roddy, I see things now as I never used to see them.'

'I think that after our time in Angola, many of us will see things differently,' Roderick responded.

'No – I mean, I've begun to think of black and Coloured people in a way I never used to think of them – no, that's not quite what I meant to say: I think I've become fully conscious of their humanity.' Blaise stubbed out his cigarette, and lighted another, his face wearing a look of slight puzzlement. 'What I'm trying to say, is, of course I always knew they were human; I never looked at our maid and our cook and our gardener in any other way, but deep down … oh! I don't know what I'm trying to say! I'm a bit nuts, you know. They have a fancy name for it: Post Traumatic Stress Disorder. Let's go for a walk.'

The two tall young men set off at a slow amble around the extensive grounds. Once in a while, one of them would speak. Often, Blaise did not respond to something Roderick had just said, but Roderick did not think that he was inattentive. Blaise smoked another two cigarettes during their stroll. He had become a heavy smoker in Valkenberg. After they had parted, Roderick promising to visit again soon, Blaise was glad that his friend had visited. He could talk to Roddy as to no other. OK – Hugh was a good listener, but Hugh hadn't been through what Roderick and Blaise had been through; Blaise knew that there was a limit to what his brother could possibly understand. He felt however that Roddy understood him perfectly.

Blaise spent more than five weeks at Valkenberg, but his father visited him only three times, each time on a Sunday afternoon. Although pleased to see his father, Blaise found that neither had much to say to the other. He almost got the impression that his father was embarrassed to have to be seen at Valkenberg. Perhaps he was just being over sensitive? But for the first time, Blaise became consciously aware that he had never been particularly close to his father, not as close as he was, for example, to Hugh. (Lawrence was another matter: poor Lawrence made it difficult for anyone to get close to him). It was his mother with whom Blaise had felt a special bond; his mother whom Blaise had loved with all his heart.

But his mother was gone! Blaise felt that now familiar hurt whenever he thought of his mother, but he was no longer crippled by grief; remembering her no longer tore him apart. He had begun recalling the happy times – the years in which she had been a comfort and a confidante to him – more often that he remembered the anguish of those last few months of her life. It would before long be a full year since she had died.

'Do you think,' Guy asked Hugh, who had been visiting his brother one afternoon in February, 'that Blaise is getting any better?'

Hugh thought a moment. Then, 'He is. That lost look he had, I don't see it on him as often now. He seems to pay more attention to what you say to him. And he talks to me quite a lot.'

'He tells me very little,' Guy responded. 'If I wasn't reading about the Angola campaign in the newspapers now – and that's not the whole story, I'll bet – I wouldn't have known about it from listening to Blaise.'

'Blaise hasn't told me everything,' Hugh told his father. 'He wont tell me what triggered this thing – whatever it is he's suffering from. He just says something awful happened.'

Hugh and his father had taken Heidi for a walk together just before sunset, and they were sitting in the den now, with a beer each. Hugh asked, 'Dad, what is it exactly that's wrong with Blaise? I'm not sure that I understand.'

'I know what I've been told by the doctors there,' Guy replied. 'It's something I had never heard of before: they called it "Post Traumatic Stress Disorder."'

'And what does that mean, Dad?'

'As best I can understand, Blaise has been traumatised by some event that he's witnessed.'

'But he does seem to be getting better!' Hugh repeated.

'I'm very glad to hear you say so,' Guy told Hugh. 'But you know, he will never get over it fully, the doctors tell me. I'm not sure that I understood correctly, but I gather that these symptoms – this withdrawal from the rest of the world – can and probably will recur at times.'

'Oh Dad!' Hugh exclaimed. 'It's a tragedy – Blaise of all people. But he was always inclined to be otherworldly at times, wasn't he?'

'If anyone in this family is ever canonised,' Guy remarked (rather oddly, thought Hugh), 'it will be Blaise. Father O'Connor at Saint Mark's is saying an intercessory Mass for him twice a week, and I know that the Brothers at the school are praying for him.'

'If you believe in that sort of thing,' remarked Hugh.

'We must believe. Sometimes belief is all we have,' Hugh's father admonished him. 'But you tell me you think Blaise is improving. Let's be grateful for that.'

'Yes, Dad. And it could have been worse. Blaise might have been injured, or worse. I gather the Cubans inflicted a shocking number of casualties.'

Nicolette Dillon, Gregory's sister, nursed an undeclared passion for Blaise, which long predated his having taken her to his Matric Ball. Nicolette was now in her third year at UCT, reading English and Sociology, and she had bumped into Blaise on campus quite often. In fact, Blaise had two or three times taken her to the cinema – but to her dismay, he had treated her much more as a sister each time than as a potential romantic partner. She was a sweet girl, still the same elfin blonde that she had been aged sixteen, and she now paid Blaise what was to him an entirely unexpected visit.

For a few seconds, Blaise had stared blankly at her, as if he did not know who she was, then recognition and pleasure lighted up his face. 'Nikki! What are you doing here?' he exclaimed.

'I've come to see you, Blaise.'

'Well, you are very welcome. It's been a long time since I last saw you.'

'Yes, it has,' Nicolette responded. In fact, she had not seen Blaise since his mother's Requiem Mass. The two sat down alongside each other on a small sofa.

'I have a gift for you,' she said, handing Blaise a package done up in fancy gift paper. Blaise took it and removed the wrapping paper. Inside was a book, *How Green Was My Valley*, by Richard Llewellyn.

'Have you read it?' Nicolette asked. 'I thought it was a wonderful story.'

'No, I haven't read it. I'm sure I shall enjoy it: I've read pretty much every book they have here. Thank you, Nikki.' He leant across and kissed her on the cheek. She was a reminder of happy times.

Blaise had in truth hardly spared her a thought since his mother's death, but he was touched and moved by her visit. What is more, he appreciated almost for the first time just how beautiful she was, and he felt the faintest stirrings of something more than a fraternal interest in her.

'Let's walk to the shop,' he suggested, the book in one hand. 'I need some cigarettes.' He donned a pair of sunglasses.

'OK,' the girl responded. On the way to the shop, she said, 'You look better than I expected, Blaise. You look well; do you feel well?'

Blaise remembered that one of the things he had liked about Nicolette was her direct manner. She said what she felt; there was no artifice in her. So he answered her question honestly.

'I feel fine, most of the time, Nikki, but occasionally I feel vulnerable, and sometimes I cannot bear to be around people, and I stay in my room.'

'But you are getting better, aren't you, Blaise?'

'I'm a lot better than I was when I first arrived here. Yes, I'm getting better.'

'I'm glad,' Nicolette responded, smiling up at Blaise. She touched his hand for a moment. They had almost reached the shop, not much more than a tuck shop, run by lady volunteers. Blaise bought a packet of twenty Peter Stuyvesant cigarettes. He did not think to ask whether he could get anything for the girl.

On their return, Blaise made them both an instant coffee in the small pantry attached to the unit. They sat on a low wall outside in the sun and drank their coffees.

'Will you be finishing your degree?' Nicolette asked.

Blaise was silent for a while. Then, 'I hadn't thought about it much. But I suppose I should. What do you think?'

'It would be a shame not to: you were in your final year.'

'Of course, I've just missed this year's intake.'

'Next year, then,' said Nicolette.

'Yeah … next year …'

Chapter Seven

Within a week of returning home (where both Anna and Magda made a great fuss of him, and he in turn was pleased to see Tinker, the Siamese cat, and Heidi, the dog), Blaise turned twenty-one. His father wished to make a bit of an occasion of his eldest son's twenty-first birthday. Guy had the wit to realise that a large party would be inappropriate, but he planned to mark Blaise's return home and his birthday with some sort of celebration, so (without informing Blaise of his plans) he invited Gregory Dillon, and his sister, Nicolette, to a birthday dinner in Blaise's honour. Even Lawrence, now almost sixteen years old, and having just begun his semi-final year at school, made an effort to enter into the spirit of the occasion, and he gave Blaise a leather bound diary for that year, 1976.

'I didn't think you would have gotten around to buying yourself a diary yet,' he told Blaise.

'I hadn't. That's thoughtful of you. Thanks Lorry.'

Lawrence gave his older brother one of his rare smiles.

Hugh (who presented Blaise with a Ronson electric shaver) had brought his current girlfriend to the birthday celebration. This could have been a bad idea: Blaise found it difficult enough right now dealing for any length of time with people he knew, let alone with strangers. But the girl (a pretty brunette) had a quiet, retiring personality, and after a short while, Blaise was able to accept her presence without feeling awkward. There were seven people sitting around the big mahogany dining table for supper. (Guy had decided not to include Blaise's grandparents in the birthday celebration; the family would visit them the coming Sunday).

Although he was not much moved by the gesture, Blaise thanked his father, amidst smiles and laughter, when he was presented with a large, decorative, silver plated key (a purely symbolic gesture: each of the brothers already possessed a front door key). However, when Magda, the cook, as the dinner was being served, gave Blaise a carefully wrapped parcel, which, when he opened it, proved to be a knitted sky blue cable pattern pullover, he felt tears start to his eyes. He stood and embraced the Cook. Kindness could still unman him.

'En hierdie, dis van my, met my gelukwensinge, Master Blaise,' Anna told Blaise, handing him a small package. Opening it he found a small silver crucifix on a chain, wrapped in cotton wool. Blaise embraced Anna too, his eyes wet.

'Dankie, Anna, dis pragtig.'

Blaise of course already wore a crucifix, the small gold crucifix that his mother had worn, but Anna was not to know that, and so as not to hurt her feelings, he slipped the top of his tie loose and undid the top button of his shirt, and fastening the crucifix around his neck, he tucked it beneath his shirt.

But throughout the dinner, Blaise kept finding himself wishing that Roddy had been there. However, no one in the family other than Hugh knew of Blaise's friendship with Roderick Boyd (and Hugh had never actually met Roderick), and Hugh had rather thoughtlessly failed to mention to his father, when the birthday celebration was being planned behind Blaise's back, that Blaise would enjoy Roderick's company that evening.

"I'll phone Youngsfield tomorrow and leave a message for Roddy," Blaise found himself thinking. "He can get a two day pass and spend the night here, and we will get up the mountain together."

Blaise's father, whom his insightful son realised was overcompensating for what he perceived to be his failing in not having managed to become closer to him (but there was also Guy's consciousness of the loss of Blaise's mother, and after that, the suffering Blaise had clearly endured while in the army), had that morning presented Blaise with a brand new, three litre V-8 Triumph Stag sports car, which a salesman from the car dealership had driven to their address. Blaise knew that he ought to have been thrilled: this was a highly sought after sports car among young men his age; he also knew that he ought to be feeling a wave of gratitude towards his father, but he felt neither thrilled nor very grateful.

"I was happy enough with my little Triumph Herald," he was thinking. But he smiled and thanked his father as profusely as he knew how, and during the birthday dinner that evening, he told Lawrence that if he wished, he could have the Triumph Herald when he turned eighteen in just over two years' time.

Saint Blaise

'I wont sell her in the meanwhile,' Blaise told his brother.

After supper, the gathering repaired to the sitting room for their coffee. There had been wine served with the meal, and although Blaise had drunk only two glasses of white wine, this had made him feel tired. He was not used to alcohol anymore, after his long alcohol-free stay at Valkenberg. After a while, Lawrence disappeared to the den, to watch the television. Nationwide public television had at last been introduced in South Africa at the start of that year. There was just one channel, alternating between English and Afrikaans. Blaise had watched some television since returning home, but he did not think very much of it. The American sit-coms which dominated the content did not appeal to him. What he wanted to do was to go upstairs, and pray. Soon after half past nine, he shook hands with Gregory and with Hugh's girlfriend, kissed Nicolette on the cheek, and thanked his friend and his sister for coming, and for the gift edition of the Catholic Missal, bound in soft white leather, that they had jointly given him.

'Please excuse me,' he said. 'I'm feeling tired.'

'May I visit again?' Nicolette asked Blaise.

Blaise blinked slowly. His eyes were tired. 'Yes,' he replied thoughtfully. 'Yes, I would like that.'

In his bedroom, Blaise fell to his knees at the oak *prie-dieu* which had belonged to his mother, and which he had acquired after her death. The kneeler was of padded red leather. On the wall above the *prie-dieu* was fixed a large crucifix made of olive wood from the Holy Land, with the figure of the crucified Christ carved of ivory, which his parents had given him many years ago, and crossing himself,

Blaise directed his eyes towards it for a minute or two. Then he said, in summons, 'Oh, Jesus, oh my Lord,' and after a while, he began to feel a wondrous peace enveloping him. Before long, Blaise was lost to the present, unconscious of his surroundings, swept up in God's love.

Blaise telephoned Youngsfield base the next morning, and Corporal Roderick Boyd was brought to the telephone.

'Roddy, it's Blaise.'

'How are you?' Roderick asked.

'I'm OK. Look, can you get a two day pass soon, and you can spend the night with us, and we can shin up the mountain the next morning?' Blaise asked him.

Roderick replied yes, he could probably do that. He would ring Blaise tomorrow.

'Good. I'll look forward to hearing from you.' They chatted for a while longer, then Roderick told Blaise that he had to go now.

'Until tomorrow, Blaise.'

'Yeah, goodbye Roddy.'

The next day was a Saturday. Roderick telephoned the Cressingham household soon after they had had their breakfast. When Anna called Blaise to the telephone, Roderick said, 'Blaise, I have a two day pass, the rest of today, and tomorrow. Is that OK?'

'That's cool, Roddy. How about I collect you at the gates to the base at about two o' clock? I'll be going to the nine o' clock Mass tomorrow morning. We can go up Skeleton Gorge straight afterwards.'

'That'll be fine, Blaise. Your father wont mind my spending the night at your place?'

'Oh, Dad wont mind. I often had friends over for the night when I was younger.'

'I'll be waiting at the gates at two then,' confirmed Roderick.

'*Ja*, it'll be good to see you again, Roddy.'

On Sunday morning, Roderick having spent the night at the Cressingham home, both young men ate a good breakfast. They would not be back in time for lunch. Blaise headed off for Mass, but he did not suggest that Roderick accompany him.

'I'll be back at about ten-fifteen,' Blaise told Roderick. 'I'll pick you up and we can set straight off. Is that OK?'

At about a quarter to eleven (Blaise had had to change out of his church-going jacket and tie, and make some coffee and sandwiches in the kitchen), the two friends set off on foot for the top gate to Kirstenbosch Garden, and once within the gardens, they worked their way north along the mountainside until they reached Skeleton Gorge and the trail known as the Smuts Track. (This was named after the great war-time statesman and South African Prime Minister, Jan Smuts, who had often employed the ascent in his old age). It was less than ten minutes' walk from the Cressingham home to the top gate of Kirstenbosch Garden, the world famous mountainside botanical gardens. It was a beautiful late summer's day, the sky a clear, shimmering blue, as if charged with an electric current, and the south-easter, that notoriously powerful summertime wind that so often visited Cape Town, was imperceptible here as the young men passed through indigenous woodland, a clear stream of water sounding musically as it leapt and fell to one side of them. The hot sun was by now high in the sky to the north, and once the two young men left the woodland behind them, they would have welcomed the cooling effects of a breeze. Both the friends were dressed in loose shorts and tee-shirts, and each wore boots: Blaise had on a pair of Lubbe's boots, top quality boots made in Stellenbosch (a town not far from Cape Town), and much favoured by the South African hiking community, beneath which he wore thick woollen hiking socks, while Roderick wore similar civilian boots of leather. Roderick wore his SADF fatigue hat, a khaki coloured floppy hat with a stiffened brim, of thick cotton, and Blaise wore something not dissimilar. Both the young men were fit (although Blaise found that he had been breathing a little heavier than he remembered from previous ascents; no doubt a consequence of his smoking. "I really should give up smoking," he thought). Roderick however was not breathing hard at all as they climbed the steep trail.

The two friends had soon left the lower stratum of granite below them, and were within the sandstone formation which constituted the upper reaches of the Table Mountain mass. It had grown warmer, with the sun at its zenith. By a quarter to one (having overtaken two groups of hikers on their way up), they had reached Breakfast Rock at the top of the gorge, a large flat rock overhanging the edge of the mountainside. Here on the Back Table they had gained an altitude of about two thousand five-hundred feet above sea level, and they were once again standing in the cooling breeze of the wind. Blaise, Roderick by his side, turned to gaze at the sublime view. Directly below them lay Kirstenbosch Garden, and

Blaise's home suburb of Bishopscourt; a little nearer Cape Town were the equally leafy, well established suburbs of Kenilworth and Claremont. Beyond Bishopscourt, just over the ridge to the south, was Constantia, a suburb ranking equally with Bishopscourt in status. In the far distance, beyond Muizenberg, they could see a great sweep of False Bay, the waters a sparkling cobalt blue, the distant shore backed by a range of mountains. Far to the east, across the low-lying Cape Flats, could be seen the blue-grey silhouette of an even more impressive mountain range, a natural barrier for several hundred years to the exploration and settlement of the hinterland.

Since about the age of eleven, Blaise had hiked times beyond count on Table Mountain, growing up as he had within easy reach on foot of a number of routes to the top, yet he never tired of the sense of god-like elevation, of the clean air, of a welcome remove from Man's shabby concerns far below. Blaise felt as close to God in a literal, tangible, physical sense, up here in the mountains, as he felt to Him in church during the Mass. Only when he walked one of the Peninsula's wild, unspoiled strands, and gazed at the incoming ocean-swell for ever reaching for the shoreline, did he experience a similar sense of intense physical proximity to God.

Each young man un-stoppered the water canteen he had slung from his shoulder, and drank deeply. Neither commented on the view. There was nothing either could say which would do it justice. But Blaise at last said, 'It's about one o' clock, Roddy. Let's have some sandwiches.'

'Good idea,' Roderick responded. The two young men sat down on the flat expanse of rock, and Blaise reached into the small satchel he was carrying and removed the Tupperware box containing the sandwiches he had made.

'I've got ham with mustard, or cheese and pickled onion, Roddy. Which do you prefer?'

Roderick smiled. 'How about ham with mustard, Blaise?'

'Good choice.' Blaise lifted the corners of the sandwiches until he had found the ham with mustard, and gave his friend two of them. He made a discreet sign of the cross with a closed fist and the knuckle of his thumb above his cheese and pickles sandwiches in blessing, then took a large bite.

After a while, he informed Roderick, 'We've got coffee in a Thermos, too, if you would like some.'

'That's great! *Ja*, I'll have some coffee, please. You're well organised, Blaise.'

They ate in companionable silence, and each had a mug of sweetened black coffee. At the finish of the simple meal, Blaise lighted the only cigarette he would be smoking during the hike. Having smoked it, and stubbed it carefully, he asked, 'Shall we walk?' and Roderick replied, 'Yeah,' and they shortly thereafter entered the forest of Scots pine which then still grew on the Back Table, following the shaded path as it made its way between the dark, resinous trees, and of a sudden, they had exited the fringes of the forest and were once again in bright sunshine, and they saw ahead of them a broad, dark, still body of water. This was the Hely-Hutchinson reservoir, built in the late nineteenth century as part of a system of reservoirs atop Table Mountain, with the aim of supplying Cape Town with water. They crossed the wide reservoir, traversing the dam wall itself, which was built of enormous cut and chiselled blocks of Table Mountain granite, and turning to their left on the far side, they followed the dusty trail to the west, another large body of water, the Woodhead Reservoir, on their left. After a while they could see the steep-sided, deep Disa Gorge opening up below them to their left, and they gazed at the view. They had passed only one small group of walkers, coming the other way. It was by now about a quarter past two; the sun was lower in the sky.

'I could do with another sandwich, and I think there's a bit of coffee left,' Blaise commented. He found a flat topped rock to sit down on, and Roderick joined him. Each young man ate a couple more sandwiches, and Blaise drank another mug of coffee.

They made their way slowly back to the head of Skeleton Gorge and the Smuts Track, beginning their descent at a quarter past three. Both young men were feeling slightly intoxicated, liberated from the world below them, and they almost bounded from foothold to foothold as they descended the gorge, the crowded world of Mankind drawing rapidly nearer. It was something of a shock to enter the gardens, busy with happy visitors that Sunday afternoon, but they were back at the Cressingham home, with its tranquil view across Bishopscourt, by about half past five.

Hugh greeted the pair in the entrance hall. 'You look like you've got some sun,' he said. Both young men showered and changed, Roderick into his army uniform, and after a cold beer each in the den, Blaise drove his friend back to Youngsfield base.

A week later, on a Saturday morning, Blaise collected him again. Roderick had a day pass. Back home, Magda packed the two young men a picnic lunch while they drank a coffee together on the terrace. The extreme summer heat was past; in some respects, thought Blaise, the weather was at its best at this time of the year. They drove together to the Cape Point Nature Reserve, at the southern tip of the Cape Peninsula, and at Platboom Beach, near the southern extremity of the reserve, they sat at the edge of the sandy beach, the only people in sight, and ate an early lunch of cold chicken, salad, bread rolls, and a large piece each of walnut cake baked by Magda. They had a bottle of Cape white wine with them, which they drank from wine glasses that Magda had wrapped carefully in napkins. Blaise lighted a cigarette afterwards, and leant back against the sand dune on one elbow, and watched the Atlantic swell through his sunglasses, as it swept in towards the shoreline. The sun shone brilliantly.

'In a place like this,' Blaise remarked, 'Angola seems like a nightmare from which I have awoken.'

Roderick was the only person Blaise could truly talk to about their time in Angola; the only person who would understand. Roderick was glad that Blaise was talking: he had not been very communicative their previous weekend together.

'Yes,' Roderick agreed, 'and that period shares with nightmares the impossibility of conveying it to others.'

'Your time in the SADF must be almost over,' Blaise said.

'I *klaar out* next month. And then I can get on with my life.'

'You haven't changed your mind, Roddy, been tempted to begin earning money, have you?' Blaise asked his friend.

'No, my folks will carry me a while longer, Blaise – long enough to get my Masters,' Roderick replied. He planned to return to university next year, and obtain first his Honours, then his Master's degrees in Psychology.

Blaise smiled at his friend. 'I wish I was as certain as you are. I'm not sure what I want to do next. I'm thinking of approaching my old school and asking whether they could use me to teach for the remainder of the year – just until I return to varsity next year and do my third year. But what comes after I've got my degree, I'm not sure.'

'You believe in God's guidance, don't you, Blaise?'

Blaise nodded.

'Then God will show you what He wishes you to do.'

'You're right,' Blaise responded. 'Of course you're right.'

Blaise felt the wrench of parting as he dropped his friend off at the gates to Youngsfield Military Base early that evening. He would miss him. But they would get together again soon, of that he was sure – and Roddy would soon have finished with the army.

Roderick turned and waved once as he walked away, a paper bag held in his left hand, a khaki canvas kitbag slung over one shoulder. Magda had baked him a large fruit cake.

'Ag, jy lyk so skraal, Meneer Roderick,' she had said, handing him the bag containing the fruit cake. *'Eet jy nie genoeg nie in die Weermag?'*

Roderick had laughed, and thanked Magda. 'You can fatten me up again the next time I visit, Magda,' he said. Magda had given both young men a huge tea at four o' clock that afternoon, with freshly baked scones, the remainder of the walnut cake, and a variety of sandwiches. Hugh had been out, but Guy Cressingham and Lawrence had joined them on the terrace. Guy approved of young Roderick, who had a clear, workable vision for his life, but he would have been happier had his son brought a girl back with him.

Blaise drove home, feeling suddenly rather sad and alone. "Dont be such an idiot," he thought. Before much longer, he and Roddy could spend as much time together as they wished.

Chapter Eight

Blaise went to see Brother Joseph O' Neill, the school's Headmaster, a week and a half after his birthday. It was now early March, and the summer was running out.

'How are you, Blaise?' Brother Joseph asked.

'Fairly well, Brother Joseph,' Blaise replied. 'I feel better every day. My father tells me the Brothers have been praying for me. I am grateful.'

'I am pleased to hear that you are feeling better, Blaise. Many people here remember you with fondness.'

The two men sat silently for a minute, Brother Joseph quietly assessing the young man across from him. He saw someone who had – literally as well as metaphorically – been through the wars, and whose features were attenuated with recent suffering. Indeed, Blaise had lost weight since Brother Joseph had last seen him: he looked, thought Brother Joseph, more than ever like an El Greco saint – or martyr. Brother Joseph was struck by a strange idea: that he might be in the presence of a holy man in the making. Brother Joseph's gift of perception was both natural and acquired; years of assessing the characters of others – both staff and pupils – as Headmaster, had honed his natural gift for discernment.

Blaise spoke. 'I need something useful to do for the rest of the year. I plan to return to university next year, to complete my degree.'

'Yes … ?'

'Would I be useful to you teaching, Brother Joseph? I was in my third year in English, History and French at university, when I left. I could teach any of those subjects up to Matric level, I think.'

In fact, Blaise could be useful, thought Brother Joseph: Brother Edward Daley, the History Master who had taught Blaise, had had to take a sabbatical while he recovered from a serious illness. He was unlikely to resume his teaching duties until much later in the year. And the English department had been getting by, with some difficulty, short of one teacher for some time. But would Blaise be able to cope with classes of over-energetic, sometimes exuberant, adolescent boys? Perhaps so – he appeared to be remarkably self-contained, and he showed no signs of nervousness, sitting here across the desk from his old Headmaster.

'Do you think you are well enough, Blaise? You remember what boys can be like.'

Blaise believed that he could cope with even the most difficult of boys, after having learned how to rub along with a very mixed bunch of men in the army. 'I believe I could manage,' he replied, but an unpleasant memory surfaced of some of the hard cases he had known in the company. The corner of his mouth twitched as he remembered what those hard cases had done towards the very end of his time in the SADF: the unspeakable horror they had perpetrated. But Blaise was only rarely now a hostage to that memory, and the Headmaster noticed nothing unusual in his expression.

'In fact, I think we could find you useful, Blaise. You would have to become, technically at least, a lay brother, and don the habit. And of course, we could not pay you.'

Blaise gave a fleeting smile. 'Money is not a problem, Brother Joseph. I wouldn't need you to pay me.'

'Well – the sooner you could begin, the better. Brother Edward Daley has had to stop teaching History for a while, due to sickness. Brother Bernard Riley (on hearing his old form master's name spoken, Blaise smiled more fully) has taken over his teaching duties, but Brother Bernard has no more than a Matric pass in History. And we could also use you in the English department.'

Blaise sat and listened. Brother Joseph continued, 'Would you wish to live in Community? You could have a room of your own (the Order no longer called the Brothers' rooms "cells"), and dine in Community.'

'I would like that.'

'Good! Can you move across this Saturday, and begin teaching on Monday?'

Blaise nodded. 'I'll do that, Brother Joseph.'

Brother Joseph stood. Blaise followed suit, and Brother Joseph said, 'God be with you,' and they shook hands.

Was God, Blaise wondered, busy mapping out his destiny? Or would this prove to be just a way-station on his pilgrimage through Life? It was not very important that Blaise knew the answer to that question, he realised. He had complete trust in God's plan for him, whatever it should prove to be.

Blaise did not have to take vows of poverty and chastity, but there was a clothing ceremony on Sunday (during which he knelt, wearing the white habit – minus the cowl – of the Order for the first time, in front of Father Justin Hurley, the Father Guardian), and he made some promises, chief of which were to obey his superiors within the community, and to conduct himself in a manner befitting the habit he was now wearing.

Blaise found that asserting his authority in the classroom was not as difficult as Brother Joseph for one had feared it might be, for in addition to the air of self containment about him, which hinted at a rigorous self discipline, there was a hint of asceticism in his angular features, which rather overawed the boys. Blaise began to enjoy teaching History and English. After a while, he also began taking a few boys for extra lessons in French. Blaise had been so recently a happily institutionalised in-patient at Valkenberg, and he now felt very much at home living as a member of the religious community. He rejoined the school choir, bringing his exceptionally pure, powerful tenor, able to take descant parts, to that body, and just as it had been as a schoolboy, lifting up his voice in praise of God brought him joy. He attended the Community's Mass every morning, along with the two school Masses each week. As often as he could, however, he joined his father – and sometimes Lawrence, although rarely Hugh – at Saint Mark's parish church in Newlands for Sunday morning Mass. The Cressingham family maid, Anna, was a Catholic, and she always accompanied Mr. Cressingham and whichever family members joined him, to Sunday morning Mass, although once inside the church, she did not sit with the family, but sat at the back with the other Coloured people attending the Mass. So Blaise did not lose himself entirely in the life of a religious; he kept up his contacts with his family.

Blaise had of course not fenced since quitting university (fencing was not a sporting priority in an army on a war footing), but he began fencing again at the school. Brother Anthony Tobin, his old PT teacher and fencing master, was glad to welcome him back, another adult to help with the tuition of young fencers and would-be fencers. Blaise cut down savagely the number of cigarettes he smoked, although he was unable to do entirely without a cigarette after lunch, and a couple in the evening, after supper.

Guy Cressingham, unhappy with Blaise immersing himself in the life of a religious, invited Nicolette Dillon to lunch at the family home one Sunday in late March. Blaise (as he often did on a Sunday) would be joining the family for lunch.

'Nikki!' exclaimed Blaise, on finding her with the family in the sitting room before lunch. 'I didn't know you were coming for lunch.'

'It's nice to see Nicolette again, isn't it, Blaise?' asked Guy.

'Yeah, it is,' responded Blaise, smiling at the girl.

Nicolette, as slight and sweet as ever, smiled almost shyly at Blaise. She had an idea that he was halfway to becoming a Religious, and she was unsure of the degree to which she could exercise familiarity with him. But he seemed genuinely glad to see her, in that respect the same old Blaise, and she relaxed immediately.

'You are looking so much better, Blaise – or do I call you Brother Blaise?'

Blaise laughed. '"Blaise" will do. Only the boys at school address me as "Brother Blaise." It's too complicated to try to explain to them exactly what my status is. I'm not sure I know myself.'

Anna, the maid, greeted Nicolette. She had known her, as the little sister of Master Blaise's best friend at school, ever since she had begun working for the Cressingham family. Then she said, addressing Guy Cressingham, 'Lunch is ready to be served, *Meneer*.'

'OK, Anna. We're coming.' The three brothers followed their father (who had taken Nicolette by the arm) into the dining room. Hugh managed to be present at most Sunday lunches. Lawrence, aged sixteen, but still the shortest and darkest by far of the three brothers, followed behind his older brothers.

Guy sat down at the head of the long, polished mahogany dining table, which had a centre piece of dried King Protea blooms arranged in a large copper basin. Just down from him on his right sat Blaise, with Nicolette to Blaise's right; opposite Blaise sat Hugh, with Lawrence seated to his left. Once everyone had a bowl of soup placed in front of them, Guy said the blessing. Having joined in the collective "Amen," Blaise added under his breath, "I love you, Mum. God keep you in Heaven," his invariable practice at the end of his father's blessing.

Magda had roasted a top rump of beef, with delicious golden baked potatoes, caramelised baked parsnips and carrots cut in half lengthwise, and fresh garden peas from

Saint Blaise

the farm shop in Constantia. (Since his wife had passed away, Guy had necessarily had to take over responsibility for shopping for groceries: he took Magda with him once a week in his brand-new Mercedes-Benz 280E, and they would shop in Claremont, and at the farm shop in Constantia).

Blaise tucked in with a will: he had regained a healthy appetite, and was beginning to recover some of the weight he had lost in Angola (and had failed to regain entirely during his stay at Valkenberg). But he still looked not a little like some Renaissance saint, thought Nicolette. (In this assessment, her response to his appearance was similar to that of Brother Joseph O' Neill, although it was unlikely that Brother Joseph thought Blaise to be, as Nicolette most certainly did, "beautiful").

The family and their guest repaired to the terrace, with its view across Bishopscourt, for their coffee. The late summer weather was still fine, although no longer as warm as it had been even a fortnight earlier. On the bougainvillea-clad north-facing terrace, they were sheltered from the wind by the bulk of the house behind them. Blaise lighted a cigarette.

'You're still smoking those damned things, I see!' Guy Cressingham exclaimed, largely for Nicolette's sake. He did not really hold any strong opinions on smoking. He himself was known to smoke an occasional cigar.

'Yeah, but I've cut down, Dad.'

Guy grinned, in a good humour induced by the company of a pretty young woman at their gathering. 'Well, cut down some more, Blaise.'

Blaise smiled. 'I'll try, Dad.'

It was the fourth week of Lent, and Blaise had cut sugar out of his diet. He shunned sugar in his tea and coffee (both of which, anyway, he drank black), and he avoided cakes and sweet deserts. While the others had happily enjoyed the sponge pudding dripping with hot syrup which had followed the roast beef, Blaise had ate an apple. He had gone without smoking during the first few days of Lent, but this had put him in such a bad mood, that he had decided that the good it might be doing his soul was outweighed by the harm, and so he had resumed smoking, although reducing fairly severely the number of cigarettes a day he smoked. He was currently lighting up no more than half a dozen cigarettes a day.

Once the roast beef lunch had settled somewhat, Blaise said to Nicolette, 'Let's go for a stroll, Nikki. We can take Heidi with us.'

'I'd like that,' responded Nicolette.

Heidi was on the terrace with the family. 'Walkies!' Blaise said to her, and stood up. Heidi leapt to her feet, her tail wagging fast, and the three of them went through to the entrance hall, where Blaise took Heidi's lead from the coat stand. The eager dog was gambolling about their feet, but she stood still as Blaise attached the lead to her collar, and they set off down the gravelled driveway, past the triple garages on their left, past the independent entrance to the guest suite above the garages, and past the gateway to the servants' court. They descended by easy stages to the valley floor below, and as they were walking past Bishopscourt itself (the Anglican Archbishop of Cape Town's large residence, set in its extensive grounds, after which the suburb of Bishopscourt was named), Blaise asked Nicolette how things were going at university.

'I'm enjoying myself, Blaise,' she replied. 'I'm a member of the Students' Dramatic Society, you know. We're going to be staging Anton Checkov's *"The Cherry Orchard"* next term. I've been cast as Dunyasha, the housemaid. It's a great part!'

'Yes, I know *"The Cherry Orchard,"*' Blaise responded. 'Playing the part of Dunyasha should be fun.'

Nicolette laughed. 'She's a character! And so over the top.'

Blaise too laughed. 'And you're not at all over the top, are you, Nikki?'

Nicolette smiled. 'I can liberate that side of my character while playing Dunyasha.'

'Let me know the dates of the performance,' said Blaise. 'I'll come watch if I can. How are you doing with your major?'

Like Hugh, Nicolette was in her third year of university studies. She was majoring in Sociology and Psychology, and although he had been two years ahead of her, she had known Roderick Boyd slightly. Blaise had mentioned his faithful friend to Nicolette. 'Have you seen Roderick recently?' she asked.

'Yes, not long ago. He stayed overnight, and we went up the Smuts Track together.'

'I'd like to come up with you sometime, Blaise,' said Nicolette, turning to him with a smile. Heidi was much taken by some interesting scent in the verges as they were passing the big varnished wooden gates to the Archbishop's residence. Blaise halted, to permit the dog to enjoy her olfactory exploration.

'Yes, we can do that, Nikki,' Blaise answered her. Nicolette lived at home, and the Dillon and Cressingham homes were of course not far apart. 'I'm busy with fencing tuition on Saturday mornings,' he continued, 'and of course there's Mass on Sunday mornings, but we could take a packed lunch with us, and leave after Mass.'

'That sounds perfect,' Nicolette responded. 'Perhaps next Sunday?'

Blaise was watching the dog. 'Come along Heidi,' he said, and commenced walking again. He turned to Nicolette. 'OK,' he said. 'I'll be at Saint Mark's for Mass next Sunday; I'll probably see you there. Why don't you meet me at our place afterwards, once you've changed, and we can set off together. I'll get Magda to pack us something to eat.'

Nicolette smiled happily up at Blaise. 'That'll be lovely!'

'It's a date then,' said Blaise.

On returning to the Cressingham home, they joined Blaise's father, who was sitting alone on the terrace. Guy had a glass of white wine on the table alongside him, and the *Sunday Times* was open on his lap. He was gratified at hearing the two young people laughing together as they came outside. He would far prefer to see Blaise married, with children, than becoming a religious – no matter which of the religious orders (as he feared was likely to be the case in the long term) eventually claimed him.

Chapter Nine

The first that Blaise knew of the Soweto Massacre on Wednesday the 16th June that year, was when edited images of the incident appeared on the SABC's single channel of TV in that evening's news. The camera would pan across the thousands of young black marchers, then across ranks of white policemen armed with pump action shotguns. The next day, during the school lunch break, Blaise read of the march by several thousand black school children in Soweto to Orlando Stadium, protesting against the compulsory use of Afrikaans as a teaching medium in black schools; a march that culminated in the police gunning down scores (later claims were made that the figure ran into the hundreds) of black school pupils.

Blaise felt a stirring of rage against the regime; the same regime that had sent him to Angola in what proved to be a useless war against Cuban troops. Despite being brought up, as middle class white children in South Africa then were, to regard the police as their allies against potential expressions of anarchic black and coloured criminality and even possible insurrection, the photographs in the *Cape Argus* and the

Cape Times, particularly those showing the police firing their shotguns into the crowd of black school pupils, horrified Blaise. The soon to be globally iconic image of the black twelve year old, Hector Pietersen, dying in the arms of his would-be rescuer, filled Blaise with rage against the system that enabled such a murderous response to black protest. The Brothers, as they smoked their after-lunch cigarettes and drank their coffee, could speak of little else. Almost everyone seemed to feel that a line had been crossed: that nothing in South Africa would ever be quite the same again. Blaise felt this particularly acutely.

In the early evening, Roderick (who was by now once again a civilian) telephoned Blaise at the school. After expressing their mutual shock, horror, and anger against the police, and against the Apartheid system that empowered them, Roderick asked Blaise whether he wished to join what would be a necessarily illegal protest (open air protests and demonstrations in Cape Town had been declared illegal since 1973) against police brutality, which NUSAS (the National Union of South African Students) would be staging on the steps of Saint George's Anglican Cathedral in Cape Town city centre the next day.

'There's a possibility we'll meet with police violence. We may be arrested,' Roderick told Blaise. 'But I cannot stand by after this.'

But Blaise cringed inwardly, as images of uniformed men, firearms raised to their shoulders, came to mind. Blaise would never fully recover from the trauma he had suffered in Angola: violence – or the prospect of violence – terrified him. And there was the Order: what would the Order have to say about a member of its school teaching staff taking part in an illegal demonstration?

'I cannot,' Blaise told Roderick. 'I made promises to the Order.'

But this was not the real reason for Blaise's reluctance to say that he would be there. After all, there were several well-known anti-Apartheid activists among the Catholic priesthood; there were Catholic priests who had been arrested. The Archbishop of Durban, Denis Hurley, for example, was a prominent South African Catholic clerical voice against Apartheid. No, Blaise was afraid not because he was by nature a coward (he was not), but because he had been so severely traumatised by events during the Angolan campaign that the prospect of violence, especially uniformed and armed violence, threatened to unman him.

Roderick was already regretting that he had asked Blaise to join him in Friday's demonstration: he should have known better! How could he have forgotten how Blaise might respond to the prospect of violent confrontation?

'Forgive me, Blaise,' he said. 'I shouldn't have asked you.'

'I'll call you back ...' Blaise responded. He put the telephone down.

Afterwards, Blaise knelt at the *prie-dieu* in his room. Above him the figure of Our Lord, carved in wood, stared down in anguished pity from his cross. Blaise felt ashamed. He prayed for strength to overcome (as he saw it) his cowardice. Early the next morning he telephoned Roderick.

'Roddy – its Blaise. What time is the protest?'

'We're meeting at eleven o' clock,' Roderick answered.

'OK. I'll be there if I can.'

Blaise did not ask the Headmaster for permission to absent himself later that morning. He merely left a message with the Headmaster's secretary, a young Brother named Gerald Quinn, saying that he would be away during the second half of the morning, to attend to a personal matter. This was remiss of Blaise, and out of character too: Blaise was usually extremely honest. But he now felt compelled to attend the protest: he had to prove to himself that his initial reluctance to participate in the event did not stem from cowardice. He was sure however that if he had asked the Headmaster for leave of absence to attend an illegal public protest in Cape Town, Brother Joseph would have refused him his permission. Shortly after ten o' clock that morning, Blaise removed his white habit, and put on jeans and a leather jacket, and set off in his sports car for Cape Town city centre.

He parked some distance up Wale Street, and walked towards Saint George's Cathedral. It was a rare fine winter's morning, a still, calm day, the sky almost clear, the sun remarkably bright for this time of year. Walking beneath bare, leafless trees, Blaise was glad of the sunglasses he wore. He found a group of young people, UCT students, already gathering on the Cathedral steps. Roderick stood out among them, his attenuated build and his height making him especially noticeable.

'Blaise!' Roderick greeted him, shaking his friend's hand. 'I wish I hadn't phoned you, but I'm glad you're here. Thanks for coming. Perhaps nothing much will happen.'

'I prayed about this,' Blaise responded. 'It seemed to me that I was meant to be here.' Roderick was not yet himself a committed Christian, but he was certainly sympathetic towards the Faith, and as a consequence of Blaise's influence (Blaise's fundamental goodness, his absolute confidence and trust in God, and his quiet certainty of the fact of his salvation, impressed Roderick), he was growing closer to making a personal commitment to Christ. Where another man might have found Blaise's statement embarrassing, Roderick accepted it as part of the Blaise he loved.

The group was growing in numbers even as the two friends stood speaking. Soon there were upwards of twenty students and sympathisers, all of them young – with the exception of the Anglican Dean, standing in his black cassock at the head of the Cathedral steps.

The group raised large home-made banners. "End Police Brutality!" was the dominant message. And at half past eleven, four police vans drew up just beyond the foot of the Cathedral steps, and armed white police officers in combat uniforms spilled from the vans. Several of their numbers blocked off Wale Street's westbound lane to traffic at the junction with Adderley Street. The police, all of them armed with shotguns, lined up in Wale Street, looking up at the protesters, who began shouting in unison, 'End police brutality!' One of the policemen stepped forward with a megaphone. He halted a few feet infront of Blaise and Roderick as they stood in the front ranks of the group of protesters; so close that Blaise could see where he had nicked his chin shaving that morning.

'This is an illegal gathering!' he declared, his voice, with its pronounced Afrikaans accent, enormously amplified. 'If you do not disperse, you will be arrested!'

The protesters shouted back all the louder, 'End police brutality!' On the far side of the street, a small group of people, including newspaper photographers, had gathered, eager to see what would happen next. Among them was an SABC TV crew with a camera. The police officer stepped back within the ranks of his men, and while the police stood, immobile, the young protesters shouted slogans and shook their signs.

Neither Roderick nor Blaise was shouting. They felt they stood out enough: both were by far the tallest people in the group, and they looked older than most of the other protesters. Blaise felt a frisson of fear, as he stared at the police line within a few feet of him, those armed men in their combat uniforms. His mind was on the verge of flipping him back in time, to the Angolan bush. He trembled slightly. Roderick put his arm around Blaise's shoulders, squeezed, then released him.

The police officer stepped forward again and raised his megaphone to his mouth. 'You are taking part in an illegal gathering! If you do not disperse, you will be arrested!' But the protesters ignored him, except to raise their voices even louder. The Anglican Dean of the Cathedral moved discreetly into the shadows of the porch. Blaise was perspiring beneath his leather jacket. The onlookers on the opposite pavement had grown in numbers. Ten minutes went by, during which the police officer had once again stepped back within the ranks of his men. Then Blaise saw him looking at his watch. Blaise glanced at his own watch: it was just after noon. The police officer yelled a command in Afrikaans to his men. The front rank raised their shotguns to their shoulders. Blaise's lips began to move as his trembling increased. 'God help us, Lord help us,' he said under his breath.

The police officer yelled another command, and there was an enormous crash of sound, as the foremost rank of policemen, aiming well above the protesters' heads, fired their shotguns. Lead shot bounced against the Cathedral's stone walls, and there was a light tinkling of broken glass from some of the lower panes of the high windows above them. Blaise, along with most of the other protesters, flinched, and several of them ducked. Grey smoke, accompanied by the scent of cordite, moved lazily in the air. Blaise felt suddenly as if he might lose control of his bowels and bladder, and quite involuntarily, he pushed back into the group, then turned, and used his broad shoulders to force a way up the steps. But he was not alone in this sudden retreat: the group began to break up, and there was a general movement up the steps towards the wide Cathedral doors. Pushing and shoving, Blaise among those in the lead, the young protesters funnelled through the Cathedral doors, seeking sanctuary within the precincts of the building. The police surged up the steps behind them, at which the Anglican Dean stepped into the middle of the entryway, his arms widespread.

'This is a holy place!' he shouted. 'You cannot enter with weapons!'

There was a loud command in Afrikaans, and the police halted, just a few feet from the Cathedral doors, and within seconds, the heavy wooden doors, with their decorative design patterned in wrought iron, were slammed shut, the Dean and the protesters behind them.

Blaise almost fell into one of the light wooden chairs which served the Cathedral congregation. He was trembling, and tears were running silently down his cheeks. Roderick pulled up a chair and sat down alongside him, and put his arm around his friend's shoulders.

'You are the bravest man I know, Blaise. But you shouldn't have come, and I shouldn't have asked you.'

Roderick had brought a bottle of water with him, and Blaise drank thirstily from it. He needed a cigarette, but he could not smoke inside the Cathedral.

Over an hour passed before the Dean was able to persuade the leaders of the protest to allow him to negotiate their exit with the police. Then he had one of the heavy wooden doors opened, and he stepped outside. The officer commanding the police stepped forward, and the two men, both of them well accustomed to the exercise of authority, spoke for a while. Then the Dean stepped back inside the building, but the door was left open behind him. After speaking with the protesters' leaders for a while, the Dean led the group towards an inconspicuous door on the southern side of the Cathedral building, and the young people followed the Dean through the door and into a range of Cathedral offices, via which they exited the building, and found themselves in the open. It was about a quarter past two, and Blaise immediately lighted a cigarette, puffing greedily at it. Many of the protesters made their way down the narrow lane named Government Avenue, and as they did so, they passed a small group of policemen. There were a number of catcalls from some of the youngsters, but no one halted to engage in an altercation with the police: they were, if truth be told, relieved to be spared arrest; their hot blood had had time to cool.

Government Avenue gave onto the corner of Wale and Adderley Streets, and Blaise and Roderick made their way back along the far side of Wale Street towards Blaise's sports car. Blaise was feeling too shaken to drive, but Roderick, who had been given a lift to the protest, drove Blaise back to the school, where he joined him in his room. They sat for a while in silence, then Blaise, a cigarette in his fingers, said to Roderick, 'I felt myself on the edge of losing it when the police opened fire.'

'I think most of us were freaked out.'

Blaise asked, 'Would you like a coffee?'

'I wouldn't mind.'

The two made their way to a small pantry which served the Brothers' domestic quarters, and here there was a kettle and a jar of instant coffee. Blaise made two mugs of coffee, both of them heavily sweetened, and he found some milk in the refrigerator for Roderick. They took their coffees back to Blaise's room.

At about half past four, Blaise drove Roderick home. Blaise felt calm now. He no longer trembled; his mind was no longer agitated; the palms of his hands were no longer damp. Having dropped Roderick off in Kenilworth, Blaise drove to the Cressingham home in Bishopscourt. He realised how lucky he had been; how much worse the entire episode might have been. God had been with him, he thought. He doubted that the police would have injured the protesters – rich white kids – but they might easily have been arrested. Nonetheless, the evidence that he was not over his trauma, distressed Blaise. He needed a few hours at home. Blaise was not yet as deeply immersed in the life of a religious as his father thought.

Blaise telephoned the school, and told them that he would not be there for supper, but that he would be back later that evening. He ate supper with his father and Lawrence – Hugh was absent – and sat with his father after supper, enjoying a large brandy with him, while he smoked another two cigarettes. It was half past ten that night before Blaise drove through the school gates and parked his car and set off for his room. Most of the Brothers, following the communal recitation of Compline, the last Office of the day, were already abed. Blaise met no one as he made his way to his room.

Chapter Ten

The short-lived protest outside Saint George's Cathedral featured in both the *Argus* and the *Cape Times* the next morning, a Saturday, and the nationwide *Sunday Times* also ran a piece on it the following day. There were several photographs accompanying these reports, and in one of them, Blaise, despite his sunglasses, was clearly identifiable. "Trouble," he thought. He was not surprised when, after his second class on Monday morning was over (this one an English class), he received a summons to the Headmaster's office.

Brother Joseph O' Neill was holding a copy of the *Sunday Times* in his hands. 'Sit down, Blaise,' he said. Blaise sat. 'You've seen the newspapers?' Brother Joseph asked.

'Yes, Brother Joseph. I've seen them.'

'And you've seen this photograph – the photograph in which you are easily identifiable?'

'Yes, Brother Joseph.'

'Blaise, I share your sympathies. But you are a member of staff at our school, and you must know that many of the parents of our boys are deeply conservative, and they would take it amiss if they knew that members of the school's staff were taking part in illegal protests.'

'I understand, Brother Joseph. But it was something I had to do.'

'Are you likely to participate in any more of these gatherings?'

Blaise was thoughtful. He had a great regard for the truth. 'Probably not, Brother Joseph,' he replied, 'but it is possible.'

'Now, I am asking you as your Superior – and please bear in mind, you made certain promises to the Order – I am asking you not to participate in any more such gatherings as long as you remain a member of this school's staff.'

Blaise considered this request. It was more than a request; it was of course a command. He understood that he was being presented with a choice: he could undertake further political activism, or he could remain a member of the school's staff. He could not do both. Which was more important to him? What would God wish him to decide?

And he remembered his near incapacitating fear on Friday, as the police fired that warning volley. He made his mind up.

'Very well,' he said, 'I will not take part in any more public protests.' Why did he seem to hear a cock crowing thrice as he spoke these words?

The Headmaster smiled. 'I'm glad,' he said. 'It would have been a waste of your talents had you decided to leave us now.'

Brother Joseph had of course always been a rather distant figure throughout Blaise's schooling, and something of the awe that Blaise had then felt for him remained still. But the Headmaster's smile was genuine, as was his pleasure at Blaise's decision, a pleasure which went some way to making Blaise feel better about himself.

'You are an extremely valuable member of staff, Blaise,' Brother Joseph continued. 'Multi-facetted. You are the only teacher qualified to take the Matric History students at the moment, and I know that the English and French departments appreciate your help too. And Brother Anthony Tobin tells me he finds you very useful during fencing lessons.'

The Headmaster stood, Blaise following suit. The older man took Blaise by the elbow as they headed for the door to the office. 'I would be very pleased if you decided your future lay with the Order, Blaise,' Brother Joseph said. 'The Father Guardian agrees with me.' Both men halted at the door.

'I think I shall finish my degree next year, Headmaster,' Blaise replied. 'But after that – perhaps …'

'Well, we'll see,' Brother Joseph responded. 'There would be much to discuss… . good … until later, Blaise.'

'Thank you, Brother Joseph.'

Blaise's future did not, however, lie with the order of teaching brothers.

During the second half of 1976, following the Soweto Massacre, the mounting unrest and racial tension across South Africa was marked by shocking levels of police brutality and violence in putting down marches, demonstrations and protests. These incidents brought into stark relief for Blaise the importance of working for social and political justice –

not only in South Africa, but anywhere in the world where social and political justice were faced with opposition from established élites. Blaise did not think the teaching order which was represented at the school was the best means of his undertaking such work. As he now realised, the school was unwilling to challenge the establishment.

In February 1977, just before his twenty-second birthday, Blaise recommenced his third-year studies at university. Blaise had become a member of the Catholic Students Society during his first year at university. He now became more deeply involved in CathSoc activities than ever before. The Catholic Chaplain at the university was a Jesuit priest, and Blaise had grown to know him well over time. Father Edmund Bartlet SJ was a fit and active man in his forties, with aristocratic English and Scottish links, and he was very popular among the Catholic students at UCT. Both Blaise and Father Edmund saw in the other an asset to the Faith. During his third year, Blaise came to know, and count as friends, the two young "Scholastics" (as Jesuit novices for the priesthood were called) who were studying at UCT, and who were living in the Jesuit community located in Christow Road in Rosebank, a suburb which lay within easy walking distance of the university campus.

By late 1977 it was clear to Blaise, and to Father Edmund (and for that matter, to Father Michael Schmidt SJ, the Christow Road Superior, a German-born priest whose full title was "Father Superior"), that Blaise would almost certainly be seeking to become a member of the Society of Jesus. As they ascended the Jeep Track from Constantia Nek on a Saturday morning in late October, Blaise was

Saint Blaise

telling Roderick, who remained his closest friend, about the spiritual direction he found himself following. They had halted to admire the splendid view across the semi-rural suburb of Constantia. In the distance they could see the blue waters of False Bay, whose far shoreline was marked by the Hottentots Holland mountain range.

'You see Roddy,' Blaise was saying, 'the Jesuits have a reputation around the world for a willingness to challenge political, economic and social injustice. Have you heard the term "Liberation Theology"?'

'Yes,' replied Roderick, 'I've come across it, although I'm not entirely sure I understand it.'

'It's a term that arose with regard to Jesuit missionary work in South America, pursuing social and political justice in the right wing dictatorships that abound in that region,' explained Blaise, 'and it embodies a belief that Christ seeks to free us from oppression not only of the spirit, but of the body too. The Jesuits recognise that it is difficult to realise the full extent of Christ's salvation if you are suffering from political and material oppression. Starving and oppressed people aren't much concerned with their souls' salvation.'

'I see,' Roderick responded. 'I can understand how that would be relevant in South Africa today.'

'Liberation theology appeals to me,' Blaise continued. 'Membership of the Society of Jesus is the best vehicle I can imagine for pursuing the objectives of liberation theology.'

'"Society of Jesus"?' Roderick interjected. 'Is that the formal name for the Jesuit order?'

'*Ja*, the Society of Jesus.'

The Jeep Track was a narrow unpaved road built for

vehicular access to the Back Table and the catchment reservoirs atop it, constructed at the turn of the century. It commenced opposite the restaurant at the crest of Constantia Nek (a *"nek"* being a pass), and ascended gradually to the Back Table. It was a lovely hike, forested with cool, dark Scots pine during its early stages, but after a while breaking free of the tall trees, and rewarding the hiker with magnificent views. The two young men were dressed – as always when they hiked in the mountains during the summer months – in shorts and tee-shirts, and both wore floppy cotton hats with stiffened narrow brims. Roderick carried a small pack on his back in which were a water canteen and a Tupperware container of sandwiches. Blaise favoured a small satchel of sturdy khaki cotton, slung across his shoulders, to carry his provisions. He had taken to using a walking stick when he hiked in the mountains, not because he had any physical need of it, but because he found it agreeable to do so.

At home, Heidi the dog (now very old indeed, but still up for a gentle stroll to Rhodes Drive and back again) would wag her tail and rise to her feet if she saw Blaise reaching for a walking stick, of which he had several, in the stand in the entrance hall.

'Not now, old girl,' he had said that morning, knuckling the thick fur between her ears. 'I'll take you out this afternoon.'

The two friends were nearing the top of the ascent, at an elevation of approximately two thousand five hundred feet. Tiny, brightly coloured sunbirds, their iridescent plumage flashing in the sun, were feeding on the nectar of proteas and other wild flowers that grew on the mountainside.

Blaise had earlier heard the barking of baboons from above them. He was content: the mountains had granted him soul's ease since his earliest adolescence, and he had by now grown accustomed to sharing them with Roderick. The two friends' shared experiences in Angola would be a bond that would unite them all their lives. For the most part, it was an unarticulated bond, as they rarely talked about their time in the SADF anymore. But they shared experiences in common that they shared with no other friend.

The two young men made their way through the forest of Scots pines atop the Back Table, pine needles and fallen pine cones beneath their feet, amidst trees which smelled of resin. They stepped abruptly into sunshine again as they reached the big Hely-Hutchinson Reservoir with its dark, tea coloured water, the smooth, rather sinister surface unruffled by disturbance, and they crossed over by the dam wall itself (a retaining wall built of enormous blocks of Table Mountain granite), and on the far side they sat beneath a lone pair of Scots pines and ate their sandwiches. They would go no further today. Both young men had academic work at home that needed tackling this weekend. Furthermore, Father Edmund Bartlet was giving a dinner this evening for half a dozen youngsters at the Society of Jesus Chaplaincy in Rondebosch: his guests (two of whom were young women) were all CathSoc members, and they included the two Jesuit Scholastics. Blaise had been invited, but first he wished to type up a clean copy of an essay he had been researching in the university main library all week, then take Heidi for a short walk, with time in hand to get ready for the dinner in Rondebosch, just a few miles from Bishopscourt via Rhodes Drive.

Generally, neither Roderick nor Blaise had much to say when hiking together; the tranquillity each experienced in the mountains would have been marred by too much unnecessary conversation; their camaraderie did not require words with which to express itself. But they exchanged a few words now, as they sat in the broken shadows of the pair of Scots pines, eating their sandwiches and drinking coffee from the Thermos flask that Blaise had brought with him. They talked about the academic work they were busy with. Roderick was working on his Psychology Honours thesis. Blaise (two years behind schedule, for he had been in his third year when he had quit his studies in May 1975 in favour of undergoing his national service) would be writing his third year finals in November.

Then, unexpectedly, Roderick announced, 'I would like to come to Mass with you tomorrow, if I may.' He had not expressed an interest in attending Mass before now.

'What brought this on?' Blaise asked, smiling at his friend.

'You talk about the Church so often, and in such a matter-of-fact fashion. It seems to be so much a part of your everyday life, and Church membership, and Mass attendance, appear to you to be perfectly normal, whereas for a majority of people, especially people our age, they're quite rare. I wonder sometimes what is about the Catholic Church, about the Mass in particular, that draws you so much. I think I need to try to find out – before you leave for the Novitiate in England later next year.'

'I'm attending the ten o' clock Mass at the Chaplaincy tomorrow morning. Could I collect you on the way?' (On a Sunday morning the Chaplaincy Mass was celebrated later than the weekday Mass, because of the number of UCT students who attended).

'Yeah, I'd like that, Blaise,' Roderick responded.

'OK then, I'll pick you up at half past nine.'

The relatively few Jesuits then working in South Africa fell under the authority of the Salisbury Mission in Rhodesia (which in turn fell under the authority of the British Province), and it had been decided that Blaise would probably be leaving South Africa later the next year for a two year stay at the Jesuit Novitiate in England. Roderick, who loved Blaise (and who would love him all his life), dreaded Blaise's absence. He knew that he would miss him very much indeed.

The two friends had descended the Jeep Track by soon after two o' clock, and Blaise had dropped Roderick off in Kenilworth by three o' clock, and was home before half past three. As he had promised her, he took Heidi for her short walk. (The dear old dog was very slow now, but she still enjoyed the interesting scents and aromas along the way, and Blaise tried not to think what it would be like once she was no longer part of his life). Afterwards, he made himself a mug of coffee in the kitchen, greeting Anna as he did so, and then he settled down to work for an hour and a half on his essay, before having to get ready for the dinner at the Chaplaincy that evening. He was looking forward to the dinner: Father Edmund was stimulating and amusing company, and Blaise anticipated enjoying the company of the other youngsters who would be there.

The Sunday morning Mass at the Chaplaincy comprised a youthful congregation. The two Scholastics of course were there, and over a dozen students, almost all of them members of CathSoc, and known to Blaise. Two or three of the youngsters also knew Roderick from the university, or they had seen him before in Blaise's company, and they greeted him cheerfully. Blaise introduced Roderick to Father Edmund before the Mass commenced.

'Father Edmund, this is Roderick Boyd, my very good friend.' Blaise smiled. 'He's an Anglican, in theory, but he cannot help that. Roderick, meet Father Edmund Bartlet, the Catholic Chaplain at the university.'

The two men shook hands. 'You are very welcome, Roderick,' Father Edmund told him. 'Will you stay for coffee and a chat afterwards?'

Roderick looked a touch alarmed. Blaise reassured his friend. 'We meet for coffee together after Mass, Roddy.'

Roderick, who had feared for a moment that he was to have to engage in a private interview with the priest, looked relieved. 'Sure. I'd like that,' he said.

Roderick, who had attended an Anglican Holy Communion service at school once a week, and had been to Holy Communion services at Anglican churches a few times since then, was pleased and surprised at how reassuringly familiar the Catholic Mass was. The liturgy was almost identical to the Anglican liturgy, and Father Edmund's vestments were in no way different to those of an Anglican priest. Roderick had not realised how "Catholic" the Anglican Church in South Africa was. He quickly relaxed, and found himself about to join the others when they went forward to receive communion, before recollecting that this he could not, as a non-Catholic, do.

Blaise introduced Roderick to Father Michael Schmidt,

the Jesuit Superior in Cape Town, after the Mass. Father Michael and his secretary, a young Jesuit Brother, had entered the chapel only minutes before the Mass commenced.

'Father Superior, this is my friend Roderick Boyd. Roderick, this is Father Michael Schmidt, the Superior in Cape Town.'

Shaking hands, the two men greeted each other. Father Michael, who had strong, rather severe features, lacked Father Edmund's ready charm, and he was considerably older than Father Edmund, possibly in his late fifties.

'How do you do, Father,' said Roderick.

Father Michael's accent was marked by his native Germany. 'You are welcome in our little community, Roderick.'

'I was surprised at how familiar the Mass was,' Roderick told Blaise as they stood drinking coffee. 'I had no idea how little the Catholic Liturgy of the Mass differed from the Anglican Liturgy of Holy Communion.'

'What did you feel during the Mass, Roddy?' Blaise asked his friend. 'Did you feel anything?'

Roderick pondered for a moment. Then, 'I felt comforted, at ease, almost embraced by the environment.'

Blaise smiled. 'That's good. That's a good way to feel during the Mass.'

'I need to talk to you sometime – I have questions to ask you, especially about … oh … what do you call it? "The Real Presence," you know, Jesus Christ actually physically present in the bread and the wine.'

'Yes, we can talk about that,' Blaise responded, 'but perhaps not right now.'

'No, of course, not right now.'

Father Edmund approached the two young men, who were both equally tall, but Roderick's shoulders were narrower than Blaise's, and he was, if anything, even thinner than his friend. But Blaise's friend had a pleasant, sensitive, intelligent face, the priest thought. 'So tell me, Roderick,' asked Father Edmund, 'what are you studying at UCT?'

'I'm in my Psychology Honours year, Father,' Roderick replied.

'That's very good,' Father Edmund responded. 'A fascinating field, so much opportunity to bring healing.'

Roderick smiled at the priest. 'I agree, Father. That's its great attraction for me: the opportunity to help people, to bring healing, as you say.'

As Blaise dropped Roderick off at his parents' home in Kenilworth some time later, Roderick said, 'I'd like to come to Mass with you again.'

'That's great. It makes me glad. You are welcome to attend Mass with me anytime, Roddy.'

'Thanks, Blaise,' and Roderick got out of the car and walked round to the driver's side. 'How about I come to Mass next Sunday?' he asked, bending to speak through the open car window.

'OK. I'll give you a ring.'

'I'll see you next week, then.'

'Yeah – keep well, and God bless you, Roddy.' Blaise smiled good-naturedly.

Roderick could not yet bring himself to offer God's blessings as casually as his friend did. Instead, he responded, 'Take care,' smiled in return, and opened the front gate to the garden of his parents' home.

Chapter Eleven

Guy Cressingham did not understand his oldest son at all. In a right world, Blaise should be showing an interest in the business, and Hugh, or Lawrence, could choose, if they wished, to enter the priesthood. But he was going to lose his first born to the priesthood; the son for whom he felt both irritation and a special love, a love in which guilt played a large part: as he had grown older, Blaise had reminded Guy more and more of Irene; he served as a constant accusation that Guy could and should have loved his wife more than he had. Blaise would not be giving him grandchildren, and all Guy's hopes for the future were now devolved upon Hugh and Lawrence.

As Guy sat in his study before dinner one evening in the second half of March 1978, he nursed a scotch, and brooded upon his children and their attributes. Hugh was perhaps too happy-go-lucky to take charge of Cressingham Retail Holdings (and anyway, he seemed set upon a career as an engineer), but Lawrence, aged eighteen (who had commenced his first year at UCT the previous month, studying for a Bachelor of Commerce), showed the sort of precise, passionless personality

– a personality in which the emotionalism shared, in different fashions, by both Hugh and Blaise, was absent – which could be trained to take charge of the family business.

Under Lawrence, thought Guy, Cressingham Retail Holdings would almost certainly flourish – but it would do so without the brilliant coups that either of his other two sons might have brought to it. But that was still in the future: Guy was only fifty-one years old, after all, and apart from a slightly raised blood pressure, he appeared to be fit and healthy.

Within a few days, Blaise would be attending his graduation ceremony – two years later than should have been the case. Hugh would also be graduating a day later, having completed his four year engineering degree. Guy would of course be present at their graduation ceremonies: he was proud of both his sons, but he recognised that Blaise had overcome considerable obstacles to attain his degree in History, English and French. (He had gained, respectively, a First, a First and a Second). Once again Guy thought of his wife: Irene had died so tragically, near the start of Blaise's then final undergraduate year, and it had been that dreadful loss that had thrown the boy so badly off course, and had led, ultimately, to the terrible traumas (the precise details of which, Guy was still unaware) that Blaise had suffered in Angola. But Blaise had recovered bravely. Only his family, who knew the tell-tale signs, would have guessed that sometimes Blaise found himself in the grip of memories so painful and so traumatic that they rendered him momentarily almost dysfunctional.

Lawrence would be accompanying his father to the

Saint Blaise

university, to support his brothers at their graduation ceremonies. And the brothers' grandparents, Ambrose and Teresa Cressingham, would also be present both evenings, as would Blaise's aunt, Fiona Denholm. Ambrose and Teresa were immensely proud of the first two of their grandchildren to obtain their university degrees. Neither Ambrose nor Teresa had been to university. Last Sunday afternoon, at the Cressingham Senior home near Fish Hoek, Blaise's grandfather and grandmother had presented him with a massive bound volume, *Young's Analytical Concordance to the Bible*, to mark his graduation.

'Your Grandmother and I are very proud of you, Blaise,' Ambrose told his grandson. 'We hope you will find this concordance useful in your future studies.'

'Grandpa, I certainly shall! It's a wonderful gift. Thank you both,' Blaise responded. His grandmother kissed him and embraced him. 'My brave boy,' she said to him. Poor Hugh: it had been rather taken for granted that he would find it no problem in obtaining his university degree. His grandfather however now took Hugh to his workshop, to show him a piece of milling work he was busy with. He was manufacturing a new part for the engine of the Phantom III. The two men, Hugh so young, his grandfather now aged seventy-six, bent their heads (one a dark honey-blonde, the other now a thinning shock of white hair) over the work bench. They discussed the work for a few minutes, then Ambrose straightened up and turned and reached for an oblong blued metal container, closed with a pair of catches, about two and a half feet long, one foot broad, and eight inches deep. It was a motor mechanic's comprehensive tool kit, and brand new.

'This is for you, Hugh. Your Grandmother and I thought you would appreciate it more than a book, or something like that.'

Hugh took the box and opened it. Inside it lay an array of gleaming, chromed motor mechanic's tools, systematically arranged, and he looked at his Grandfather and grinned happily. 'Thanks, Grandpa! This is great!'

'The world needs men who look after our souls,' Ambrose Cressingham remarked, 'but it also needs men who know how to keep the world turning.'

Blaise had met his family for Sunday lunch at the rambling old stone house, far down the Cape Peninsula, a few days before the brothers' graduation ceremonies. Blaise always enjoyed visiting his grandparents: their home was redolent with happy memories for him. He had not been living at home since January: instead, he was now living in community at the Jesuit establishment below the university, in Rosebank. Although not yet formally a Scholastic, he was being treated as such. The plan had been that he would set off for England in September, to commence his two years at the Novitiate.

Blaise however was having second thoughts (no, not of his calling; of that he was certain, but rather, of where he ought right now to be). A month earlier, he had chanced upon a newspaper report of Jesuit missionary activity in Rhodesia, a country which was then being torn apart by an armed struggle waged against the minority white government; a struggle pursued by two distinct black nationalist organisations, ZANU and ZAPU. (The former had as its tribal base the majority Shona people, and its armed wing, ZANLA, was materially supported by the USSR; the latter drew support from the minority Ndebele tribe, and its armed wing, ZIPRA, was backed by Communist China). This longstanding armed struggle was known as the "Bush War."

Since having written his finals the previous year, Blaise had been working as a lay assistant at Saint Michael and All Angels Catholic Church in Athlone, a large Cape Coloured township on the Cape Flats, whose priest in charge was Father Francis Sullivan SJ. Blaise's energy, his enthusiasm, his charm, and his clear delight in the Lord (not to mention his near-angelic good looks) exerted a powerful attraction on many of the parishioners with whom he came in contact, and he created a particular stir among young (and not so young) female members of the parish. The Coloured suburb of Athlone represented a considerable shift in experience from Bishopscourt, Kenilworth, Rondebosch or Rosebank, those comfortable white suburbs with which Blaise was so familiar. Laid out on a flat, sandy plain, with sparse vegetation, Athlone was very much a working class district, much run down in places, with frequent indications of poverty and material struggle. Blaise however was extremely fond of the Cape Coloured parishioners, who were unfailingly courteous and resolutely cheerful.

But as he read the piece in the *Cape Times* about German Jesuit missionary activity during the ongoing Rhodesian bush war, he had experienced a revelation: it was as if God had spoken to him directly; he felt an overwhelming certainty that Rhodesia was where he was meant to be. Permeating this revelation was a sense of great urgency.

Nonetheless, "I must pray about it," he thought.

Blaise had sworn no vows as yet, but he was expected to live as if he had, and he wore a lay worker's black cassock with a closed collar when engaged on pastoral duties.

'I feel as if I were already a member of the Society of Jesus,' he told Nicolette Dillon, whom he had met for coffee in Claremont one Saturday afternoon, a week before Easter, and a few days before his graduation.

Sitting on either side of a small table in the coffee shop, the two looked as if they might be brother and sister: both were of an age, with their pale blonde, straight hair and their fine features. Nicolette, who had been awarded her degree in March the previous year, had been working at an art gallery in Cape Town for over a year.

'But you have sworn no vows yet, have you? You are still a lay person?'

'Of course, you're right. I could back out now without breaking any formal promises. But I know I am on the right track; I am meant to become a Jesuit.'

"And I," thought Nicolette, "ought to let go of my extreme attachment to Blaise, and find a nice, normal young man who will father my children." In fact, that nice, normal young man might even be Blaise's brother, Hugh, for during the last few months, Hugh had several times met up with Nicolette, either inviting her home for lunch or supper, or on two occasions, taking her to the cinema. Hugh bore little superficial resemblance to his older brother, yet, thought Nicolette, you would know straight away that they were brothers: they had the same grey eyes; the same set of the jaw, even, at times, the same smile.

As she matured, Nicolette was becoming a truly beautiful

young woman, but Blaise was so God-maddened that he was able to acknowledge the physical attraction he felt for her without having to put up any great struggle against it: this attraction was but a feeble thing when set against the raging fire of his love of God and Christ (a love which, for Blaise, now ruled out any but the most chaste affection for a women. Gone was the compulsive indulgence in casual sex of his first two years at university).

'And there's something else, Nikki,' continued Blaise. 'I think I'm supposed to be in Rhodesia. Right now. I've been sure of this for about a week.'

'Rhodesia? But the country is at war!'

'Perhaps that's why I need to be there.'

'Why are you so sure you need to be in Rhodesia?' asked Nicolette.

'God spoke to me,' answered Blaise, in a matter of fact tone.

"Oh, Blaise!" thought the young woman, staring at his fine, sensitive face. "God certainly loves you, but He often deals badly with those for whom He has a great love."

'And you have no doubts at all of this?' asked Nicolette.

'I'm as certain of it as anything I've ever felt,' responded Blaise.

'But what about your plans for the Jesuit Novitiate in England?'

'I'll have to put those off for a while.'

'Blaise, have you spoken about this with Father Edmund?'

'I'm praying for discernment, to be sure I heard God aright. I'll talk to Father Edmund and the Father Superior after my graduation – after Easter.' Blaise and Hugh were to graduate in a few days' time, on the Wednesday and Thursday of Holy Week.

'Oh Blaise, I think you may have taken leave of your senses.' Nicolette reached out and unconsciously touched Blaise's hand for a moment. 'But most of God's greatest servants have been mad, haven't they?' she continued, with a wry smile. But Blaise merely sat and stared at her, a gentle half smile on his lips.

Since then, Blaise had seen Nicolette once more, this time at his graduation ceremony. She was there with her brother, Gregory, who had been Blaise's best friend at school, and with whom Blaise had remained in amicable, but irregular, contact ever since. Surrounded by people who loved him, Blaise did not speak privately to Nicolette on this occasion, and the subject of his going to Rhodesia did not again arise.

In fact, Blaise spoke first to Father Anthony O' Connor, soon after Easter, rather than speaking either to Father Edmund or to the Father Superior. Father Anthony was the parish priest at Saint Mark's, the Cressingham family church, and Blaise had known him since his boyhood.

'This consciousness of my being needed in Rhodesia is so powerful, Father, that I am certain it is truly God's will,' Blaise told Father Anthony.

'If it is truly God's will that you go to Rhodesia,' Father Anthony responded, after some moments' thought, 'then no barriers will be set in your path. Have you spoken with your superiors in the Society of Jesus?'

'Not yet, Father. I wanted to talk to you first,' Blaise replied.

'Well, speak with them. And I shall pray for you, Blaise.'

Chapter Twelve

Blaise next spoke with Father Edmund Bartlet, who was his spiritual director. This was a term the Jesuits used, and it referred to the priest appointed to assist an individual in discerning God's will for him, and in deepening his faith and guiding him towards more generous service to others.

'This may sound weird, Father Edmund,' began Blaise, 'but I believe that God wishes me to go to Rhodesia.'

Father Edmund smiled, and Blaise relaxed just a little, and continued, 'In February I came across a report in one of the newspapers about Jesuit missionary work in Rhodesia. As I was reading it, I was struck by an overwhelming sense that that was where I was meant to be.'

'This "overwhelming sense." What did it feel like?' asked the priest.

'It felt as if God was commanding me.'

Father Edmund blinked. Assertions made by others of having received a direct command from God were not entirely outside his experience, but they were rare. Coming from Blaise, however, he should not have been surprised. He had sometimes suspected that Blaise was conscious of God as few others were. He had seen his face transfigured during the Mass two or three times; shining, radiant, almost as if illuminated by an inner light; and he had thought, "This young man is close to God." Certainly, it did not sound as if Blaise were mad: he was not claiming to have heard a voice from Heaven.

'So,' responded Father Edmund, 'you wish to join one of the Jesuit missions in Rhodesia? But what of our plans to send you to the Novitiate in England later this year?'

'Yes, Father, I do wish to join one of the Jesuit missions in Rhodesia,' responded Blaise. 'I was thinking, it wouldn't be for ever – perhaps a year or two – and I could continue to the Novitiate afterwards.'

'I see,' said Father Edmund. He sat in thought for a while, Blaise sitting silently opposite him. Then the priest said, 'Obviously, you need to discuss this with the Father Superior. Would you like me to talk with him first?'

'I would be grateful, Father Edmund. Yes, please.'

'Leave this with me for now. I will talk with Father Michael very soon.'

'Thank you, Father Edmund,' said Blaise, grateful the priest had not dismissed his request as either crazy or utterly impractical. But he thought that it was important that he impress upon his spiritual director the sense of urgency he felt. 'You do understand,' he continued, 'I'm possessed of a strong sense of urgency in this.'

The Chaplain, who could remember a time when he too had felt as certain of himself, of the course he must take, as Blaise now felt, smiled again. 'As I said, I will talk with Father Superior very soon, Blaise, and come back to you shortly.'

Saint Blaise

'Thank you, Father Edmund.'

Three days later, after the early morning Mass, Brother John, the Superior's secretary, approached Blaise. 'Father Superior can see you this morning, Blaise.'

'That's excellent. What time?'

'Ten o' clock will do,' Brother John replied.

So Blaise telephoned Father Francis at Saint Michael and all Angels in Athlone, to tell him that he would be in much later than usual today, and as he waited for ten o' clock to come, he felt himself growing tense with anxious anticipation. It was almost April, and the summer was waning fast. Blaise was wearing a light pullover. But the days were still lovely, filled with sunshine, and even as Blaise desired above all things to heed what he was sure was God's call, and quit the Cape for Rhodesia, he was aware that he felt an intense love for Cape Town and the Cape Peninsula: this was Home; it was where he had grown up; his time in the SADF aside, and two or three childhood trips to England by sea with his family, it was all he had ever known.

Yet he prayed, "My God, if You truly wish me to serve You in Rhodesia, then help me gain Father Michael's support."

When Blaise entered the outer office, Brother John, who was busy typing, looked up and told him to go through directly. The door to the Superior's office was open, but Blaise still knocked at the door before entering. Father Michael looked up from the papers he was reading. 'Blaise,' he said. 'Be seated,' and he waved at a chair opposite him. Blaise sat; there was a desk top between him and the Superior, who said, 'You wanted to see me, I believe?'

Wondering how much Father Edmund had told Father Michael, Blaise drew a breath, and began. 'Thank you for seeing me, Father Superior. Has Father Edmund spoken to you?'

Father Michael's features did not alter their rather severe expression. 'He has. I want to hear it from you.'

'As you know, Father Superior, the plan was that in September I was to travel to England, to commence my two years at the Novitiate. I wish to put that off by at least a year.'

'Yes? Why is that, Blaise?'

'I feel an overwhelming conviction that I am meant to be in Rhodesia right now,' answered Blaise.

Father Michael stared at the young man. He saw an absolutely honest, open face across the desk from him. Blaise continued, 'I believe that God wishes me to go to Rhodesia.'

The Superior sat silently for a while, staring at Blaise, who returned his level gaze. 'You say that God wishes you to go to Rhodesia. Has God spoken to you, Blaise?'

Blaise thought for a moment. Then he replied, 'Not in so many words. I mean, I did not physically hear God speaking to me, Father Superior. But I felt His wish for me as clearly as if I *had* heard Him speaking to me in words.'

Father Michael took his responsibilities very seriously indeed: he was responsible for the welfare of every Jesuit brother and priest in Cape Town, and for the work they did. Two questions were in his mind: could it be possible that this young man had indeed discerned God's particular will for him, and if so, how should he, the Superior, respond? As to the first question, there was a long tradition within the Church that God's servants sometimes felt Him communicate His wishes to them clearly; as to the second question, there would be many ways in which a mission station in Rhodesia might find an enthusiastic, pious, intelligent and energetic young man of use. Indeed, the Superior had already spoken to his titular superior in Rhodesia, and there was a mission near Umtali, in Rhodesia's Eastern Highlands, which had been staffed by two elderly priests, one of whom had recently died. A young man like Blaise could be very useful there. However, Father Michael had reservations about granting Blaise his permission to go to Rhodesia, unless he was fully aware of the potential dangers he would be facing there: since June 1972, almost forty missionaries had been murdered in Rhodesia by guerrilla forces, who seemed to harbour a particular hatred of European Christian missionaries.

'You are of course aware that a war is raging in Rhodesia?' Father Michael asked Blaise. 'Missionaries have been targeted in the past by guerrillas. Do you think – after your experiences in Angola – that you would be able to cope with a posting to Rhodesia?'

'Father, I honestly cannot say,' answered Blaise. 'But if, as I believe, God wishes me to be in Rhodesia right now, then He will surely equip me for the task.'

The Superior pondered for a while. The issue of delaying Blaise's novitiate a year or two was neither here nor there: there was no urgency in that regard. Indeed, if it came to that, the time Blaise might spend working on a Jesuit mission station would count towards his formation. So he said, 'There is a possibility you could be useful to the Society in Rhodesia right now. Let me look into it, and I will come back to you.'

'Thank you, Father Superior.' Blaise stood, a smile on his face. It seemed that Father Michael would not be opposing him.

The following Saturday morning, Blaise, showing his Alumnus card at the front desk, visited the main library on campus, to see what he could find out about the Rhodesian bush war. The reports of missionaries being murdered particularly concerned him. Was he ready for possible violence, for visits by armed men? Was he out of his mind to consider putting himself in danger of such confrontations? He prayed some more about it. "Lord, if this is what You wish me to do, please give me the strength to do it."

That Sunday, Hugh approached Blaise at their grandparents' home, where the family was gathered for lunch. 'Feel like a stroll, Blaise?' Hugh asked.

'OK.'

The brothers followed a path through patches of scrub, large areas of *fynbos*, and occasional stands of Scots pine, in which Cape turtle doves were calling, their cooing the very soul of Africa. The path led ultimately, via a circuitous course, to the Fish Hoek – Kommetjie road, and it was a trail Blaise had often followed on horseback. As the path took them through a stretch of *fynbos*, that low ground cover indigenous to the Western Cape, the air was rich with herbal scents released by the sun. Here there were small flocks of brightly coloured sunbirds feeding from the proteas and the flame coloured *fynbos* aloes, from the late flowering yellow Capegorse, and the pink blossomed ericas in their final bloom before the coming of autumn proper.

'Nikki told me you were thinking of working on a mission in Rhodesia,' Hugh began. Blaise frowned. 'No – don't be angry,' Hugh said. 'Nikki is worried for you. She thought she could tell me. Are you really planning to join a mission in Rhodesia? Do you think you're up to it, Blaise – after what Angola did to you?'

Blaise did not answer immediately. The two young men continued with their walk. Then Blaise said, 'I know. It must seem as if I've lost my mind. How can I describe my absolute conviction that I am meant to be working on a mission in Rhodesia? If I am wrong, obstacles will be placed in my path that I cannot overcome.'

'We – the family, your friends – will worry about you. And Dad and I know how long it took you to get over your experiences in Angola. They say one is never really over something like that. Blaise, please don't do this thing, for Dad's sake if for no one else's!'

Sounding as if he were in pain, Blaise responded, 'I *must!* Dont you see? It is what God wants of me!'

'I'm no expert on God, and what He wants,' his brother retorted, 'but I don't know how you can be so sure that it is what God wants.'

Blaise halted, and turned and looked his brother full in the face. Both young men had earnest expressions. 'You must accept that I do know it is what God wants of me. I cannot evade His wishes for me. I *cannot!*'

'Well,' said Hugh, 'I guess that if it is what God wants you to do, He'll take care of you.'

'Yes, He will.'

In the distance could be heard the sound of the luncheon

gong. The brothers turned around, and made their way with some haste back to the house. Neither mentioned the subject of Blaise going to Rhodesia again. And Blaise was not angry with Nikki: he knew that it was loving concern which had prompted her to talk to Hugh about his wish to join a mission in war-torn Rhodesia.

"I am lucky to be loved by so many people," he thought. But Hugh, like their father, although he loved Blaise, felt he hardly understood him. Blaise was not like other people. Hugh felt no powerful urge to religious observance; piety was not a part of his character. Since leaving home he had attended Mass only infrequently, and he rarely gave any thought to God. Hugh was an entirely practical man, which was why he had studied civil engineering at university, and why he, along with a friend from university, had launched a civil engineering consultancy with an office in Cape Town. He planned to make use of the contacts he had cultivated in the City Council engineering department during university vacation work in order to obtain contracts, and in early March, before even his graduation ceremony, he and his partner had obtained their first contract from the City Council. Guy Cressingham was enormously proud of his second son, set to do well in a career his father could relate to. Neither Guy nor Hugh could begin to relate to Blaise's wish to be ordained a priest. They could not understand why Blaise was God-mad; such a condition was beyond their comprehension. But they loved him anyway, and wished him happiness.

But the month of April passed, and May arrived, and the leaves of the oak trees (that tree that for many, residents and visitors alike, was emblematic of Cape Town) began to turn bronze, then the first sustained cold front hit the Cape Peninsula, and for over a week a cold rain fell from lowering dark skies. Blaise wondered whether the Regional Superior had forgotten about his request, but he reasoned that these things took time, and so he pursued his normal routines: early morning Mass at the Community's chapel, breakfast, then the drive to Athlone and Saint Michael and All Angels, where he spent the rest of the morning, then he had lunch with the parish priest, Father Francis, and between half past three and four o' clock (unless there was a function for parish youngsters scheduled for the evening, in which case Blaise would stay behind), he drove back to the fat, comfortable suburbs amidst which he had grown up. If the evening found him at the Jesuit Community in Rosebank, he would have supper there, followed at half past eight by Compline, the final Office of the day, recited in community. Then, in early June, Father Michael, the Superior, took Blaise by the arm after early morning Mass and said, 'Come walk with me, Blaise.'

'Father.'

In the damp garden, beneath grey skies, the priest halted and turned to Blaise. 'There is a mission in the Bvumba Mountains,' he said, 'in the Eastern Highlands – Saint Joseph's – a few miles from Umtali, which at present has only one serving Jesuit missionary left. He is an elderly priest, Father Joachim Schneider, a German like most of the Jesuit missionaries in Rhodesia. He would welcome your help, at least until the Order in Germany sends out another priest.'

Blaise's eyes lit up. 'Will you be sending me there, Father Superior?'

'Yes, if you still wish to go, Blaise. The mission is almost on the Moçambique border. It is always at risk of guerrilla visits, for they have camps across the border. So far, they have not harmed anyone at the mission. Are you prepared to put yourself in the way of possible danger?'

Blaise did not need to think at all. He answered immediately, 'Yes, Father Superior.' Blaise was certain that he would be held in God's hands, able to deal with whatever challenges God sent his way. And so, preparations were set in hand. It was planned that Blaise would travel north in early July. And then, on Monday 26th June, terrible news reached the Regional Superior's office via Jesuit channels of communication, of a horrifying massacre of Protestant missionaries in Rhodesia the previous Friday. On Friday 23rd June, eight adults and four children had been brutally axed, battered, and bayoneted to death by Robert Mugabe's ZANLA guerrillas at the Elim Pentecostal Mission in the Bvumba Mountains, not far from Saint Joseph's Mission. As if this event were not shocking enough, two German Jesuit missionaries had been murdered to the west of Salisbury, on the Sunday immediately following.[*] Blaise received a summons to the Superior's office on Tuesday, shortly after his return from Athlone in the late afternoon.

'Good afternoon, Blaise. Sit down please.'

Blaise sat opposite the Father Superior, whose features looked more than usually drawn. Blaise anticipated further

---

[*] Both these events are historical, documented fact.

instructions regarding his planned move to Saint Joseph's mission in the coming month, but instead, Father Michael handed him a copy of the previous day's *Cape Argus*, and asked, 'Have you read this report?' He pointed at the report in question. It was titled, "Brutal Massacre of Missionaries in Rhodesia's Eastern Highlands."

'No, Father Superior, I haven't.'

'Please read it, Blaise.'

Blaise read the report. It stated the number of missionaries already murdered in Rhodesia (there were more than forty such martyrs), before what was being referred to by the newspapers as the "Vumba Massacre" had taken place. The murder of children at Elim Mission – and the brutal manner of their deaths – particularly horrified Blaise.

'This is dreadful news, Father.'

'Elim Mission is only a few miles from Saint Joseph's Mission. What is not reported in the newspaper is that on Sunday, only two days ago, two Jesuit priests were murdered by guerrilla forces to the west of Salisbury. If you go to work at Saint Joseph's, you will be putting yourself into real danger, Blaise.'

'I'm needed at Saint Joseph's, aren't I, Father? I will surely be in God's hands.'

'Yes, Saint Joseph's Mission would find you very useful, that is true. But are you absolutely certain that you still wish to go? I want you to pray some more about it. Come talk to me again next week. If you still wish to go, then I will arrange it.'

Father Michael Schmidt wished he could be sure that Blaise was not merely being wilful and misguided, mistaking his own wishes for those of God, but the priest was, after all, in the business of acknowledging that God sometimes communicated His will very clearly to His servants, and he dared not forbid Blaise outright, for fear that the young man was truly heeding God's will. Blaise was, after all, so certain of this!

'Thank you, Father Superior. I will pray some more.'

And Blaise did pray some more, but by Tuesday the next week (his further prayers having served only to reinforce his conviction that God wished him to work at Saint Joseph's), he had told the Superior that he was absolutely certain he was meant to be going to Rhodesia. Plans for his departure were then set in motion once again. On Friday 14th July (in less than two weeks' time) he would be flying to Salisbury, and from there, via Air Rhodesia, to Umtali, where Father Joachim Schneider would meet him at the airport. Blaise felt almost transfigured with joy at his certain knowledge that he was fulfilling God's will for him. His family's horror at his plans barely registered with him. Guy Cressingham came close to begging his eldest son to drop his plans for working on the mission in Rhodesia.

'Cant you see how crazy it is?' exclaimed Guy, exasperated at last after almost fifteen minutes of fruitless efforts at dissuasion.

'Dad, it is God's will for me. How can God's will be crazy?'

'Yah? Well, I think you've lost your bloody mind!'

But Blaise just sat there, a serene half smile on his lips.

'I'm almost glad that your mother isn't here to see you do this lunatic thing,' Blaise's father declared. 'It would break her heart.'

'Dad, I wish I could obtain your blessing before I leave,' Blaise responded.

'Well, you wont damn well get it!' exclaimed Guy, who stood up and left Blaise sitting alone in the study.

After dinner that evening (a strained gathering, for Blaise's father was silent, and Lawrence spoke but rarely at the best of times), Hugh, who was also paying a visit to the family home, said to Blaise in the den, 'I'm angry with you. I think you're out of your mind. But I am going to be praying for you every single day you're in Rhodesia.'

'I will be grateful for your prayers, Hugh.' Blaise knew that prayer did not come easily to his younger brother.

Later that evening, Hugh joined his father in the study (Guy Cressingham had not joined his sons in the den after dinner), while Blaise and Lawrence watched some quickly forgettable programme on the television in the den. 'I feel as if I've already lost a son,' Guy told Hugh. 'Blaise seems to inhabit another planet now.'

'I agree with you, Dad. He's difficult to reach these days, and he's totally beyond reasoning with. I think we're going to have to accept that he's his own man – or God's – and pray for him. I've never been much of a one for prayer, but I've told Blaise I shall be praying for him every single day he's in Rhodesia.'

'Yes,' Guy agreed. 'We must pray for his safekeeping. I will ask Father O' Connor at Saint Mark's to pray for him also. Prayer is all that's left to us once Blaise leaves for that country.'

On Sunday 9th July, Guy and his three sons had lunch at the Cressingham Senior home near Fish Hoek. Teresa

Cressingham, Blaise's grandmother, had embraced him upon his arrival, saying, 'Blaise, are you sure you know what you're doing?'

'Yes, Granny. I know what I'm doing. God wishes it of me.'

Teresa Cressingham's eyes were awash with unshed tears. She hugged Blaise again. 'Your Grandfather and I shall be praying for you every day.'

'Thank you, Gran. I know I will need your prayers.'

Ambrose Cressingham shook Blaise's hand upon his arrival, something he rarely did. 'I expect we will be proud of you, wont we, Blaise?'

Blaise thought this was rather an enigmatic thing to say. 'I hope you will, Grandpa,' he responded. Blaise's aunt, Fiona Denholm, kissed him on the cheek, and his uncle by marriage, Jeremy Denholm, greeted him, 'Hullo old son!'

Over lunch, thus far an unusually quiet meal, Hugh suddenly spoke up. 'Come on you lot!' he exclaimed. 'This isn't a wake! Rhodesia is full of missionaries of all ages doing wonderful things. We should be proud that Blaise will be joining them. And it probably wont be for more than a few months anyway – until the Jesuits send out another priest or brother for the mission. Cheer up, everyone!'

Hugh's grandfather smiled. 'Hugh is right. Let's drink a toast to Blaise, and to his safe return home in due course.'

The bottles of wine were passed around the table, and when each of the family present had recharged their glasses, Ambrose rose to his feet and declared, 'Here's to Blaise, whom we all love. May God keep him safe, and bring him home to us soon.'

Saint Blaise

'Amen,' said Teresa Cressingham, and Guy, also on his feet, echoed the Amen, as did Hugh, Lawrence, and the Denholms. The toast had become a prayer, the first of many for Blaise by his family and friends over the many months to come.

Chapter Thirteen

On Tuesday, three days before departing for Rhodesia, Blaise and Roderick (who was now studying for his Masters in Psychology) went hiking in Silvermine Nature Reserve. Blaise collected Roderick at his digs in Rosebank just after breakfast, and they drove south along the Simon Van Der Stel Freeway, and then began climbing towards Silvermine via the steep Ou Kaapse Weg. (This was the same route that Blaise usually took for his grandparents' farm, avoiding many miles of the far slower Main Road route via Muizenberg and Fish Hoek).

Roderick had been to Mass, both with and without Blaise, many times by now: he was now undergoing instruction in the Catholic faith under Father Edmund Bartlet, the university's Catholic Chaplain. Roderick was to become Blaise's first convert to Catholicism, but there would be many more such in the years ahead. The two friends exchanged a few words during their drive, but for the most part, they remained silent. Blaise waited until he had parked the car near the entrance gate to Silvermine Nature Reserve, and they had set off on foot, before telling Roderick that he was due to leave for Rhodesia in a few days' time. It was one of those rare mid-winter days when the sun shone in a clear blue sky, and there was almost no wind, but at about one thousand feet above sea level it felt cool, and both young men were wearing pullovers. Blaise had a walking stick with him.

On hearing Blaise's news, Roderick halted. 'Oh, Blaise!' he exclaimed. 'So soon!'

'I'm afraid so.'

'But you're *not* afraid, are you?' Roderick asked Blaise. 'This is what you wanted.'

'No, I'm not afraid, and perhaps I ought to be. Plenty of people have been telling me I must be mad. Perhaps I am mad. But if I am mad, then it's a divine madness.'

'But I worry about you, Blaise,' Roderick said. 'I remember how you were after Angola.'

Blaise laughed. 'I'm not going to war, Roddy!'

'But you are going to a country torn apart by civil war.'

But Blaise did not respond. They were walking to one side of a shallow valley, through the bottom of which ran a small stream, the water descending in musical rills and sudden falls, and they were ascending gradually as they walked. They heard baboons barking, and they halted and looked towards the sound: they could make out the animals moving along the lip of a low *krantz* on the far side of the valley. Scattered Scots pines grew either side of the stream, becoming a narrow belt of woodland as they approached the Silvermine Dam. The path was still following the high ground to the right of the valley, and they halted and turned around. The view was already stupendous: far to the south,

Cape Point lay under a bank of cloud. The weather would be changing soon. Nearer to hand, on the western shore of the Peninsula, the gentle curve of Long Beach, the sand gleaming white in the sunshine, was visible, and to the south-east they could see the blue waters of False Bay, with its mountain ranges beyond.

'There couldn't be anywhere else in the world so beautiful,' remarked Roderick.

'Yes,' agreed Blaise. 'I love it.'

'Then why are you going away?' asked Roderick.

'Because I must,' Blaise responded. He smiled at his friend. 'And anyway, I'll be back.'

It was approaching eleven o' clock. The two young men sat down together on a low granite outcrop, gazing towards the south and that magnificent view, and Blaise reached into his satchel and withdrew a Thermos flask of black coffee, heavily sweetened. 'Would you like some coffee, Roddy?'

'*Ja*, thanks.' The two drank their coffee, and then stood and continued on their way. Descending the valley slope – it was not far to the bottom – they crossed the stream just below the dam, and followed a path climbing diagonally across the opposite slope. They rounded a spur, turned abruptly west, and all the time, they were gaining in altitude. Their destination was the lookout point, where they intended eating their sandwiches. They could see the Atlantic, a brilliant blue, and the far horizon where ocean and sky met, a gentle curve. The lookout point, at an altitude of nearly eighteen hundred feet above sea level, below which the ground fell almost sheer, was a tumble of rocks, amidst which grew tall, spiky Fynbos Aloes, their scarlet blooms a splash of colour. These aloes flowered only between late June and the end of August. The splendid vista rewarded the young men's efforts: the waters of the Atlantic were a deep turquoise, and they could see several ships far off, rounding, or having just rounded, the Cape of Good Hope. Gazing to the north they could see the fishing village of Hout Bay beneath it's sheer sided mountain, the Karbonkelberg. There was a light breeze blowing up here, and the two friends began to cool down after their exertions. The sense of elevation, of a god-like perspective, was a heady one. The young men sat in silence for a while.

After perhaps ten minutes had passed, Roderick reached out his sandwiches wrapped in greased paper. Blaise did likewise, opening the Tupperware container in which the ham and mustard and cheese sandwiches he had made in the Jesuits' communal kitchen that morning, were stored. He made a fist of his right hand and with the knuckle of his clenched thumb he blessed his meal discreetly with the sign of the cross, giving thanks for the food. Roderick, despite his considerable advance in the Faith, had not yet begun to bless any but his main sit-down meals, while Blaise gave thanks every time he ate.

'I read that report in the papers, Blaise,' remarked Roderick. 'The Vumba massacre. I didn't want to say anything to you at the time. Is the mission you'll be going to nearby?'

Blaise did not wish to alarm his friend, but he could not lie. He hesitated a while, staring at the beautiful view. Then he answered, 'Yes, Saint Joseph's is not far from the scene of the massacre.'

Roderick's features looked stricken. 'I am going to be worrying about you every single day you're away, Blaise.'

'You needn't worry about me, Roddy. I will be in God's hands.'

Despite his (relatively recent) acquisition of faith, of belief in a loving, caring God, Roderick knew that he would be unable to cease feeling concern for his friend. Perhaps, he thought, my faith is not as strong as that of Blaise. But then, how many people possessed Blaise's huge measure of faith?

'Come home for tea, Roddy,' Blaise suggested, once the two friends had reached the car again, around three o' clock.

'OK. Thanks.'

Anna was pleased to see Blaise, as was Magda, the cook. Neither addressed him as "Master" anymore. Blaise had long ago put a stop to that. On entering the family home, he had taken Roderick through to the kitchen, where both servants greeted the young men fondly. They knew Roderick well by now.

'Anything nice for tea, Magda?' asked Blaise.

'You young men, always hungry,' responded Magda. '*Ja*, I baked a fruit cake this morning.'

'That's great,' Blaise said. 'We'll be in the den.'

On the way to the den, Blaise knocked on the open door of his father's study, then stepped inside, Roderick standing in the doorway behind him. Guy, seated in his leather upholstered armchair, looked up from the documents he was studying. The room smelled of cigar smoke.

'Blaise! I wasn't expecting you!'

'We were hiking at Silvermine,' Blaise told his father. 'I thought we'd stop by on our way back.'

'It's good to see you – and you too, Roderick.'

'How are you, Mr. Cressingham?' asked Blaise's friend.

'I'm well thanks. And how are you both?'

'We had a good hike,' Blaise responded. 'But the weather is changing.'

Blaise was right. It was already too cool and overcast to want to take their tea on the terrace.

'Stay for dinner, both of you,' Guy said.

'Thanks, Dad, but Roderick has to get back. You'll see me tomorrow evening.'

Blaise would be having dinner with the family the next day, Wednesday. Thursday he would spend at the Community in Rosebank, packing for his journey the following day. Tomorrow evening might be the last time he saw his family for a long time.

Anna had lighted a fire in the den, and the room was welcoming, warm, infused with the scent of burning pine logs. Both young men tucked eagerly into the fruit cake that arrived with the tea things. They were still at an age when they could eat prodigious quantities of food without gaining any weight.

When Blaise dropped Roderick off at his digs not far from the Jesuit Community, he got out of the car and followed his friend to his front door, where he shook hands with him.

'Dont worry about me, Roddy. I'm in God's hands,' he said.

Roderick tried to smile. 'I know. Just take care, Blaise.' And the two friends parted, neither knowing when next they would meet.

For the family dinner at the Cressinghams the

following evening, Magda had served grilled kingklip for the fish course. (Guy had driven Magda to the fishmongers in Claremont that early afternoon: they necessarily did most of the household shopping together, as the nearest shops were too far for Magda to reach on foot, and there was no bus service). This was followed by roast chicken, with plenty of the golden baked potatoes that Blaise and his brothers loved so much. A Cape sauvignon blanc accompanied the meal. Steamed pudding dripping with syrup was served for desert, and a cheese board was passed around the table, accompanied by Bakers cream crackers and a Hannepoot desert wine. This dinner combined all the family's old favourites; the sort of simple fare that boys enjoyed. For to Magda, the Cressingham brothers were still boys.

When at about ten o' clock that evening, Blaise took his leave of his family, he made a point of hugging the now very elderly Heidi the dog, and he picked up Tinker the Siamese cat – who was just as old as Heidi, but aging rather better than her – and cuddled him. He not only shook hands with his father and his brothers, he was moved spontaneously to embrace each of them in turn, and he was immensely gratified when his father returned his embrace. And when he said goodbye to the two servants – so much more than mere servants after so many years with the family – he kissed each of them on the cheek.

'*God seën jou*, Blaise,"* Anna told him.

'*En jy ook*, Anna,' responded Blaise.

---

* Afrikaans – "God bless you, Blaise."

Saint Blaise

'Make sure you eat enough,' Magda advised him. Blaise laughed.

'I will, Magda.'

The two servants came outside and joined the family as they waved goodbye to Blaise. Then he was gone, the sound of his sports car disappearing up the street. Despite Guy Cressingham's earlier protestations, Blaise had left with his father's blessings. On Friday morning, Blaise would be leaving his car keys with Father Edmund, who would give them to Roderick, whom Blaise had said could use the car in his absence. His brothers had no need of it: Hugh had his own car, and Lawrence still drove Blaise's old Triumph Herald.

The Cressinghams had no idea that Blaise had begun his journey to Calvary, but perhaps, in some deep part of his soul, Blaise knew that his destiny awaited him – and if so, he went out anyway, praising God.[*]

---

[*] Luke 23:33

Chapter Fourteen

As dawn was breaking on Friday 14th July, Father Edmund drove Blaise to D.F. Malan Airport outside Cape Town. It was almost eight o' clock. The underside of the clouds which hung low above the mountains on the eastern horizon glowed a fiery red, and Blaise felt cold as they set off. It had rained during the night, and more rain was threatening. "I can still call this whole thing off," thought Blaise.

"Vade retro me Satana," he said under his breath. How easy it would be for him to evade God's will. All he need do was say, "Turn around!" and Father Edmund would head for home again. But Blaise kept silent, and they sped down the highway towards the airport. Blaise was wholly in the hands of Providence now.

The shuttle flight reached Jan Smuts Airport outside Johannesburg at about midday, and here, Blaise caught the South African Airways flight for Salisbury in Rhodesia. Blaise had never before travelled far from home alone. As the aircraft rose into the cloudless Highveld sky, he thought of his mother, then of his brothers, then of his father. He knew that fear was best conquered by prayer, and that prayer was best said for others. As the aeroplane gained rapidly in altitude, soon rising far above the Johannesburg winter smog of traffic fumes and cooking and heating smoke, he said a prayer for his family: he prayed for his mother's soul (but he knew that she was in Heaven), and he prayed for his grandparents, and for his father, for Hugh, and for Lawrence. Then he prayed for Roderick, whom he knew would be missing him in the months to come, and would be anxious for him, and for good measure, he prayed for Nicolette Dillon also. Crossing himself, he opened his eyes, to find an air hostess drawing nearer, pushing a trolley down the aisle in front of her.

'Would you like anything to drink, Sir?' she asked, smiling at this rather striking young man. 'Tea, coffee, cold drink, a beer, something stronger?'

'No thank you – oh, yes, I'll have a coffee please.'

Blaise was surprised to find that the airport building at Salisbury Airport was patrolled by a contingent of black troopers, with a number of European officers. Blaise had imagined that the Rhodesian war was a struggle between entirely white Rhodesian security forces, and black guerrillas, but by this stage of the war, the majority of units within the Rhodesian security forces were manned predominantly by blacks. The men Blaise was now looking at were members of what he would learn was the British South Africa Police (initially a mounted police force founded by Cecil John Rhodes, now a paramilitary police force), and they were armed with rifles which Blaise recognised as Lee-Enfield bolt actions.

From Salisbury Airport, Blaise took an Air Rhodesia flight for Umtali, the capital of Manicaland Province in the east of the country. It was a flight of only just over forty-five minutes in duration, and he made his final landing of the day soon after five o' clock. Shortly before landing, it had been announced over the intercom that the temperature at Umtali was seventy-seven degrees Fahrenheit. The Eastern Highlands were always cooler than the rest of the country. Blaise knew from the reference works he had consulted in Cape Town on Rhodesia's climate and ecosystems that this was the region's dry season, and he was not surprised to find that there was comparatively little humidity in the air.

Father Joachim Schneider was a tall, gaunt, white bearded and moustached figure, perhaps in his late sixties. Unmistakable in a black cassock, he was waiting for Blaise in the tiny arrivals hall at Umtali Airport, which was patrolled by a small unit of white British South Africa Police Reservists armed with automatic rifles.

'Greetings!' the priest boomed. 'Greetings and welcome!' His grip when the two men shook hands was as powerful as his deep voice. His accent still held a trace of his native Bavaria, although he had been working as a missionary priest in Rhodesia since the late nineteen-forties.

'Is that all your luggage?' he asked. Blaise was carrying a leather suitcase, which still had several partially torn steamer labels adhering to it from childhood voyages to Britain with his family, and he had a large gym bag slung over one shoulder. 'We must hurry: it will be sunset soon.'

Father Joachim's Land Rover was parked just in front of the tiny airport, and he drove surprisingly fast along the tarred road, and the hills in the south and the south-east grew steadily nearer. 'We are located at the foot of the

Bvumba Mountains,' he told Blaise. 'The military swept the road this morning, so I can afford to hurry.'

'"Swept the road," Father?' asked Blaise. 'You mean, for landmines?'

'That is right. The guerrillas lay landmines at night.'

They were crossing a wide, shallow vale, in whose large fields crops were growing, but Blaise was ignorant of their nature. He knew almost nothing about agriculture; he could recognise maize, but little else. After a while they began passing through hilly country, the hillsides already dark with shadow. Then the priest began to slow, and swung the vehicle sharply off the road to the left, and they began to follow an unsurfaced road, descending gradually. Father Joachim did not however reduce his speed by very much: he was racing the clock.

A wide swath of flat bottom land, indistinct in the fast fading light, opened up ahead of them, beyond which, in the east, a range of mountains (the tops of which caught the last golden rays of the sinking sun in the west) reared high against the rapidly darkening sky behind them, and after a while they slowed and drove between a pair of tall brick gateposts. A large signboard was arched above the gateposts, and Blaise assumed the words "Saint Joseph's Mission" were probably painted on it, but it was already too dark to tell. They followed a dirt driveway lined with tall eucalyptus trees (known locally as "blue gums") towards a huddle of low buildings with corrugated iron roofs, amidst which was a small church with a single, flat-topped bell tower, whose smoothly plastered, white painted walls made it stand out in the fast gathering twilight. The time was now a quarter to six, and the sun had set about ten minutes ago. Soon it would be fully dark. They were seventeen miles from Umtali.

A middle-aged black man, dressed in baggy shorts and a loose short sleeved shirt, met the Land Rover. Father Joachim greeted him in Shona, then turned to Blaise and said, 'This is Malachi Tangwena. He works in the house.' The priest resumed speaking in Shona, and Blaise was aware that he was being explained or introduced to Malachi, for his name occurred once, then the black man extended a hand, and shook Blaise's hand in that typical triple grip so common throughout much of sub-Saharan Africa. He said something to Blaise in Shona. Blaise smiled at him. Then Malachi switched to English.

'I greet you, *saBlez*,'* he said, his words quite heavily accented. Blaise smiled again. 'And I greet you, Malachi,' he responded.

'I help you,' Malachi told Blaise, who was reaching for his suitcase and gym bag, which Father Joachim had removed from the back of the Land Rover. The black man picked up Blaise's bag and slung it over one shoulder, then reached for the suitcase, but Blaise said, 'Dont worry,' and grabbed hold of its handle first.

Even as Father Joachim led the two men into the main dwelling (probably, thought Blaise, the original mission house, for it was larger and taller than the rest of the buildings, and he could see that it had a wide, roofed veranda on three sides, and Blaise thought that beneath the

---

* Shona language – the prefix "va" before a male name, signifying seniority or respect, becomes "sa" in Manyika, the local dialect, thus "saBlez."

eaves he could make out small square windows, designed to let the heat out and aid with ventilation), it was growing rapidly darker. The mountains looming to the east were a dark mass now. The sun went down very fast, here in the tropics. Father Joachim spoke to Malachi again in Shona, then said to Blaise, 'Malachi will take your bags to your room.'

Blaise put the suitcase down, which the black man now took.

'Thank you,' Blaise told him. Malachi grinned at Blaise and disappeared with his suitcase and shoulder bag. Blaise followed the priest through to a small chapel located inside the house, and Father Joachim said, 'We shall say Vespers together, then I can give you something to eat and drink.'

Since the death of his fellow priest at the mission, Father Joachim had almost always recited the Offices of the Day alone; very occasionally, however, he would say one of the Offices with one or two of the black mission staff, although they struggled to read, let alone pronounce, the Latin text. Father Joachim was looking forward to reciting the remaining two Offices tonight with a fellow Jesuit (for thus he regarded Blaise, although Blaise's situation was anomalous, and he had as yet taken no vows).

The two men, one so young and fresh-faced, the other weathered both by age and the climate, recited Vespers together, not in English (or for that matter in German or Shona) but in Latin, each holding a thick Latin Breviary, in which the Offices of the Day for an entire church year were laid out. (Blaise had not had occasion to read much Latin since matriculating; although moderately able in Latin, it had not been his favourite subject at school). Vespers said, the priest took Blaise through to a bedroom at the back of the house. Blaise suspected that its single window (with a small square window above that, directly beneath the high ceiling) probably looked out onto the mountains. There was a single bed, utterly plain, but made up, and it was covered with a cheerful bedspread in tones of yellow and orange. At the head of the bed was a small bedside table, upon which stood a candle in a candle stand, with a box of matches next to it. The curtains on either side of the window were patterned in large yellow sunflowers, and the walls were painted a pale yellow. Someone had once made an effort with the surprisingly cheerful room. There was a bookcase with a few hardbound volumes in it, which Blaise was to learn were for the most part written in German, but among them was a Jerusalem Bible in English and a Missal in English. Blaise placed the Latin Breviary that Father Joachim had lent him alongside the latter. There was a plain wooden table with a hard wooden chair, and on the table was placed a paraffin lamp. On one wall was fixed a rather beautiful crucifix of wood, about one foot tall, and in front of it was a *prie-dieu* of some dark wood with a cushion on the kneeler. There was also a wash stand, with a large porcelain bowl painted with sunflowers and cornflowers on the marble top, and a large tinned enamelware jug next to it. Fixed to the wall above the wash stand was a small mirror. A towel hung on a rail nearby. A chest of drawers completed the room's furnishings. There was no wardrobe: across one corner (behind a curtain of material which matched that of the window curtains), a metal rod was fixed at head height, from which hung half a dozen or more wooden coat hangers. Perhaps, thought Blaise, moths were not a problem here.

Blaise's suitcase and gym bag stood on a somewhat worn rug laid on the floor alongside the bed.

'This is your room,' Father Joachim told Blaise. 'Come, I will show you where the bathroom and toilet are.'

These were located along a corridor, not far from Blaise's bedroom. Then Father Joachim led Blaise to a large kitchen in which a wood-fired range took up most of one end of the room, and sat him down at a scrubbed wooden table of some size standing in the middle of the room.

'I will heat up the soup which Thomas made at lunchtime,' Father Joachim told Blaise, 'and there's plenty of bread and cheese.' So saying, Father Joachim placed a wooden bread board, with half a home-baked loaf of brown bread on it, on the table, along with some butter. These were accompanied by a covered crockery container which proved to contain cheese. These were followed by some cutlery and a soup bowl each.

'I'm making coffee,' the priest said. 'It is a great weakness of mine. Would you like some, Blaise?'

'Yes please, Father Joachim.'

The priest placed two mugs of black coffee on the table, returned to the range, then shortly thereafter poured a thick beef broth into each soup bowl. Sitting down, he pronounced a blessing over the meal and immediately set to. After a while he paused, saying, 'We have our main meal of the day at lunchtime. Do you speak any Shona?'

Taken aback, Blaise answered, 'I'm afraid not, Father.'

'Never mind. I will teach you, and you will pick up the language from Thomas and Malachi and the people here.'

'I have brought a Shona language primer with me, Father.'

'*Ja* – that is good. But to pronounce the words correctly, you must hear them spoken. You will learn. Until you can speak some Shona, you will not be much use to me.' But the priest smiled at Blaise as he said this. 'Do not be downhearted!' he continued. 'It is not so difficult a language to learn, and you are young. It will come quickly to you.' Father Joachim sat back and lighted a cigarette. Blaise was to learn that he only ever smoked after supper. Blaise lighted one of the half dozen or so cigarettes he still permitted himself a day.

The priest poured himself a second mug of coffee. 'You would like some more coffee, Blaise?'

'No thank you, Father.'

Having smoked his cigarette, Father Joachim stood, picking up his mug of coffee. 'Come! We will go to the sitting room.' He led the way to a large room, somewhat haphazardly furnished with a rather shabby, over-stuffed sofa covered in floral chintz, and three equally elderly, mismatched upholstered armchairs. A low table sat in the middle of the room. There was a large bookcase crammed with books against one wall. But there was no desk, nor was there a telephone. Father Joachim must have a study elsewhere, thought Blaise. Between the skirting boards and the dado rail, the walls were panelled in some rich, dark, reddish-brown wood. There were only two decorations on the walls: a crucifix of very dark wood with a yellowed ivory figure of Christ in His agony, fixed above the fireplace (Blaise thought that the crucifix was probably quite old, and he wondered whether it had come from Germany), and a coloured oleograph of an Alpine scene, perhaps representing a vista from Father Joachim's native Bavaria. The fireplace had a clean-swept hearth; it had clearly not been used at all recently. Blaise could not imagine it ever growing cold enough to justify a fire being lighted, but perhaps after over half a lifetime here, your blood grew thin. The two French windows, which Blaise realised must open onto the veranda, were hung with heavy brocade curtains, again, showing their age. These curtains remained open to the night. Blaise had the impression that this room was not much used. Indeed, he was to learn that during Father Joachim's rare moments of leisure, if he was not praying in the chapel, he was more likely to be found sitting in the kitchen, speaking fluent Shona with Thomas and Malachi and any of the local people who dropped by, than taking his ease in the sitting room. It was only in the early evening that Father Joachim might be found in the sitting room.

This rather spare, even austere, clerical environment, in which no hint of a woman's touch was evident, did not strike Blaise as particularly alien: indeed, he felt in some measure as if he already knew it. He felt drawn to Father Joachim, who, in between talking about Saint Joseph's Mission and the people who lived in the surrounding district, was asking him questions about his education and his future plans. The priest was drinking what he told Blaise was Schnapps, sent him from Germany. He offered Blaise a glass, but Blaise declined, accepting instead a glass of Cape red wine. At about half past eight, Father Joachim led Blaise to the small chapel once again, and they recited Compline, the day's final

Office, together. This done, the priest said, 'I will see you in the morning. We will say Prime together at seven o' clock, *ja*? Afterwards, I celebrate the Mass in the church. There will be quite a few local people there. We can talk again over breakfast after the Mass.' Father Joachim smiled at Blaise. 'So, I say good night, and may God bless you.'

'Good night, Father Joachim.'

The two men parted, each headed for his bedroom, and no doubt, prayers.

Chapter Fifteen

The next day was a Saturday. There were fifteen local people at Mass that morning. All were black. The majority of these were women, but there were at least five men present, including Malachi, and a young black man who assumed the role of altar server during the Mass. Blaise (now wearing a Jesuit's hoodless habit) aroused much curiosity on the part of the people attending the Mass, and after the Mass many of them approached him, greeting him in Shona, but when they realised he spoke no Shona, they switched readily enough to sometimes fluent – if strongly accented – English. Blaise knew that it would be a while before he could put names to all these friendly faces.

Nonetheless, "I feel at home here," he thought.

Blaise was introduced to Thomas, the Cook, in the kitchen. Breakfast was a generous meal of fried eggs, grilled beef sausages, fried tomatoes, baked beans, and toast and marmalade; a very British breakfast in what might have been thought to be a German household, but clearly, after so many years in Rhodesia, the priest had picked up the colonial habit of starting the day with a hearty breakfast.

During breakfast, Father Joachim said to Blaise, 'Michael, who was serving for me at Mass today, cannot come during the week; he is still at school. You will be able to serve for me, not so?'

Blaise smiled, remembering how he had been an altar server as a boy. 'Of course, Father.'

'I am busy for much of today,' continued the priest, 'but after supper, I can begin teaching you some Shona. You can come with me this morning. I shall be visiting some of the villages in the district.'

'I would like that, Father.'

And indeed, Blaise enjoyed his morning with Father Joachim. It was, he thought, a beautiful region, the rocky hillsides covered with shrubs and grass, and on some of the eastern slopes and in the valleys, could be found dense, high canopied indigenous forest. As they drove through one such area, Father Joachim told Blaise that these forests were inhabited by the blue monkey, and its sub-species, Sykes' monkey. 'But they like to stay in the forest canopy,' the priest said. 'I would be surprised if we see any.'

They followed narrow single tracks deep into the Bvumba Mountains, splashing through numerous streams and often engaging four wheel drive, visiting four widely scattered villages in all. At each of these, the people crowded around the priest, who was clearly liked and respected. *'Mauya! Baba Yokim!'* they would cry. *'Mauya!'*

Father Joachim had his medical bag with him, and at each village, although he had no formal medical training, he treated minor ailments and injuries.

'If there had been any serious medical problems,' he

told Blaise afterwards, 'I would have taken them to Umtali Hospital. However, I have had to set a few broken bones in these mountain villages, when haste has been all-important. What I really need here is a missionary doctor. But you can sit in on my main clinic of the week, this afternoon, and begin to learn from me.'

Blaise thought that this would be interesting, and he could imagine no more useful skills for a rural missionary in Africa to acquire than medical skills.

They were back from their mountain village tour by two o' clock, and they sat down to a late lunch: this consisted of leek soup, pork sausages with sauerkraut, string beans and pumpkin – the greens grown by Thomas in the Mission's kitchen garden – and potatoes baked in their jackets. (Potatoes did not grow well in these Eastern Highlands, and were obtained during Father Joachim's weekly shopping trip to Umtali). They had fruit salad for dessert. Blaise realised that he would not be going hungry here. Father Joachim drank two glasses of South African red wine with his meal, but Blaise drank just one glass. Unlike his brother Hugh, who worked hard, played hard (he still played rugby), and drank hard, Blaise had never acquired much of a fondness for alcohol.

By half past two, a score or more people were waiting outside the mission house beneath a large Msasa (or Zebrawood) tree for medical treatment. Malachi had set up a table in the shade on the deep veranda, behind which he placed two chairs. When Blaise and Father Joachim, who had given themselves time for a mug of coffee and a cigarette each after lunch, sat down at the table, with Malachi standing behind them, the waiting group quickly formed itself into a queue, approaching the priest at the table on the veranda one by one. Ailments ranged from bad cuts, which Father Joachim cleaned, treated with disinfectant, and bandaged, to colds and coughs – for which, Father Joachim handed out Aspirin, vitamin C tablets, and bottles of patent cough mixture. Two women from the same village brought babies with respiratory problems to the priest, and he told each woman that he would take them to the hospital in Umtali at the end of the clinic. At this, both women in turn looked anxious and fearful. One of them tied her baby onto her back with the large shawl she used for this purpose, and left hurriedly. The other, however, agreed to wait, and the priest instructed Malachi to make her a cup of tea, after drinking which, the woman retreated to the shade of a large Mobola Plum some distance from the house, bared a breast, and began to suckle her infant.

'Other than for emergency treatment, I will not treat children below ten years old,' Father Joachim told Blaise. 'I always advise the mothers to bring the infant to hospital. But some of them do not like the idea of visiting the hospital.'

The clinic was finished by half past four. Father Joachim and Blaise each drank some tea and ate a slice of fruit cake baked by Thomas, then the priest said, 'Come. We must take that poor woman and her child to the hospital.'

The woman, her child clutched to her breast, sat on the left hand side of the Land Rover's cab. Blaise took the middle seat, next to Father Joachim. During the seventeen mile drive, the baby cried for much of the time, but above its grizzling, the priest asked Blaise, 'Do you drive?'

'I do, Father.'

'That's good. Once you know your way around, you can take the burden of this sort of chore from me.'

The two Europeans left the anxious woman and her baby at the hospital in Umtali, reassuring her that they would tell her husband where she was. She would spend the night at least with her child there. Father Joachim had given her some cash, with which she could buy cups of tea, and some food, from the vendors outside the hospital. The hospital staff knew Father Joachim well, and they would be able to telephone him should need arise. On the way back, having left the main road, the priest drove to the woman's village, near the mission, and informed her husband of this development, reassuring him that all would be well. It was well after dark, the curfew in place, the air full of the sounds of night creatures (above all, the constant electric whine of millions of cicadas, which the mind soon blanked off), before they had reached the mission again and parked the Land Rover in its lock-up garage. Thomas and Malachi had disappeared to their quarters, but after Father Joachim and Blaise had said Vespers together in the chapel, the priest heated up the remainder of the leek soup from lunch, and put out bread, butter and cheese on the kitchen table. He also made a pot of coffee. After their simple supper, the priest said, 'I will give you a lesson in Shona, Blaise.' They sat at the kitchen table, Blaise with a notebook and a second mug of coffee, and Father Joachim with a glass of Schnapps in front of him. The priest took him through simple phrases: greetings, goodbyes, enquiries after health and suchlike. Blaise had always been fairly good at languages at school, and he was able to pick up the correct pronunciations of the words very quickly. In the background could be heard the deep, rhythmic thudding of the electricity generator, which Malachi had fired up before ending his day's work, but Blaise soon ceased to be consciously aware of the sound. At half past nine the generator's automatic timer would close it down for the night, and if illumination was needed during the night, candles or paraffin lamps would have to do.

'Next time,' said Father Joachim, 'I will teach you some basic requests and commands: expressions like, "Bring me …," "Fetch that …," and so forth. But you will learn most by listening to the people talking.'

Later the following week, it was Blaise whom Father Joachim sent in the Land Rover to collect the woman and her child from the hospital at Umtali. Blaise was picking up some Shona already, but he could not yet begin to conduct a conversation in the language. He had a good sense of direction and a good visual memory, and on the way back he found the woman's village near the mission without any problems. The woman, clutching her baby (who seemed much happier), was profuse in her thanks when Blaise dropped the two of them off. *'Wazviita saBlez, wazviita!'* she declared, bobbing her head. Blaise smiled at her, and at the children who had gathered upon his arrival.

'*Sara mushe,* goodbye,' said Blaise, waving at the woman and smiling at the children who had gathered on his side of the car, before reversing carefully and heading back to the mission.

The month of August passed, and with the coming of September, the glow of grass and brush fires could be seen at night on the hills. With the arrival of the rains in October, the weather changed dramatically. There was often a dense mist in the morning, and later in the day there would be a heavy downpour lasting several hours. Despite the rains, it grew very warm, with temperatures reaching almost eighty Fahrenheit during the day. The air, to Blaise at least, felt intensely humid. One day Blaise found that his black leather shoes (which he rarely wore, preferring to wear sandals with his black cassock) had acquired a green mould on the leather.

Blaise's command of Shona improved enormously, and by November he could conduct simple conversations in the language. Father Joachim now found Blaise much more useful than he had in the past, and Blaise was able to take on some of the burden of pastoral work from the priest. He was also appointed to be one of the readers (in Shona) during the Sunday Mass. Returning from a solo shopping trip to Umtali one late afternoon, the Land Rover in four-wheel drive once he had left the main road, for the unsurfaced road was slick with mud, Blaise realised that he felt as if he was coming home.

"I'm happy," he thought. He offered up a prayer of spontaneous thanks to God, for His bountiful blessings, and for the sense of purpose He had gifted him with. Blaise often prayed when he was alone in the car. These were almost always prayers of gratitude, but sometimes he would pray for some particular member of the local congregation who was sick, whom he had thought of suddenly while driving, or for one of the people whom he knew needed God's special help and blessing. He could put names and personalities to many of the faces now.

Back in Cape Town, Father Michael Schmidt, the

Superior of the Cape Town community, was gratified at the reports he had been receiving from Father Joachim: Blaise was fitting in well, and was proving useful. Blaise in the meanwhile kept up a regular correspondence with Roderick, a less frequent correspondence with other friends of his, and an irregular but not infrequent correspondence with his family. At home, Guy Cressingham said to his two younger sons, 'Blaise seems genuinely happy in his letters. Perhaps this thing is right for him after all.'

'Yeah, but I still pray for him every day, Dad, like I promised I would,' commented Hugh.

'Yes, we must all pray for Blaise,' Guy agreed. What Lawrence thought, who could say? Lawrence had always kept his thoughts to himself. As a teenager, Hugh would tease his younger brother with the words, "How's the world takeover plot going, Lorrie?" And Lawrence would smile distantly.

Blaise, in his letters to his family, had made no mention so far of guerrilla activity in the region, but he was more forthcoming when he wrote to Roderick. Roderick knew therefore that guerrilla bands came and went, and that there had been several hot pursuits by Rhodesian security forces into the Bvumba Mountains. So far, however, the ZANLA guerrillas (it was these men, members of ZANU's military wing, who were active in the region) had not targeted the Mission, perhaps because they feared alienating the local people, who valued the Mission's presence in their lives. This hands-off policy on the part of ZANLA was to change, however, with the appointment in March 1979 of a new ZANLA commander for the Eastern Highlands, "Brigadier" Solomon *"Nzou"* (Elephant) Karuru.

Saint Blaise

Solomon Karuru, now in his forties, was mission educated. The Christianity did not take: on the contrary, over time he was to form an abiding hatred of European missionaries. He was a clever, sensitive, cruel and ruthless man, and he had felt at school that his intelligence was not properly recognised by the European missionary teachers, who, he believed, had patronised and talked down to him. He had come to regard Christianity as a tool of colonial racial oppression. Some years spent studying in the USSR had grafted a rudimentary Marxist framework upon his hatred of European Christian missionaries, and when he returned to Rhodesia, he was seething with an anger and hatred which owed as much to his own angry, bitter nature as to the partially digested Marxist ideology he had acquired.

Upon his appointment as ZANLA regional commander, he decided to send a message both to the local people (whom he regarded as collaborators) and to the Rhodesian white colonial regime, by attacking Saint Joseph's Mission. He waited until Good Friday, the 13th April, then, at dawn, he left his camp of a week's standing, which was located deep in a hidden valley high in the mountains, and with fifty men, all armed with Russian-made Kalashnikov (AK 47) 7.62mm automatic assault rifles, he made his way via narrow paths, avoiding the few villages, until he descended from the foothills into the wide flat lands below, amidst which Saint Joseph's Mission was located.

But now Solomon Karuru could no longer entirely avoid observation, for the villages were too many, and particular note was paid to his passage, and to the direction the guerrillas were taking, by the headman of one of the villages on the approach to the Mission, The headman thought it worrying that the guerrillas marched rapidly past his village along a track that led to Saint Joseph's Mission. This astute old man, Timothy Chitepo, owned a fine horse, and he instructed his eldest son, Robert, riding this horse, to circle ahead of the ZANLA band, and warn Father Joachim of the approach of a large body of guerrillas, whose purpose and intent he feared.

Chapter Sixteen

Good Friday was of course a public holiday in Rhodesia, and the schools were closed, so the Mission church was packed with children; there were indeed perhaps more children present than adults. The members of a visiting builders' crew from Umtali (who were camping in two large tents in the mission grounds, and eating their meals with Malachi and Thomas), there to erect a new wooden church hall on brick foundations for the Mission, were also present – whether Catholic or not – for the Good Friday service. There would be no Mass celebrated today: on this day, Jesus had died, His body laid in the tomb. He could not be brought down in the form of bread and wine. But the Good Friday service was an intensely moving one, for the Passion reading began with Luke 22, verse 54, ending only with Luke 23, verse 46.[*]

By the end of the Passion recitation, many of the women in the congregation were weeping, and the entire congregation was kneeling, most with bowed heads and clasped hands.

---

[*] Luke 23:46: "Jesus cried out in a loud voice saying, 'Father, into your hands I commit my spirit.' With these words he breathed his last."

Blaise, along with two of the regular Sunday Mass readers, had been reading their respective passages in Shona, each taking a different part, during the lengthy Passion recitation. Blaise wore a layman's black cassock, cinched in at the waist with a leather belt. Blaise now snuffed the candles in the brass candlesticks standing on the altar, and removed the brass altar crucifix and the candlesticks while Father Joachim stripped the altar of its purple altar cloth, folding the cloth and laying it to one side in the sanctuary, where Blaise had placed the crucifix, and the candlesticks with their dead candles. Then Father Joachim opened the tabernacle, and removed the Host within, and Blaise took the silver paten and its contents and the brass crucifix through to the vestry, where he locked them in a cupboard. Then he returned to the sanctuary to fetch the candlesticks and the folded altar cloth, and put them away in the vestry. Then the priest turned down the wick in the red sanctuary lamp until the flame had been snuffed. The large Easter Candle in its tall brass candle stand, standing to one side of the altar, remained unlighted. The church was now symbolically empty of the Lord's presence, and would remain so until Easter Sunday.

And the village headman's son, Robert, had just mounted up and was digging his heels hard into the horse's flanks, headed for the Mission.

Father Joachim and Blaise were chatting outside after the service with members of the congregation, when Robert galloped up and hauled on the reins, making the horse rear up extravagantly and paw the air with its hooves.

'Baba Yokim!' the young man cried. *'Baba – !'* and he

Saint Blaise

spoke rapidly, and somewhat breathlessly, in Shona. The priest listened to him, as did several of those around, including Blaise, who could by now follow the gist of the young rider's words.

Father Joachim took no time to think. 'Blaise, you stay here and urge the people to go home,' he said in English, when Robert had finished speaking. 'I will telephone the police in Umtali.' So saying, he headed for the house.

Robert, the village headman's son, spurred his horse and left for home. He did not wish to be around in the event of trouble. Word spread fast, and the majority of those assembled outside the church began to disperse, headed for their villages – all but a dozen or so, who seemed loath to abandon Blaise and Father Joachim to their fates.

'You must go home,' Blaise urged them. 'I think there will be trouble here.' He spoke in Shona. But in addition to the builders' crew, who had nowhere else to go, and Malachi and Thomas (both of whom were afraid, but their loyalty to Father Joachim overrode their fear), there were still half a dozen of the congregation who would not leave. Blaise was not sure what to do next. He felt a frisson of fear. It was the uncertainty: he did not know what lay ahead of them, but the air of crisis was pronounced. Unable to persuade the remnant still gathered in front of the church to leave, he went to the house and found Father Joachim in his study, where he had just completed making a telephone call.

'The security forces will be here very soon,' the priest told Blaise. 'Have the people left?'

'Most of them have gone, Father Joachim. Some will not

leave. Do you think we should be worried, then, Father?' Blaise asked.

'I did not like the sound of the message Robert Chitepo brought us. Timothy Chitepo is a sensible man. If he thinks there is reason for concern, we would be foolish to disregard his warning. I think the best thing that we can do now is pray.' So saying, Father Joachim got to his knees, and Blaise followed suit – and they thus saved their lives, for before the priest could commence his prayer, the glass in the study window, and in the windows of the sitting room next door, shattered, and the rapid metallic clatter of automatic gunfire sounded, so close it seemed as if the air was being torn apart.

'Gott, hilf uns!' Father Joachim exclaimed. He got to his feet as the gunfire ceased. They heard shouting outside and the priest made for the front door, determined to meet danger head on. Blaise, following him, was trembling: he had been shocked by the all too familiar sound of automatic gunfire, but he was not witless with fear. He noticed that the elaborately carved Black Forest cuckoo clock in the hallway was now showing a quarter to eleven. They should have been sitting down to a very late breakfast right now. Since waking at quarter past six that morning (he had recited Prime with Father Joachim in the chapel at seven o' clock), Blaise had drunk two mugs of coffee, but neither man had yet had anything to eat.

The two men opened the front door and stepped onto the veranda, and they saw below them a large group of armed men, dressed in shabby civilian attire. Neither the priest nor Blaise spoke, and as they stood there, they saw two armed men returning from the builders' camp with all but two of the builders being driven ahead of them at gunpoint. Another two armed men were returning, having rounded up the people who had remained in front of the church. Malachi and Thomas were among them. One of the guerrillas stepped forward and shouted in Shona to Blaise and Father Joachim as they stood on the veranda.

'You! White men! Come down!'

'Do as he says,' Father Joachim told Blaise. 'God help us, but I think we are about to be martyred.' The two men descended the short flight of stairs to the sparse lawn. Solomon Karuru stepped forward, raised his arm, and backhanded the priest viciously across the face. There was a low moan from the people whom the guerrillas had assembled to watch these proceedings. Father Joachim staggered, and Blaise stepped bravely in front of him, very afraid. Then he was knocked off his feet as Solomon Karuru struck him hard on the side of the jaw with a clenched fist. The guerrilla leader was a big man, powerfully built – thus his *nom de guerre*, *"Nzou."*

Solomon Karuru screamed at them in English, 'You white filth! You agents of oppression! You Christian jackals!' He paused to draw breath, then continued, his features contorted with hatred, 'Your god died on this day, yah? Now you will die like he did!'

Blaise had no doubts but that he was about to die. Strangely, his fear had diminished, although he continued to tremble: instead, he felt God's presence as surely as ever he had experienced it. He got to his feet. 'Spare the priest,' he said to the man who had struck them both, speaking

English. He switched to Shona. 'Spare the old man. He is old enough to be your father!'

For a moment, Solomon Karuru's features acquired a puzzled look, then he responded, also speaking in Shona, 'The old man can live. I will take you, you young white *bere* (hyena).' He clicked his fingers and waved a hand, and two of his men stepped forward and grabbed hold of Blaise by either arm. '*Uya!*' ('Come!') the guerrilla leader commanded them, and the whole group made their way towards the building site. Solomon Karuru had done this before, although his was a spontaneous decision this morning, triggered by the presence of the building site, which he had not known of. He knew what he was looking for now, and he found them: some eight inch nails that the builders intended using to fasten the massive roof timbers together. Next he found a heavy hammer.

He had his men cut the black cassock from Blaise, and in so doing, their sharp knives cut the skin of his chest, and the singlet he was wearing beneath his cassock was immediately stained with blood. The two men stripped the cassock from him, and Blaise was naked but for a singlet, a pair of underpants and his sandals. One of the men kicked his feet and pointed at them. Blaise bent and unfastened his sandals. He had a momentary recollection of the Passion recitation of that morning, of the humiliations Jesus had suffered before His crucifixion. The man then snapped in Shona, 'Take off the vest!' Blaise removed his singlet, revealing the twin cuts to his chest, which were marked by thin runnels of blood on his white skin. The two men then made two low stacks of bricks, each about a foot high, and spaced five feet apart, against one of the completed wooden walls, across which they placed a sturdy wooden plank, pushed up against the wall. Solomon Karuru spat at Blaise, 'Stand on the plank – no! – with your back to the wall, you white pig.'

And Blaise realised then what his subconscious had known for a while. An almost crippling fear swept over him. He had to brace his legs, or he would have collapsed. 'Jesus, Jesus,' he said, loudly enough to be heard by the men immediately in front of him. But he knew that this bitter cup could not – for Father Joachim's sake, and for the sake of the people from the Mission – be avoided.

'He calls to Jesus,' one of the men remarked in Shona. 'Perhaps Jesus will save him.'

Blaise was trembling violently now, and his breath grew short. He hoped it would not take long before he died. But his mind could hardly comprehend the horror of what was about to happen.

The guerrillas had assembled the people, with Father Joachim at their centre, in a half circle in front of the wooden wall. The group was covered by men holding automatic assault rifles. The guerrilla leader harangued the people loudly in English – perhaps because he was using words for which there were no Shona translations: they were (he shouted at them) reactionaries, counter revolutionaries, *kulaks*, collaborators, and they all deserved to die, but he would show them mercy; he would take the life only of this young white *bere*.

Solomon Karuru snapped out some commands in Shona, and one of the guerrillas stepped forward a pace and held the muzzle of his automatic assault rifle a few inches from Blaise's naked stomach. Blaise's upper limbs and torso looked very white. One of the men climbed onto the plank. He seized hold of Blaise's left arm, raised it, and held it against the wooden wall. A second man stepped onto the plank, holding the big hammer. He reached into his pocket and withdrew one of the enormous eight inch nails, the point of which he placed against Blaise's wrist. (Solomon Karuru, whose particular hobby this form of murder was, knew that nails pounded through the palms of a man's hands could result in the weight of the body causing the hands to tear free).

Blaise gave a terrible scream of agony and his body convulsed, as the huge iron nail was pounded through his left wrist. The guerrilla standing with the muzzle of his rifle inches from Blaise's stomach shoved it hard against his belly. Some of the people watching cried out, *'Jesu! Tenzi!'* ('Jesus! Lord!') Most, including Father Joachim, were now on their knees. The women had begun to weep. Then the two men turned to Blaise's other arm, and with brutal efficiency, Blaise's right arm was raised and held against the rough wood of the wall, and he shrieked again as the massive iron nail was driven through his wrist. Father Joachim cried out in Shona, 'Have mercy! For the love of God, have pity!'

The guerrilla leader kicked the priest hard with his booted foot, and commanded him to be silent. The horror was gathering pace, for now, Blaise, who was groaning in pain, felt his legs lifted and bent at the knees, and immediately, his full weight hung from his nailed wrists. He cried out again. The men and women who had been gathered as witnesses also cried out, in sympathy. One of the guerrillas, using both his

Saint Blaise

hands, held Blaise's bare feet together, one foot over the other, supporting his weight, and his companion hammered a third eight inch iron nail through Blaise's flesh, fastening his feet together against the wall. The plank was kicked free. Blood, bright scarlet, ran an inch or two down Blaise's wrists, then dripped on the ground below; blood still oozed from the two cuts on his chest; and blood ran in a thin stream from his nailed feet, pooling on the earth below.

The only way that Blaise could relieve the agony in his wrists and shoulders was to press down against the nail through his feet, and the only way that he could draw a deep breath was to do likewise.

'Oh God, oh Father, help me,' he managed to say, his voice shuddering. Malachi Tangwena, the houseboy, fell face forward in the dirt, his arms outstretched. A terrible anguished keening arose from the people watching Blaise's crucifixion, interspersed with cries to Lord Jesus.

And at this moment there came the sound of automatic gunfire not far away, and two of Solomon Karuru's men, who had been among the small contingent guarding the track to the Mission from the Umtali main road, came running back, shouting. Solomon Karuru began barking commands, and his men commenced to flee in different directions. The guerrilla leader then aimed his Kalashnikov at the crucified figure of the young white missionary, and squeezed the trigger, but there was only a dull metallic click: the gun's firing mechanism had jammed. Karuru swore, turned, and made off at a lope. Twice that morning, a miracle had saved Blaise's life.

Just a few minutes after Solomon Karuru had joined his

men in flight, uniformed white member of the British South Africa Police Reserve were making their way cautiously from the Mission perimeter to the scene of horror. Father Joachim shouted at the first of them, 'Help me! We must get him down!' He cast around, frantic with haste, repeating the words, 'My God, my God,' and whether because God heard him, or whether through good fortune, he saw the heavy sledgehammer he had noticed a day or two earlier, standing upright in a corner.

And all the while, a terrible groaning came from the crucified figure each time he tried to draw a full breath. The police reservists, who had in their time seen some terrible things, had come across nothing like this before. This was new to them. But the officer leading them realised what the old priest was about, and he seized the heavy sledgehammer from the dirtied, black cassocked figure, and ran towards Blaise and began to swing the sledgehammer against the wall, first to Blaise's left, then to his right, and with a creaking and snapping sound, the wooden timbers began to break, and the wall behind Blaise began to fall towards the security officer. But several of his men were there with him, and they ensured that the wall went down slowly backwards, with Blaise spread-eagled on top of it, flat on his back. The company's medic administered morphine via hypodermic injection into Blaise's upper arm while Father Joachim knelt at his side, holding one of his trapped hands.

Captain David Parry, the BSAP company's commanding officer, was not a religious man. The religious symbolism of the ghastly situation – on this particular day – evaded him; the man's suffering was all.

'You poor bastard,' he told Blaise. 'You poor bastard, we'll have you out of this soon.' He turned his head and spoke in Shona to Malachi, who, among the black onlookers, was now standing close by. 'We need to get the nails out,' he said. 'We need pliers.' He did not know the Shona for the word "pliars" (if there was such a word in Shona), but he mimicked extracting a nail, and Malachi understood what was needed, and ran to the shed behind the garages, where tools were kept, returning with a large pair of pliers.

The police reservist officer called one of his men forward, a big man, strongly built, and he handed him the pliers, while he held Blaise's left forearm firmly against the wood it was attached to. And Blaise moaned as the pliers gripped the head of the nail against the flesh and, with a side-to-side twisting motion, the nail was slowly withdrawn. Then his right wrist was freed, and now the two men turned to his feet. The reservist officer had to call two men to help hold Blaise still, as the big man extracted the enormous nail from his feet.

Blaise no longer moaned. Instead, he was making a child's whimper. 'Water!' the police reservist officer cried. And Blaise was given water to drink from a canteen while the officer held his head up. He gulped greedily, the water running down his chin. The police reservist commander removed the bandana from around his neck and wiped Blaise's sweat-soaked forehead with it. The medic cleaned and disinfected Blaise's terrible wounds, which were still bleeding, and bandaged them, then gave him an anti-tetanus injection, and another injection also, this one of antibiotics.

'How long was he up there?' the medic asked the old priest. 'How much blood has he lost?'

The priest looked almost beside himself with anguish and shock. He could not answer the questions. Instead, he just shook his head.

At a command from his officer, the big police reservist picked Blaise up, cradled in his arms like a child, and carried him to one of the Buffel mine-protected armoured troop-carriers (all three of which had been radioed forward from further up the track) in which the police had made the journey from Umtali. Blaise was laid on the floor of the vehicle, on a blanket which Malachi had fetched from the house, with a rolled up tunic behind his head, and the medic set up a saline drip, which one of the men held. Then the vehicle set off for the hospital at Umtali. In addition to Blaise, it was carrying four police reservists, the priest, and the company's medic in the back, and there were an additional two armed men in front with the driver, one of them a police reservist lieutenant.

Blaise had spoken not a word since being taken down from his cross, but despite the morphine, he whimpered with every bump in the track. The bandages around his wounds showed patches of blood blossoming beneath them. The men inside the vehicle were sweating with nervous tension. The air was very warm and humid. The going was smoother once they reached the tarred main road into Umtali, and they increased speed, the vehicle's headlights on bright. Twenty-five minutes later they were pulling up in front of the hospital. They were expected, for they had radioed ahead, and half a dozen hospital medical staff were waiting outside the main entrance, including two black orderlies with a wheeled stretcher.

Back at the Mission, a BSAP unit led by a lieutenant was left behind to guard against further trouble, while the remainder of the company set off in hot pursuit of Solomon Karuru's band. But he and his band, the members of which had scattered, had had a head start, and they had not been found by sundown. By dawn the next day they had regrouped in the mountains.

Chapter Seventeen

Blaise spent a week in the hospital in Umtali, during which time his condition was stabilised. Father Joachim visited him every day, bringing with him the sacraments from the Mass, so that he could give Blaise Communion. Blaise took the bread and the wine meekly, but whether he understood what he was doing, remained unclear to Father Joachim, for Blaise remained silent. The priest was not a sentimental man (excessive sentiment was not much admired by the Jesuits), but a practical, down to earth shepherd of his flock, but he felt something akin to veneration for Blaise, who had, he knew, saved his life – and perhaps that of many others – through his sharing in the Lord's crucifixion, and he prayed on his knees by the young man's bedside. But Blaise made not a sound, except when he fell into a doze, and then he would often whimper like a hurt child.

After a week in the hospital at Umtali, Blaise, accompanied by a doctor and a nurse, was flown in a Rhodesian Air Force Douglas DC-7 transporter in three stages (Umtali – Salisbury; Salisbury – Johannesburg; Johannesburg – Cape Town) to Groote Schuur Hospital in Cape Town. Here, his family were able to visit him. Blaise's father and both his brothers were his first visitors, on Saturday afternoon the 21st April. They found a shockingly changed son and brother, his face yellowed beneath the tan, his cheeks sunken, his flaxen hair cropped short (for he had worn it short on the Mission), his arms by his side on top of the sheet, the wrists heavily bandaged. There was some sort of arched frame over his feet, for the sheet was raised above them.

'My boy! My poor boy! What have they done to you?' his father exclaimed. He pulled up a chair alongside the bed, and reaching tentatively for Blaise's hand, the fingers of which were visible beneath the bandaging of the wrists. Hugh and Lawrence, solemn faced, stood together on the other side of the bed, staring down at their brother.

Guy Cressingham had of course been told what had been done to Blaise (and he in turn had told his two younger sons): they had treated him as Jesus Christ had been treated; they had crucified him, driving nails into his flesh, and he had not spoken a word since. The Cressingham family found themselves facing a situation which left them confused and bewildered. Blaise's sufferings, replicating as they did those of the Lord, caused his family to regard him with something like awe. Neither Guy nor his two younger sons ever spent much time reflecting on their Catholic faith; they were not very pious; now they simply did not know how to approach Blaise. And Blaise, who neither spoke, smiled, nor even met his family's gaze, made it no easier for him. As they had gathered either side of his bed, Blaise's glance had merely flickered across their faces, then slid away. Only when they were leaving, did he look, briefly, directly at them again.

It was Hugh who gave voice to their feelings, on their way home after that first visit. 'God must love Blaise more than any of us could ever understand, to have made him suffer what Jesus suffered for our sakes.'

'If that is God's love,' Lawrence, usually so silent, remarked, 'then I am glad that God pays me no attention at all.'

Guy Cressingham had undergone something very like an epiphany as he had sat by Blaise's bedside, holding his son's fingers: he, who rarely prayed except by rote during the Mass, felt an overwhelming need to pray, and he wished to get home and retreat to the privacy of his study. He understood Blaise no better than he ever had, but he knew now that his eldest son was sanctified, holy, someone very special in God's eyes. He felt confusion: why Blaise; why *their* family?

The next day, for the first time in a long time, Guy and both his younger sons attended Sunday Mass together as a family at Saint Mark's in Newlands. That afternoon, Father Edmund Bartlet, the university's Catholic Chaplain, and Blaise's spiritual director, had visited Blaise. He brought with him the Host from that morning's Mass, and Blaise obediently but silently took the bread, and swallowed a sip of wine. On Monday morning, Guy Cressingham visited Father Anthony O' Connor, the Priest at Saint Mark's.

'I do not know what to say to Blaise when I visit him in hospital, Father,' Guy told the priest. 'I feel as if I were trying to talk to a saint. But whatever I – or anyone else – has to say, he remains silent. But this is my boy, my eldest son! I have known him all his life! Why am I afraid – no, that's not quite the word – why am I in awe of him?'

Guy spent almost an hour with Father Anthony, and the final ten minutes of that visit were spent in prayer with the priest.

Father Anthony O' Connor visited Blaise at Groote Schuur later that Monday afternoon, where he found Guy and Hugh already by Blaise's bedside. An hour later, as Blaise's father and brother were departing, the Father Superior, Father Michael Schmidt, arrived. Left alone with Father Anthony O' Connor by Blaise's bedside, he (a supremely practical administrator, generally unmoved by spirituality) got to his knees on one side of the bed and began to pray. Father Anthony, on the far side of the bed, followed suit. The nursing staff, who of course knew that Blaise had been crucified, and were almost as much in awe of him as his own family was, left the two priests and Blaise undisturbed; they did not wish to break into this tableau, which reminded some of them of the sacred images they had seen on Christmas cards and suchlike religious iconography. Even the most irreligious among them was strangely moved, and some, who had not been to church in years, felt a need to attend a church service the following Sunday.

Blaise, despite his silence, was evangelizing those who came in contact with him. His very presence was putting those long ignorant of heartfelt prayer – beginning with his own father – and those ignorant of recent religious observation, in mind of God again.

Hugh contacted Blaise's friend, Roderick, whose postal address and telephone number he had found in Blaise's address book (which Father Joachim had packed, together with his other belongings, before he had left the hospital at Umtali for Cape Town). Hugh knew that Roderick was closer to his brother than anyone else was. He also spoke to Nicolette Dillon, to whom (despite their relationship having cooled somewhat) he himself was still close. As a consequence, both Roderick and Nicolette happened to visit Blaise on the afternoon of Tuesday 24th April. Seeing Blaise's tortured appearance – that yellowed and sunken-cheeked, but still beautiful face, so full of pain, and the bandaged wrists – Nicolette felt love and compassion threaten to overwhelm her. She had to fight back tears. "Oh, my dear, darling Blaise," she thought.

Blaise did not withdraw his fingers when Nicolette took them. Nor, when Roderick appeared not long after, did Blaise resist the grasp of his friend's hand on his fingers, and Roderick was appalled at the stark evidence of his friend's suffering. But both Nicolette and Roderick felt that Blaise was not wholly there. It was almost as if he had found some other plane, some other dimension than this earthly one, within which to retreat from the horror he had suffered. Both these visitors loved Blaise; both felt their hearts breaking for him, and each felt constrained in expressing their love for him. Nicolette refrained from an over enthusiastic demonstration of her love because she understood that Blaise had been consciously living for quite some time as if he had sworn the three basic vows, one of which was chastity; Roderick, because if what he truly felt for Blaise were ever to be made known, society would ostracise and scorn him.

The two visitors soon found that it was much more difficult to talk to someone who remained silent, who did not meet your gaze, than they had imagined. After a while they found themselves chatting with one another across Blaise, each holding Blaise's fingers, and casting glances sometimes at his face, hoping to see some recognition on his part, but Blaise was far away from them.

'I think we should pray,' said Roderick, after some time had passed.

'Yes, let's pray,' Nicolette agreed. The two sat either side of Blaise's bed, each clasping their hands together in their laps, and Roderick, so recently (thanks to Blaise) a convert to the Faith, surprised Nicolette by beginning to pray out loud. 'Oh Lord,' he prayed, 'please heal our friend Blaise. Please bring him ease from his suffering. Please deliver him from the memories that torment him, and please set him free from hurt.' And Nicolette responded, 'Amen.'

Then she began to recite the Lord's Prayer, and Roderick immediately joined her. Each crossed themselves afterwards. They caught each other's eye, and a moment of true amity and accord passed between them.

Over the coming weeks, Blaise was to receive numerous visitors: friends from university; friends from CathSoc; the priests and scholastics from the small Jesuit community in Rosebank; his family's parish priest, Father Anthony O' Connor; Father Francis Sullivan from Saint Michael and All Angels in Athlone, where Blaise had been undertaking pastoral and youth work before departing for Rhodesia; and of course, visits from his family (although Hugh was a far more frequent visitor than Lawrence was). Blaise's grandparents and his aunt Fiona were also among his visitors. But the most diligent visitors were undoubtedly Nicolette and Roderick, who often arrived together. After a while, they became so well known to the ward staff that adherence to the hospital's strict visiting hours was waived in their case.

And Blaise spoke not one word; nor did he meet the eye, except in passing, of those who ministered to him or visited him. But he was not in a vegetative state: it appeared that he could hear others when they spoke to him, if they repeated themselves several times, and he co-operated with those who nursed him, obeying requests made to him – all except the request to speak.

From the second week of May, Roderick and Nicolette began to push Blaise in a wheelchair to a small enclosed garden, a secret garden the nurses had told them of, where the nursing staff sat and gossiped and smoked during their breaks. In fact, none of the three young people smoked: neither Roderick nor Nicolette had ever acquired the habit, and Blaise had not smoked since having given up his cigarettes for Lent, and although his father had brought him a couple of packets of Peter Stuyvesant and a box of matches on his first visit, the cigarette packets had remained unopened.

The garden was protected from the wind, but it caught the afternoon sun. Roderick told himself that Blaise enjoyed these visits to the garden. There was a single oak tree growing in it, and as the month of May progressed, its leaves began to turn bronze. Then the first winter cold front hit Cape Town, and it rained for day after day, and that was the end of these trips to the secret garden.

In late May, Roderick – Nicolette could not make it that afternoon – was sitting with Blaise in the small patients' lounge attached to the ward, having pushed him there in a wheelchair, when, to his amazement and utter joy, he heard Blaise speak his name: 'Roddy.'

Roderick turned his head and looked at his friend; there was a remarkable change in his appearance. Blaise's gaze was focused; his features had regained colour – indeed, there was almost a radiance about them – and he held Roderick's eye, and smiled at him.

'Oh thank God!' Roderick exclaimed, his voice breaking. 'You're back!' He smiled broadly, his eyes damp, and reached for Blaise's hands, which he could grasp fully now, for only light bandaging remained on his wrists.

'I've been away,' Blaise remarked, in an almost conversational tone. 'But I'm back now. How are you, Roddy?'

'Dear God, I cannot begin to tell you how happy I am that you've come back, Blaise! How do you feel?'

Blaise looked thoughtful. 'I'm OK, I think. Perhaps a little tired though.'

'Blaise, do you know where you are?' asked Roderick, suddenly afraid that Blaise might not be entirely cognisant of his circumstances.

'In hospital, I presume,' Blaise answered. 'Brother Ass needed healing, and my mind needed resting.' He smiled again at his friend. 'You've been here almost every day, haven't you, Roddy?'

Roderick was still holding his friend's hands. 'Yes, I have. Oh, Blaise, I feel like getting on my knees and thanking God!'

'Then do so,' said Blaise. 'God is pleased when we give Him thanks.'

And Roderick got to his knees in front of Blaise, who placed a hand on top of his friend's head, saying, 'God bless you, Roddy.'

Roderick knelt like that for three or four minutes, his head bowed, close to weeping with joy. He quite forgot his surroundings, sparing no thought for the other patients and their visitors in the lounge, who must surely be finding this scene a strange one. He knew that Blaise had been touched by God.

When they returned to the ward (for after a while Blaise told Roderick that he needed to rest), the Ward Sister was thrilled to hear Blaise speak to her, and the doctor who visited him a little later was equally delighted, even if the psychiatrist, who arrived not long after the doctor, urged caution.

But Roderick was quite certain that Blaise had returned for good. 'Ward Sister,' he asked, 'are you able to phone Blaise's family and tell them the good news?'

And the Ward Sister found Guy Cressingham's telephone number, and began to dial it.

In Bishopscourt, Guy said, 'Thank you! Thank you! Dear God, I am so happy!'

'We are all delighted,' the Ward Sister responded.

'And Blaise knows where he is?' asked Guy. 'He knows who he is? Can he remember what happened to him?'

'It's early days, Mr. Cressingham. How much Blaise remembers, I do not yet know. I'm sure the doctors will be able to tell you more when you visit.'

'I'm coming now!' declared Guy. 'I'll be there soon.'

'That's good. I'll make sure that Doctor Blair talks to you.'

Doctor Blair was the psychiatrist handling Blaise's case. He and Guy had spoken together frequently during the previous weeks. When in forty-five minutes' time Guy rushed up to the ward, he was greeted by a son who looked, as Guy later put it, "all there." Roderick withdrew from Blaise's bedside, to leave father and son alone, and went to wait in the patients' lounge.

Blaise knew his father, and smiled at him in welcome, and held his father's hand for almost half a minute. Exercising what was for him a rare sensitivity, Guy did not seek to establish how much Blaise actually remembered. Instead, he talked about home, about the family, and he made a joke about hospital food, and he told Blaise how much he was missed by so many people.

'Roderick tells me I have had a lot of visitors, pretty much every day,' responded Blaise. 'I'm touched at people's concern for me.'

'Of course they're concerned, Blaise!' his father declared. 'A great many people love you.' And as Guy spoke these words, he thought, "That's true: Blaise is loved by a great many people."

Halfway through the visit, Doctor Blair arrived, shook hands with Guy Cressingham, and smiled at Blaise. 'How are you feeling, Blaise?' he asked. 'Not too tired, I hope? No headache?'

'I'm fine, Doctor,' Blaise replied. 'I'm glad to see my Dad.'

'Can we talk afterwards in my office, Mr. Cressingham?' the psychiatrist requested. And when, later, Guy was sitting in Doctor Blair's office, the psychiatrist said, 'Your son is rational, and comprehends his surroundings. How much he remembers, we cannot be sure yet. One has to be careful in cases such as this: you do not want to revisit unassimilated trauma on the patient.'

'But you think he will remember everything that happened to him?'

'I cannot say,' the psychiatrist answered. 'Sometimes the patient never regains his full memory of the traumatic incident. Time will tell. The important thing is, not to force the issue. Do you understand, Mr. Cressingham? Please do not ask your son too many questions. We take things one day at a time now.'

'I understand,' said Guy.

But a few days later, Roderick put a question to Blaise, 'You told me, almost your first words, that you had been away, Blaise. Can you tell me, where had you been?'

Blaise did not respond immediately. He seemed to be thinking. Then at last he turned and looked at Roderick, and his eyes were gentle. 'You will not yet understand, Roddy.' He touched his friend's hand. 'We will not talk about it now.'

Roderick was at a loss to understand what Blaise meant by these words, but he trusted his friend and he loved him, and he did understand that this was not a subject to pursue – not yet, anyway. 'It doesn't matter,' he responded. 'What matters is that you're back, and I thank God for it.'

'Dont worry, Roddy. I shant be going away again.'

Chapter Eighteen

By early June, Blaise was able to move for short distances on his damaged feet using just a pair of crutches. He grew rapidly stronger, and every few days he was able to walk a little further with the aid of his crutches. In mid-June the doctors decided that he could go home. Guy, Hugh and Lawrence came to collect him, and when they got home, Anna and Magda were waiting to welcome him.

'*Welkom* Blaise!' they greeted him. '*Hierdie is n' gelukkige dag!*' [*] exclaimed Anna. Blaise, supporting himself on his crutches in the hall, submitted to a careful embrace by each of the servants in turn.

Only now did Blaise learn that while he had been in hospital, Heidi had finally had to be put to sleep. She had been a very old dog. But this chapter of childhood was not yet quite closed: Tinker the Siamese cat, who was as old as Heidi had been, but was carrying his age well, was still at home, and it was with pleasure that Blaise welcomed him onto his lap in the den.

---

[*] Afrikaans – 'This is a happy day!'

'They have cats and dogs in Heaven, you know,' he remarked. Guy blinked, wondering where that had come from, but Hugh smiled.

There was a celebratory dinner that evening, to which Roderick, and Blaise's old school friend, Gregory Dillon, and his sister, Nicolette, had been invited. (Gregory had been among Blaise's many visitors in hospital). Guy asked Blaise to say the blessing before the meal, and this Blaise did. His was not a formulaic blessing, but heartfelt and poignant. He thanked God for His bountiful blessings, for the love of family, for friendship, and for recovery from sickness. He thanked God for the meal, and asked Him to bless to His service those who partook of it. The "Amen" around the table after the blessing was a fervent one. Then Guy Cressingham opened a bottle of Robertson Winery sparkling wine (a South African made alternative to French Champagne), and when everyone's glass was charged, he proposed a toast to Blaise, who afterwards thanked everyone there for their love and kindness. Blaise basked in the warm, secure embrace of his family, of people who loved him, and although this would not serve for long to provide him with all that he required from life, right now, it was exactly what he needed.

Blaise appreciated the trouble Magda had gone to. This was his first home-cooked meal in what seemed a very long time, for in the intervening period, he had been to Hell, and to Heaven – and come back again. The meal commenced with a thick chicken broth, then moved on to grilled yellowtail. (The fish was fresh from the Hout Bay quayside the previous day, and had been kept refrigerated overnight and through the course of today). The main course was that classic Cape dish which Magda prepared so beautifully: it was named *Bobotie*, and was made of spiced mince beef with plump, succulent sultanas, and a creamy egg and milk topping, all baked together in the oven. After this spicy main course, chocolate mousse, or a fruit salad alternative, were served for dessert, and at the end of the meal, a cheese platter with crackers made its way around the table, accompanied by a semi-sweet Cape dessert wine.

Blaise had of course not drunk any wine since his time at Saint Joseph's Mission, and although he had had only one glass of sparkling wine and one glass of dessert wine, by the end of the meal the alcohol had gone to his head, and he was feeling sleepy. Only Anna noticed that he had ate in fact very little: as she collected the plates after each course, she saw that Blaise had barely touched his food. The rest of the family, and Blaise's three friends, were far too happy, and (thanks in part to the two bottles of sparkling wine) were talking far too animatedly, to pay any attention to how little Blaise was eating.

Blaise joined the others in the sitting room for a while, where an aromatic pinewood fire was crackling and spitting. Anna served them coffee. Guy lighted a cigar, and Hugh and Gregory joined him, accepting happily a Romeo y Julieta cigar each which Guy handed around. Blaise and his youngest brother, however, declined; Blaise no longer smoked at all. Guy said, with a smile, 'I don't suppose you would like one, Nicolette?' He laughed.

Nicolette joined in his laughter. 'No thanks, Mr. Cressingham!'

'Come on! I've told you before; you must call me Guy!' he reminded the young woman.

'Alright – Guy,' Nicolette responded.

No one troubled Blaise with questions about events from the recent past, and no one asked him what his plans were now. It was a happy gathering, and they stuck to light hearted topics. When Blaise stood and excused himself, saying that he was tired, they were solicitous for him, quick to understand.

'Thank you all for coming,' Blaise told his friends. 'I've enjoyed myself.' And he went upstairs to his childhood bedroom, which he was now to occupy once again. His father wanted Blaise close to hand, and there had been no suggestion that he move back into the self contained guest flat above the garages. Blaise was happy enough with this arrangement. Right now, he needed very much to talk with God. He still struggled to kneel, so he sat in an armchair, his back straight, crossed himself, folded his hands on his lap, closed his eyes, and began. Before long, he felt God's presence, and a dialogue commenced, which would have been a silent one, had Blaise not occasionally made small sounds of deep contentment. He was still there an hour later, oblivious to the passage of time. When he returned to himself, he blinked a few times, crossed himself again, and taking his crutches, he stood up and went to his bed. His feet were almost healed, although they would remain horribly scarred. Tomorrow he would see if he could get about the house without the help of the crutches, using only one of the walking sticks he had always taken with him when hiking in the mountains.

Father Michael Schmidt, the Cape Town Superior (soon

to become the Regional Superior), and Father Edmund Bartlet, the Catholic Chaplain at the university, and Blaise's spiritual director, spoke together at length about Blaise and his future. Father James Nolan, the current Formations Director, was also present during these discussions, but he did not know Blaise as well as Father Bartlet did, and he had little to contribute. Father Michael Schmidt expressed his concerns that Blaise's mind might not yet have fully recovered, but Father Edmund believed that Blaise had made an almost total recovery.

'We can never expect such an experience as Blaise has endured not to change a man, Father Superior,' he conceded, 'but I believe that Blaise is one hundred percent himself again. As to what his future in the Society may be, Blaise himself has told me that he wishes to minister to the poor, the marginalised, above all, to the oppressed, and he and I both understand that by this, he means that he wishes to work with black and coloured people. I am not a psychiatrist, but I believe that this alone indicates that he is not suffering from lasting … uhh … I think the word is "unassimilated"; from unassimilated trauma.'

The Superior of the Cape Town community looked thoughtful. Then he said, 'In light of what you tell me, I am considering allowing Blaise to work with Father Peter O' Leary at Saint Raphael's in Gugulethu.' He paused, then continued, 'Blaise's situation is somewhat peculiar: the way I see it, Blaise has in effect already begun his novitiate …'

'Yes, Father Superior,' Father Edmund interjected, 'he certainly has. He has been living in community, one way or another, for well over a year already, and during that time he has been engaged in Apostolic activities: there's the time he put in at Saint Michael and All Angels, then the nine months he spent with Father Joachim at the mission in Rhodesia …'

'Precisely,' Father Michael Schmidt agreed. 'I know it is irregular – if I may use that word – but sending Blaise to the Novitiate now would be a backward step…'

Father James Nolan, the Formations Director, interrupted him at this point. 'If I may say, I wonder if this is wise, Father Superior – depriving Blaise of the structured and disciplined communal life lived at the Novitiate?'

Father Michael Schmidt pondered a while, before responding, 'I believe Blaise has already learned more than the Novitiate could teach him.' Then he turned to Father Edmund, saying, 'I have one small doubt, though: you do not think that perhaps Blaise may be suffering from spiritual pride – a sense of Election – as a consequence of his terrible experience?'

'Oh gosh, no, Father!' the Chaplain exclaimed. 'I doubt I have ever found so much self assured humility in one so young. Blaise is self confident, certainly, with a rock solid faith, and a powerfully developed spirituality – but of pride, I discern no evidence at all.'

'I am glad to hear that. I think perhaps I agree with you, but you know him so much better than I do. I wanted to be sure.'

And so it was agreed that once Blaise felt himself ready to resume his duties within the Society, he would live and work with Father Peter O' Leary at Saint Raphael's in the vast black township of Gugulethu, located near D.F. Malan Airport.

Saint Blaise

'At the end of the year, Blaise can take his First Vows. Next year, he can become a Scholastic,' the Father Superior continued. 'Please ensure that he has submitted an application for the undergraduate course in Philosophy next year, Father Edmund. In due course, he can study Theology at some other location. But until that time, he will be living here in community.'

'Certainly, Father Superior.'

Father Edmund was pleased. He hoped that the course in Philosophy might serve to temper the highly individualistic streak of mysticism in Blaise of which his spiritual director was becoming aware. He was pleased also at the prospect of Blaise remaining a member of the Rosebank community during his further studies at the University of Cape Town. Not only was Father Edmund extremely fond of the young man, he was intensely curious to witness the development of Blaise's powerful spirituality, and hopeful of helping shape its direction.

Blaise had been under discipline within the Society since at least early 1978, when he had begun living in community in Rosebank, and neither priest doubted for a moment that he would fall in with their wishes for him.

At Saint Joseph's Mission in Rhodesia's Eastern Highlands, a cult of venerating Blaise's memory had already arisen. At first, Father Joachim had been troubled by this, but on reflection, he had decided that no harm would come of it, and so he did not actively discourage it. The local people were sure that Blaise was a living saint, and that even while he yet lived, he could intercede for them with God. A large wooden cross was fixed to the wall where Blaise had been crucified, and there were always flowers left at its foot, and often, one or two people would be seen kneeling there, praying. Curiously, some of the people insisted that Blaise had in fact been dead when taken down from his crucifixion, and that he was already with God in Heaven. This belief was strengthened by Blaise's disappearance immediately after he was taken down from his cross, and his failure to have been seen since. Father Joachim attempted to disabuse such people of this belief, but despite there being plenty of witnesses to hand who had seen that Blaise yet lived after being taken down from his cross, this belief in his having passed on persisted among many in the district. Father Joachim observed how, since that terrible Good Friday, the numbers attending the Sunday Mass had swelled, and he had made more than half a dozen new converts to the Faith before the end of 1979. Even in his absence, Blaise was bringing people to God and to the Church.

In July of 1979, Robert Chitepo, the eldest son of the headman Timothy Chitepo, whose warning to the Mission on Good Friday had allowed Father Joachim to telephone the security forces minutes before the guerrillas' arrival, was thrown from his horse. He landed on his head on the hard, rocky ground, and when he was found some hours later, he was unconscious. Father Joachim, whom Timothy Chitepo had asked for help, rushed the boy, accompanied by his father, to the hospital at Umtali, but the prognosis for recovery any time soon was not good. The doctors warned the priest that the boy might not come out of his coma, but this, Father Joachim kept from the boy's father. He remained with the grieving father and the unconscious youth for much

Saint Blaise

of the afternoon, but he had to return to the Mission before the dark descended from the mountains in the east.

At about nine o' clock that night, Friday the 13th, exactly three months after the Good Friday on which Blaise had been crucified, Timothy was kneeling by his son's bedside, and he was praying to *Sent Blez* (as Blaise had already become known in the district) to help his son. Afterwards, Timothy Chitepo described to Father Joachim in these words, speaking in Shona, what followed: '*Sent Blez* appeared, his face shining, at my son's bedside, and I fell to the floor, but I looked up and I saw the bleeding wounds in the wrists and feet of *Sent Blez*, and I saw him lay his hand on my son's head, and then suddenly, *Sent Blez* was gone again. But my son sat up in bed, and was fully conscious, and he spoke to me, and asked me, "Where is *Sent Blez*?"'

The priest sought the views of the doctors at the hospital. 'I would not say that Robert's sudden recovery was miraculous – such sudden awakenings from a coma, though rare, have happened before – but it was certainly extremely unusual, and most unexpected,' one of the doctors told Father Joachim. 'Curiously, there was no mark on the young man's head, no indication of any injury, and that I cannot explain.'

Father Joachim wrote to Father Michael Schmidt (now the Regional Superior of the newly created Dependent Region of South Africa) in Cape Town, describing the incident. The Regional Superior received this letter towards the end of July. Having read it, he took the letter and went to find Father Edmund, and said to him, 'Please read this. It is a letter from Father Joachim Schneider at

Saint Joseph's in Rhodesia, where Blaise served – and tell me what you think.'

Father Edmund saw bewilderment written on the Regional Superior's face, but as he read the letter, he himself felt little surprise, only wonder. When he had reread the passage describing the visitation at the young man's bedside in hospital, he sat and thought for a while. Then he spoke, 'It would be interesting to find out from Blaise what he was doing at about nine o' clock on the night of Friday the 13th July.'

He was thinking of that famous Franciscan priest and mystic, Padre Pio, who had, his followers claimed, been able to bilocate – that is, to be in two different locations at the same time. He dismissed these thoughts; there had to be some other explanation, most likely, that the injured youth's father had experienced an hallucination – but then, why had the boy, on coming out of his coma, asked his father where *"Sent Blez"* was? And how did one explain the absence of any sign of an injury?

The Regional Superior spoke again, 'This is to go no further than the two of us, Father Edmund, you understand? Well – the three of us, if we speak to Blaise about it. Though Father Joachim in Rhodesia will of course have told his superiors about the incident.'

'Of course, Father Superior,' Father Edmund replied. But he knew that a story such as this one would soon spread, first across Rhodesia's Manicaland Province, then across the rest of the country, and sooner than later, into South Africa. Stories such as this one were impossible to silence. He resolved to talk to Blaise, to try to find out what Blaise had been doing at nine o' clock on the evening of Friday 13th. 'Will you permit me to talk to Blaise, Father Superior?'

'Very well. I think we need to know whether there is anything to this story, Father Edmund.'

Two days later, after Sunday morning Mass, the Chaplain asked the young man, 'Blaise, can we talk?'

'Yes, Father Edmund.'

The priest led Blaise to his study and asked him to sit down. Father Edmund wondered where to begin. He sat quietly for a minute, smiling at Blaise, who stared back at him, perfectly composed.

'Blaise,' the Chaplain said at last, 'I know you have a rich prayer life. Can you cast your mind back to nine o' clock on the evening of Friday 13th, about two weeks ago? Were you perhaps praying at that hour?'

Blaise thought a while. 'Yes,' he replied. 'I pray for an hour or so every night after Compline.'

'Did anything unusual happen during your prayers that evening?'

But Blaise would struggle to answer such a question: he was hardly conscious of himself at all when he prayed; he communed, wordlessly for the most part, with the triune God. However, he now remembered receiving a particular directive from the Lord during prayer about two weeks ago.

'Yes … there was someone the Lord asked me to pray for, Father Edmund, now that I come to think of it – if we're talking about the same night – a very clear instruction from God,' Blaise replied after a while.

'We have received a rather extraordinary report from Saint Joseph's Mission,' Father Edmund continued. 'It seems that one of the parishioners claims that you appeared before him at about nine o' clock that evening of Friday 13th and healed his seriously ill son.'

Blaise smiled, a happy smile which lighted up his face, and remarked, 'That was Robert, then, a nice kid. And you say that he is recovered?'

Father Edmund Bartlet felt the wind sucked from his lungs. He closed his eyes. "Lord," he prayed silently.

'Blaise, were you there, in the hospital at Umtali, as the boy's father claims you were?' (What an insane question, the priest thought!)

Blaise took no time to consider his reply. 'Of course I wasn't there, Father Edmund,' he answered with a smile. 'But yes, I remember Jesus asking me to pray for Robert Chitepo, who was, He told me, very ill, and needed my prayers, and that is what I did: I asked the Lord to heal him. So you say that he is well, then?'

Father Edmund was dumbstruck. For all of three minutes he sat silently, staring at Blaise, aware that he was in the presence of a true mystic, if not in fact a saint. Then at last he spoke. 'Yes, the boy is fully recovered.'

'I am glad to hear it,' remarked Blaise. 'I must thank the Lord.'

The priest gathered the scattered strands of his reason and tried to knit them together again. After a while, he said, 'Let's keep this between ourselves, eh, Blaise?'

'OK, Father Edmund. Oh – I was meaning to ask, when may I begin working with Father Peter at Saint Raphael's in Gugulethu? I think I'm up to it, now.'

Father Edmund stared. It appeared that Blaise had not

even registered this extraordinary event as being particularly remarkable. He made an effort to calm his thoughts. 'If you feel up to it, I don't see why you may not begin immediately. But the decision is the Regional Superior's to make. Let me talk to him, Blaise.'

Blaise smiled again. 'Thanks, Father Edmund.' He stood. 'Was there anything else you needed to talk to me about?'

'No – no; that's all for now. Will you be seeing your family today?'

'*Ja*, we're having lunch at my grandparents.'

'Give them all my regards,' the priest said. Of course, he knew Guy Cressingham quite well by now, and he had met Hugh, Lawrence, and Blaise's grandparents on a number of occasions.

'I shall do, Father Edmund.' Blaise thought a moment, then he said, 'Why don't you join us all, Father? I'm sure my family would be glad to see you.'

The Chaplain smiled. 'That's kind of you, Blaise, but perhaps some other time, when your family is expecting me.'

Blaise left the priest sitting behind his desk, an expression compounded of bewilderment and thoughtfulness on his face. Father Edmund was wondering what to tell the Regional Superior – if indeed he should tell him anything at all. It might be better for Blaise and for the Society itself, if he kept this between Blaise and himself. But had he the right to keep this from Father Michael?

"I must pray about this," he thought. He proceeded to do so.

Chapter Nineteen

Guy Cressingham was wondering why Blaise seemed to be drawn to living and working in dangerous parts of the World. Gugulethu was notorious for the shockingly high number of murders which took place within its environs. But it was not danger which drew Blaise; it was poverty, marginalisation, and need. If he had thought that Athlone had been bleak and poverty stricken, then he was to think again once he saw Gugulethu for the first time: compared to Gugulethu, Athlone was a bourgeois garden suburb. Gugulethu was a vast, sprawling black township of mean houses built on sandy ground, within a near treeless environment lacking almost any signs of aesthetic beauty. This, thought Blaise, is where people are robbed of the hopes they once entertained; hopes which had drawn them from the rural Eastern Cape homelands of Transkei and Ciskei to the outskirts of Cape Town. Which is why Saint Raphael's amazed him: dating from the mid nineteen-sixties, the church's interior was minimalist (some would call it stark), and its immediate surroundings were no less bleak than the rest of Gugulethu, but its congregation – made up mostly of women – was fervent and committed, and Father Peter O' Leary, an Irish Jesuit who had arrived in Cape Town about thirty years ago, was an energetic sixty year old whose ebullient spirit, and determination to find something good in everyone and everything, won Blaise's admiration.

On a cold and wet morning during the second week of August, Father Francis Sullivan, with whom Blaise had worked in Athlone, collected him at the Jesuit house in Rosebank, and they drove to Saint Raphael's. Blaise would not have his own car with him: it would almost certainly have been stolen.

Father Peter welcomed Blaise. 'I have been looking forward to your arrival, Blaise! You will be a tremendous help to me. Do you speak Xhosa?'

'I'm afraid not, Father Peter. I speak Shona, but I understand it doesn't bear much resemblance to Xhosa.'

The priest smiled at Blaise. 'Well, here's your first lesson in the language: it's *Xhosa*.' (He pronounced the "Xh" with an explosive, clicking sound). 'See if you can manage that, young Blaise.'

Blaise did not do too badly. 'Well done! You will soon pick up the language,' Father Peter told him. 'I will teach you whenever I get the time. Now come inside, both of you. I am sure you could do with a coffee – eh, Father Francis?'

The two men, both wearing their cassocks (although the collar of Blaise's layman's cassock made no allowance for showing the white band that ordained ministers wore at their neck), followed the cheerful Irish priest into the priest's house, which was attached to the church. Here they met Catherine Mxenge, Father Peter's housekeep.

'But much more than just my housekeeper!' the priest announced with a laugh. 'Catherine knows the names of every single member of our congregation, and their family histories.'

The woman smiled somewhat shyly at the two newcomers. Blaise returned her smile, and said, 'I am very glad to meet you, Catherine.' In due course, Blaise would learn what her Xhosa given name was: it was "Esihle," which meant someone who is beautiful, and it was an apt name for this ever courteous woman with a gentle, helpful nature and a sweet smile.

Father Peter lighted a cigarette and chatted away cheerfully while Catherine made them coffee. Father Francis would be staying for an early lunch before leaving them. Blaise was thinking that he could get on with Father Peter – unless he was to find over time that the priest's relentless good cheer was to become overwhelming. But Blaise felt that a cheerful, optimistic spirit was needed in such a location as Gugulethu. He reminded himself that he had asked to come here, for here he would find the people whom he could hope to help: people ground down by poverty and by the oppressions of Apartheid.

Blaise spent the next four and a half months living in Gugulethu. During this time, he saw little of the outside world, for, lacking a car of his own, and forbidden by the Apartheid laws from sharing the black transport facilities in and out of the township (indeed, merely by living in Gugulethu on a permanent basis, Father Peter had had to obtain special dispensation from the Department of Home Affairs), Blaise had to rely on a rare lift to the Rosebank community from Father Peter, or on an equally rare visit from one of the priests from outside, and once in a while, he borrowed Father Peter's car and drove to Cape Town city centre, to visit some official or other at the City Hall on behalf of one or another of the families of the parish. But he did not linger in Cape Town: Father Peter usually needed his car back as soon as possible. (Thrice, however, Roderick braved the drive into Gugulethu, a potentially dangerous journey for a white man, to collect Blaise and take him out for the day, bringing him back in the evening). On Father Peter's advice, Blaise always wore his cassock when he walked in the township; it afforded him some safety, and not only because people would know then that he was carrying nothing worth stealing.

Within three months, with daily help from Catherine Mxenge, occasional lessons from Father Peter, and the guidance of his Xhosa primer, Blaise had learned to speak Xhosa at least well enough to conduct a basic conversation in the language, and long before that, he was able to greet people, ask after their health, and respond to their enquiries after his. The warmth and charm of his personality (characteristics which became more and more pronounced as he grew older) made up for his linguistic deficiencies. He came to know several township families, parishioners who invited him into their homes, and with whom he sometimes shared a meal. He came to admire their pride in their little homes, which were generally spotless inside, and their bravery in the face of great economic adversity.

Blaise felt happy and fulfilled. His mission, as he saw it, was to fight these people's corner; to act as their representative with the white authorities; to agitate for such small help from the City Council and the state as they were occasionally entitled to; to bring them the comfort and hope that faith provided; to express solidarity with them, and to live as simply as they did. Living in Gugulethu, Blaise could see the distant silhouette of Table Mountain in the west: that symbol of another life, of another society; a life with which he was intensely familiar, but with which he felt little emotional sympathy anymore. Within a short time, Blaise had acquired a name in Xhosa: it was *"Ubuso Ukhanyayo,"* which meant something like, "Radiant Face." The people of the parish could see that Blaise's face shone with an inner light. During the months of November and December (by which time he could hold a simple conversation in Xhosa), Blaise was responsible for bringing three people – two women and a young man – into the Faith, and Father Peter began their formal instruction.

Talking to the Regional Superior during a visit to Rosebank, Father Peter told of these three conversions, and of Blaise's part in them. Father Michael Schmidt was gratified; he had been right in sending Blaise to Saint Raphael's, and the young man was going to be a credit to the Society. He seemed to have a particular rapport with people of colour.

However, shortly after Christmas, Blaise had to say goodbye to Father Peter, to Catherine Mxenge, and to the people of Gugulethu, and he returned to the Jesuit community in Rosebank. Next month he would become a university student once again, becoming formally what was termed a "Scholastic" within the Jesuit formation process.

'Are you glad to be home again, Blaise?' Father Edmund Bartlet asked the young man.

'I wouldn't say that I'm glad, Father Edmund,' replied Blaise. 'I was happy at Saint Raphael's, but yes, this is "home" for me, and I am content. But I will be content wherever the Lord directs me.'

'Yes, of course. But this is a world you know well, eh?'

'It's a very different world to that I came to know in Gugulethu.'

This was pretty much the only world that Father Edmund had ever known. He was personally unfamiliar with the grinding poverty and hopelessness that afflicted Gugulethu and other black and coloured townships. This comfortable white South African society was one in which Father Edmund felt thoroughly at home. He asked for no other. He admired Blaise on many levels, one of which was the apparent ease with which Blaise acclimatised himself to other, far harsher societies. But Blaise was (Father Edmund was becoming convinced) probably a saint, and the priest was anticipating further proof of his intense spirituality. Indeed, further proof of Blaise's particular sanctity was to come towards the end of January, with another extraordinary episode.

Shortly after the New Year, Blaise made his Perpetual Simple Vows of poverty, chastity and obedience, as well as affirming his determination to persevere to final profession and ordination. Blaise was now sworn to a lifestyle he had in any event been living for a while.

Weekday morning Mass in the Rosebank community was celebrated at half past seven, to be followed by breakfast soon after eight o' clock. This Mass was usually attended by the entire community, which included Blaise, and the two scholastics who were busy with postgraduate studies at UCT. One of these, a young man named Christopher Nolan, had quickly become close to Blaise. He was a quiet, thoughtful, studious young man who wore glasses, and Blaise found his companionship both emotionally restful and intellectually stimulating. Indeed, he exhibited much the same characteristics that Blaise appreciated in his friend Roderick.

Blaise utterly lost himself in the Mass. As the bread and wine were consecrated by the priest, and during the subsequent Elevation of the Host – now become the body and blood of Jesus Christ – he seemed to sway almost imperceptibly in ecstasy from side to side. Had this motion been any more extreme, it might have constituted a disturbance, but no one could call it such. There were no pews in the chapel, only backless, polished wooden benches, with ample space in front of each within which to kneel. Christopher Nolan was kneeling behind Blaise's bench during the Mass on Monday morning the 7th January. Mark Dennington, the other scholastic studying for a postgraduate degree, was also kneeling not far behind Blaise. During the Elevation of the Host, Christopher was astonished at what he thought he saw: Blaise appeared to be levitating, still in a kneeling posture.

Christopher blinked several times, and even shook his head, but he was not imagining things: Blaise was levitating, hovering several inches above the floor. Had Mark seen what he had seen? He was afraid to ask him after the Mass, lest it sound as if he had lost his mind.

Some days later, however, as Christopher and Blaise were sitting together on a bench in the garden, shielded

Saint Blaise

from the hot January sun by an oak tree in luxuriant full leaf (and gazing with little conscious awareness at a half lifesize, painted stone statue of Our Lady, set in a grotto shrine), Christopher said to his friend, 'Blaise, during the Mass – are you ever conscious of levitating?'

Blaise laughed. 'Of course not!'

'I ask, because I'm sure I saw you rise several inches from the floor on your knees during the Mass on Monday,' said Christopher. 'Was I seeing things?'

Blaise looked at Christopher. 'I'm certainly unaware of doing any such thing,' he responded. 'But please, Christopher, if that's what you think you saw, keep it to yourself for now.'

'If that's what you wish,' Christopher answered. 'But I think Mark may also have seen you. Are you truly unaware of doing such a thing?'

'I'm totally unconscious of any such action,' replied Blaise. Christopher was aware however that Blaise had not denied the possibility outright, but had merely denied any awareness of such an event.

Blaise thought he now understood the strange looks he had been receiving from Mark during the last few days. He did not think it at all unlikely that he was capable of levitation during the Mass: sometimes he experienced such an intense consciousness of Jesus Christ's presence during the Mass, it did not surprise him that even his body might have to express the ecstasy he felt. His hopes that Mark might have kept to himself having witnessed any such occasion, were, however, forlorn, for unlike Christopher, who had come to Blaise first, Mark had spoken with Father Edmund.

Father Edmund, however, would not be drawn on his views of such an extraordinary event; instead, having listened quietly to Mark's account, he thanked him for coming to him, and then asked him to keep this between themselves. 'We have to think of the good of the Order,' he told the young scholastic. 'It would not necessarily benefit the Society if reports of something such as you describe were to become widespread. You do understand, Mark?'

'Yes, I understand, Father. I shall do as you say.'

During the coming months, Father Edmund himself witnessed no further inexplicable phenomena during the Mass. To be sure, Blaise sometimes seemed transfigured with joy, but the priest had seen this with others a few times before. He did not share what Mark had told him with anyone else. He was tempted indeed to dismiss Mark's report as an hallucination of some sort, except that he (along with the Regional Superior) knew of the story of Blaise's miraculous bilocation and healing the previous July, a story which was now becoming ever more widespread across eastern Rhodesia, according to reports received by the Regional Superior.

And these reports bothered Father Michael Schmidt in Cape Town. Blaise was certainly an asset to the Society – but how long would he remain an asset, if stories of miracle working were to become widely attached to him? The Regional Superior was troubled. The wise course would be to cut Blaise loose, to distance the Society from him, but he could not help feeling that Blaise would be a credit to the Society: he possessed a gift for bringing about conversions (the first having been the young man's own friend, Roderick

Boyd, of whom the Regional Superior had been made aware by the Chaplain) that was remarkable in one so young. (Blaise was then only twenty-four).

And Father Michael Schmidt, for all his pragmatic outlook, felt that the Society owed Blaise its support and care. Very few members of the Society of Jesus within recent years had suffered so terribly as Blaise had; he had come close to dying, as Jesus had, on a cross. Father Michael felt an emotional commitment to Blaise. Nor was he immune to the almost tangible air of sanctity that Blaise projected. And so, he felt that God wished the Society to claim the young man as one of their own.

Chapter Twenty

Hugh Cressingham, Blaise's brother, now had a flat on the mountainside above Clifton, on the far side of Table Mountain. His first year as a consultant civil engineer had been a successful one. His father was enormously proud of Hugh, the son after his own heart. But where Guy Cressingham felt a distance between himself and his eldest son, Blaise, Hugh remained far closer to Blaise, despite their characters being so very different. Hugh would sometimes call in at the Jesuit community in Rosebank on a Sunday late morning, and pick his brother up, so that they shared the drive together, either to the family home in Bishopscourt, or to their grandparents' home near Fish Hoek for the extended family lunch.

Hugh, having grown up with Blaise, having known him, faults and all, all his life, was not at all in awe of his brother, and Blaise, who was sometimes aware that people regarded him with wonder for what he had suffered in Rhodesia, found Hugh's down-to-earth familiarity refreshing. He especially enjoyed the long, scenic drive to the farm with Hugh. He felt then as if he were on holiday. (Blaise had in fact been permitted by his superiors within the Order to keep the use of his car, although, in order to live his vow of poverty, the legal ownership of the car had had to be transferred to the Society. Blaise needed to retain his mobility, so he – probably the only Jesuit anywhere in the world who drove a Triumph Stag sports car! – was not in fact without his own transport).

A week after Easter, that April of 1980, the two brothers were sharing the journey to the farm. Blaise asked Hugh whether he was seeing anyone at the moment.

'No one serious – no,' replied Hugh.

'What about Nikki? The two of you were close once.'

'We're friends, good friends,' Hugh answered, 'but that's all there is to it.'

'I think that's a shame,' Blaise remarked. 'I think Nikki is a lovely girl, a sweet person.'

'So she is,' Hugh agreed. 'But Nikki has someone else she's seeing right now.'

'Oh! Who's that, Hugh?' Blaise remained extremely fond of Nicolette Dillon; he was interested in her life.

'Some bloke who owns an antiques shop in Cavendish Square,' Hugh replied. Cavendish Square was a stylish and expensive shopping centre in Claremont. It was not very far from the Cressingham and Dillon homes in Bishopscourt.

'I hope he's a decent sort,' Blaise said.

'If he isn't, you and I will sort him out!' responded Hugh. Both brothers laughed.

As they were descending from Silvermine on the far side of the mountains, the blue seas of the Atlantic bright under the sun, Hugh said, 'I love these visits on Sunday to Gran and Grandpa.'

'So do I. It makes me feel that childhood never really ended after all.'

Hugh smiled. '*Ja*, you're right. You and I – we're fairly dissimilar characters, I think, but our childhood is the bond we share.'

'And that bond will be there all our lives,' Blaise agreed. 'Do you think that Lawrence is happy?'

'Who knows?' Hugh responded. 'I've never really known what goes on in Lorrie's head. Have you?'

'No, not really.'

'I expect he's happy, in his way. I'm glad he's here to take over the business once Dad retires. Neither of us would have wished to.' Hugh laughed again. 'Dad has a son for every occasion: you will be able to confess us, and marry us when the time comes; I can – I don't know: just be happy, and, I hope, successful, doing something I enjoy; and Lorrie can make sure the source of the family's wealth doesn't dry up.'

Blaise smiled. 'Yeah, the good old family wealth …' Blaise was indifferent to wealth, but then, he had never known want. In this, Blaise was more alike to many rich white youngsters in South Africa than he realised. It was from this class of young white people in South Africa that the social and political activists were drawn: they had both the political rights and the material means to become politically active on behalf of those with no political rights and few material means.

A glorious autumn, filled with sunshine and golden days, during which Blaise and Roderick managed to get up into the mountains for a day, became suddenly a dour, damp, cold winter, as the first of the winter cold front struck

Cape Town. During the long university winter break of five and a half weeks' duration, Blaise was sent to Saint Raphael's in Gugulethu again. It was with happiness that he greeted friends and parishioners he knew from the months he had spent at Saint Raphael's the previous year, and his Xhosa returned with a rush. Once again he was without a car: he got away only twice, once when Father Peter had business in Cape Town for the day, and took him to the Jesuit community in Rosebank in the early morning, collecting him again in the late afternoon, and once when Roderick collected him for the day. The weather was foul that day, so they did not spend it in the mountains, but at Blaise's family home, where they had lunch and a very early supper at which Guy Cressingham and Lawrence were present. Despite the weather, the two friends went for a walk around Bishopscourt in the early afternoon, and Blaise wished there were a dog he could have taken with them, but Heidi had not been replaced.

Dr. Roderick Boyd Psy.D., who had obtained his doctorate late in 1979, was now working with the Department of Justice, attached to the Cape of Good Hope Division of the Supreme Court as a consultant psychologist. Only a year older than Blaise, Roderick was now way ahead of him in terms of professional status, but neither young man was at all bothered by this: Roderick regarded Blaise as his spiritual master and mentor, and he loved Blaise no less than he had when he had first known him in the SADF in 1975.

Blaise in turn counted Roderick as his closest friend, and he still shared with Roderick thoughts and feelings he did not even share with Father Edmund Bartlet, his spiritual director. The bond that was forged between the two young men in the SADF, during that terrible time in Angola, was an unbreakable one.

Blaise and Roderick were discussing their work: Roderick found his job fascinating, assessing the condition of mind of individuals remanded for psychological evaluation, whose cases were due to be considered by the Supreme Court; Blaise was just as enthused by his vacation work among the people in Gugulethu, work which seemed to him to be so much more vital than his Philosophy studies. Each friend could relate to the other's enthusiasms.

'I'm not clear though, Blaise: how many years are you from eventual ordination as a priest?' Roderick asked him.

'My gosh! It could be years yet!' Blaise responded. 'The Society will wish me to study Theology for at least three years, before the issue of ordination as a deacon even arises – and after that, I may still be studying for my masters, even a doctorate, before ordination as a priest.'

'So I've still got quite a wait before you can hear my sins and give me absolution,' smiled Roderick.

Blaise returned Roderick's smile. 'I'm sure you have little need of absolution, Roddy.'

Blaise was not unaware of contemporary political issues in South Africa. The struggle against Apartheid was gathering pace, and at university, Blaise had joined the National Union of South African Students, and he had several times participated in demonstrations against conscription organised by the Union. In 1983 (by which time he was located in Pretoria), he was to join the End

Conscription Campaign, for he felt a hatred for compulsory military service.

But during what would prove to be his final three years as a student at the University of Cape Town, Blaise concentrated on two things: one was of course his desire to achieve a good pass in his Philosophy course; the other was his pursuit of a mystical, intense prayer life, accompanied by his devotion to the Mass.

Each year, during the mid-year and end of year vacations, the Order sent Blaise to join Father Peter O' Leary at Saint Raphael's in Gugulethu. During the month of January in 1983 (it was intended that Blaise would commence studying for his honours degree in Philosophy at UCT in February), Blaise made a point of visiting the family of Elizabeth Sandile, a parishioner whose one and a half year old daughter was completely blind due to cataracts. South Africa had the highest incidence of cataracts among children in Africa. Surgery had recently been advised, but Elizabeth was terrified at the idea of her daughter undergoing surgery, and she had asked Blaise to visit and pray with her family. The Sandile home was not much more than a one room shack of corrugated iron, located on a sandy piece of ground, and hemmed in by equally poor dwellings either side. Elizabeth's husband, Dumisa Sandile, eked out a precarious living as a labourer, with much of his earnings being swallowed up by transport costs between the township and various locations in and around Cape Town; the family were among the poorest in the congregation.

'Wamkelekile, Ubuso Ukhanyayo!' Elizabeth greeted Blaise as he entered her tiny home. It had taken him a while

to find it, and he had only managed to do so thanks to his growing command of Xhosa, for, wearing his black cassock, he had had to ask directions in the mean neighbourhood three or four times. Dumisa Sandile was away at work, but the room Blaise entered was full of children, ranging in age from the one and a half year old daughter, Princess, to a seven year old boy. Elizabeth made Blaise some tea on the wood burning stove which stood against one wall, which he accepted with thanks. Princess, the little blind girl, was crying in one corner of the room, lying in a cot made from a wooden box.

The corrugated iron walls, Blaise could see, had been painted a long time ago, but the peeling paint was overlaid by smoke stains, the original colour impossible to ascertain. The room was sparsely furnished: there was an ancient, near broken down, two seater sofa with two stuffed cushions arranged on it; in addition there was a very worn armchair, in which Blaise was seated, and between the sofa and the armchair was a small table on which stood a trading store paraffin lamp. There was a single metal bedstead pushed against one wall, with a plain coverlet across the bed, and a single mattress, made up with bedding, was laid on the floor. (Blaise imagined that the older children slept here). To one side of the stove was a wooden work top and a stained porcelain kitchen sink fed by a single tap. Above these were some handmade, unpainted wooden shelves fixed to the bare corrugated iron wall. A few cooking pots hung from hooks beneath the lowest shelf.

In one corner of the room stood a large zinc tub, which probably doubled both as laundry tub and bathtub. There were two rather small, square windows with four panes of glass in each, framed by cotton floral print curtains so many times laundered that the material was almost see-through, the floral pattern a mere ghostly hint. There was a plain wooden table, scrubbed clean, partially covered by a table cloth, with an unadorned paraffin lamp standing on it. There were three wooden chairs, one of them with a cushion on the seat, pushed against the table. At one end of the table stood the only indication that there was some sort of electric supply to the shack: an antiquated Singer sewing machine. Astonishingly, there was an earthenware vase on the table, with three dried protea blooms in it. How had they found their way so far from the mountains, to this barren place? What a triumph of the Human spirit, of hope and beauty over despair and ugliness, they represented! There was no television in the room, but a coloured print in a simple wooden frame, about twelve by nine inches in size, of Our Lady with the baby Jesus in her arms, was fixed to the wall above the bed.

As he registered a superficial awareness of the room's contents and furnishings, listening to the little girl crying, and to Elizabeth's anxious concern that the tea she had given him was to his satisfaction, Blaise was seized by a swelling emotion of pity. His heart was suddenly overwhelmed by compassion for this desperately impoverished family, and for the little girl in particular. He became in that same moment intensely aware of the presence of Jesus Christ, and he closed his eyes.

'Oh my Lord, please help us,' he prayed silently, crossing himself. Then, speaking in Xhosa, he said, 'Bring Princess to me.'

The mother fetched the child, and Blaise took the tiny creature in his arms. The child immediately ceased to cry, and Elizabeth smiled at Blaise as he held her daughter. Blaise began to recite the Lord's Prayer in Xhosa, *'Bawo wethu osemazulwini, malingcwaliswe igama lakho ...'* and Elizabeth immediately joined him in the recitation of the prayer.

With the "Amen," Blaise gently closed the little girl's sightless, milky eyes with a finger and thumb, holding them closed for some seconds, and, still speaking in Xhosa, he said to Elisabeth, 'The child will be well now.'

And Blaise knew that this was so.

That afternoon, having borrowed Father Peter's car in order to accompany a very elderly and somewhat infirm parishioner and her granddaughter to the Gugulethu Community Healthcare Centre for a routine check-up, Blaise was away when Catherine Mxenge, Father Peter's housekeeper, brought him a woman with a small child held in place on her back by a shawl. The woman was exclaiming in praise and joy and demanding that she see *Ubuso Ukhanyayo*, so that she could pay him honour.

"*Honour* Blaise?" wondered Father Peter. Elizabeth had used the same word employed to indicate veneration of a saint: *"ukuhlonela."* Did she wish to venerate Blaise?

With Catherine's help, the excited woman, whom the priest had recognised as one of his parishioners, explained that Blaise had healed her child of blindness.

Father Peter gaped. Had he heard aright? Blaise had healed this child of blindness?

Further questioning elicited that the child had been

totally blind with cataracts; that Blaise had visited the family this morning, and had held the child, prayed, then touched her eyes. The child had then gone to sleep in her cot, and when she awoke, her eyes were clear of their milkiness, and the baby could see, and Elizabeth showed Father Peter: the child's eyes followed its mother's finger as she moved it from side to side in front of its face.

'*Baba*, it is a miracle!' the mother declared. And Catherine Mxenge joined her in her cries of joy and wonder.

But the priest (although he had heard of the supposed miracle performed in Blaise's name in Rhodesia) struggled to believe that Blaise had worked a miracle. "There must be a rational explanation," he thought, as he gazed at the child's clear, dark, responsive eyes. His mind was not equipped to contend with the possibility that Blaise had worked a genuine miracle. So he gave the woman a cup of tea, and gave her – and the child also – a blessing, and sent her on her way again, and he did not speak of this thing to Blaise when the young man returned to Saint Raphael's later that afternoon. Instead, he instructed his housekeeper to say nothing of this to Blaise, and he sought out one of the young medical doctors who manned the Gugulethu Community Healthcare Centre, and told him the story.

The doctor could give no rational explanation for the phenomenon.

'It sounds as if you have a miracle worker at Saint Raphael's, Father Peter.'

This was not what the priest wished to hear. After some days had passed (during which Blaise wondered why Catherine Mxenge was treating him strangely, almost as if she was in awe of him), and Father Peter had brooded on the affair, the priest reported it to the Regional Superior. Father Michael Schmidt wished that he had not been told. But such a report could not be ignored, particularly as Father Peter told him that that following Sunday, the church had been jam-packed, overflowing with people who had brought their sick and their maimed loved ones with them, eager for *Ubuso Ukhanyayo* to bring them healing.

'We will have television crews here next, Father Superior,' said Father Peter O' Leary over the telephone. 'I am very fond of Blaise, but I think it would be wise if you recalled him.'

And so Blaise left Gugulethu two weeks earlier than planned, and the Regional Superior subjected him to a rigorous interrogation upon his arrival at Rosebank.

'Yes, the little girl definitely had cataracts: that was clear to see,' Blaise told the Regional Superior. 'But I did nothing; I just held her and ran my fingers across her eyes. She still had cataracts afterwards, as far as I know.'

'But the child's mother is claiming that after you had visited the family, and held the child, and touched its eyes with your fingers, the little girl was healed,' said the priest. (Indeed, Father Peter had told the Regional Superior that when the child's mother had brought the little girl to him afterwards, there had been no evidence that she had ever suffered from cataracts).

'Blaise, tell me: did you heal the child?' asked Father Michael Schmidt, half afraid of the answer he might hear.

'No, Father,' answered Blaise, his frank gaze so open, one would struggle to disbelieve him – were it not for the evidence which belied his denial. 'I did not. I am not a miracle worker: it was the Lord who worked this miracle; I was merely His instrument.'

'So the child *was* healed as a consequence of your visit?'

'It could look that way,' replied Blaise. 'I have seen the little girl since; her eyes are certainly clear of cataracts now.'

'How were you feeling after this supposed miracle had taken place?' asked the Regional Superior.

'I know how I was feeling at the time, Father Superior: I felt the Lord's presence. I felt His compassion and love,' replied Blaise.

'Yes, but were you feeling tired – drained – afterwards?'

'No, Father,' answered Blaise, 'I felt physically no different. Why should I? I had done nothing.'

'You claim to have done nothing, but the people in Gugulethu claim that you are a miracle worker. Tell me Blaise, what am I to do with you?'

'I honestly don't know, Father Superior. Must you do anything with me?'

'Of course I must!' snapped the priest, who was feeling uncomfortable, and confused in his own mind. 'You have become a … a disturbance. We cannot have you in Cape Town any longer, a magnet for pilgrims. I think we are going to have to send you away.'

Blaise felt distressed. 'Father Superior,' he asked, 'what about my Philosophy Honours course?'

'I think it is time you began your study of Theology,' Father Michael Schmidt declared. 'I have decided to send you to Saint John Vianney Seminary in Pretoria. You can obtain a Bachelor of Theology degree there. It is a residential institution, run by the Order of Friars Minor.'

'Do we – the Society – do we have a presence in Pretoria?' asked Blaise.

'I am afraid not,' replied the Regional Superior. 'There is the Jesuit house in Auckland Park in Johannesburg – you could spend your vacations there – but you would have to stay at Saint John Vianney while you were studying.'

Blaise did not feel ready to leave Cape Town. There was too much that he loved here; too many people who were dear to him. He was not convinced of the rightness of a move now, as he had previously been convinced of the rightness of his departure for Rhodesia. And although Blaise knew that a Jesuit must not become overly attached to a particular locality or community – that he must always be ready to move on if so instructed by his superiors – his spirits were low as he left the Regional Superior's office. "I must pray for strength and comfort," he thought, and he made his way to his room, and there, he knelt before the crucifix on the wall, and commenced to pray.

Chapter Twenty-One

Commencing his Theology studies at Saint John Vianney Seminary in Pretoria the next month, Blaise could not help experiencing a somewhat infantile emotion: he felt as if the Society had betrayed and abandoned him. This was of course not in fact the case, and with his rational mind, Blaise knew this. His formation had not been discontinued; he was still very much a member of the Society of Jesus, even if he was not at present living in a Jesuit community. But this young man, who had spent almost his entire life in and near Cape Town, felt that he had been cast into an alien environment – far more alien, strangely enough, than either Saint Joseph's Mission in Manicaland had felt, or Saint Raphael's in Gugulethu. The difference was, he realised, that he had felt called to work in the then Rhodesia, and at Saint Raphael's in Gugulethu he had found a place to which he could make an emotional commitment. But Blaise felt no emotional or spiritual ties to Saint John Vianney Seminary, no sense of belonging at all in Pretoria, and so he felt homesick for the Jesuit community in Rosebank, homesick for the sight of the mountains of the Cape Peninsula, homesick even for the University of Cape Town.

This obligatory exile to Pretoria was the first real test of Blaise's willingness to practice his vow of obedience within the Society.

Saying goodbye to his family late in January 1983, he had felt the full weight of the parting. But the Order had permitted him to take his car with him to Pretoria (he would need it, if he was to be maintain ties with the nearest Jesuit community, in Auckland Park in Johannesburg), and he had made the journey by car. (The car of course was no longer legally his possession: when he had made his vows of poverty, chastity and obedience three years earlier, he had had to relinquish ownership of the car. He had signed over ownership of it to the Order, but he had been permitted to continue using it.

Blaise broke his journey at Beaufort West in the Great Karoo, spending the night at an off-road motel. He resumed his journey after a good breakfast the next morning, and the road ran almost dead straight, mile after mile beneath the burning sun, disappearing into the dancing heat-haze on the formless horizon. This was arid, desert country, and in January, the temperature was at its highest. Blaise felt pummelled and made stupid by the buffet of the hot wind and the roar of the tyres on the road through his open window, and even with his window down, the air felt as if it was coming from an open oven. Blaise had a four litre plastic bottle of water with him on the passenger seat, and he drank copiously from it, with little need to urinate during his journey.

But the countryside began slowly to change after Colesberg, and eventually Blaise left the Karoo behind, and found himself driving past widely spaced farms in which maize was the dominant crop, although animal husbandry in the form of beef cattle was also common. He passed relatively few other vehicles during this long drive; often, he could see no vehicles ahead of him, and none in his rear-view mirror either. Johannesburg, with its multi-storey city architecture, its dense, congested traffic, its noise, came as a shock to him after this lonely journey. How alien this busy city seemed by comparison with Cape Town's gentler, less frenetic city centre!

It was late afternoon by the time Blaise had navigated his way across the city and come to a halt in the elegant, tree-lined suburban street in Auckland Park in which there was a large Jesuit house and community. He would be spending a while here, before proceeding to Pretoria, which lay about thirty-five miles north of Johannesburg. He found himself to be one of several travellers, both Jesuits and laymen, and like them, he was given one of the guest rooms. He met the community's Superior at dinner that evening, and he was introduced to most of the nine permanent members of the community, two of whom were elderly retired priests, and two of whom were Scholastics, studying at the nearby university. He chatted for a while with these two young men during recreation after dinner. One of them in particular, he thought, might have become a friend in time, given the opportunity. Like Roderick, and like his particular friend in the Rosebank community, Christopher Nolan, James Maclean (whose ancestors came from the Inner Hebrides) was a quiet, calm, thoughtful young man, who extended to Blaise a friendly welcome. It would be the next morning, after the Eucharist (as it was named in this community) and then breakfast, before Blaise had a chance to explore the grounds, which were beautifully laid out, well maintained, and extensive. The original house was rather grand, Blaise thought, and looked as if it dated to the early years of the century. There was, Blaise was surprised to find, a large swimming pool in the garden. This would be an enjoyable base during his vacations!

Blaise spent almost two weeks at Saint Ignatius, the Auckland Park community, before continuing his journey the short distance to Pretoria and Saint John Vianney Seminary. What a pity, he thought, that the University of the Witwatersrand, located near Saint Ignatius, did not offer a classic Theology degree. Instead, Blaise was to spend the next three years at Saint John Vianney Seminary in Pretoria (although some of his vacations were to be spent at Saint Ignatius in Auckland Park, where he was able to renew friendships with the Jesuit priests and Scholastics he would come to know).

Blaise obtained his Bachelor of Theology degree at Saint John Vianney at the end of 1985. The Society had been careful not to send him to work in poverty-stricken black communities during his vacations: the Regional Superior, back in Cape Town, hoped that by so doing, he might reduce the possibility of Blaise working any more miracles. And this policy appeared to be effective, but at what cost to Blaise's spirit? Harkening back to his pastoral and youth work years earlier in Athlone, Blaise spent his long summer vacations engaged primarily in assisting the Jesuit priest in pastoral and youth work at Saint Xavier's in Rivonia, a parish in one of Johannesburg's well heeled white northern suburbs. He understood and related to the parishioners: they came from a similar social and economic background to his own. But where was the challenge in such work? Where the deep sense of fulfilment he had experienced when working with poor and powerless black people at Saint Raphael's in Gugulethu?

Blaise was still politically conscious, and, the possessor of a University of Cape Town Alumni card, he joined the End Conscription Campaign's University of Pretoria branch, and he renewed his membership of the National Union of South African Students, but of course, a residential student at Saint John Vianney during term time, he was unable to participate in demonstrations against Apartheid and conscription, the majority of which took place outside the University of the Witwatersrand in Johannesburg during term time.

Blaise was almost unique among the seminarians (most of whom were Franciscan novices), in possessing a car, and this gave him a freedom denied them. He joined the Tuks Fencing Club at the University of Pretoria. The University's Groenkloof campus was situated only three miles from the Seminary, so Blaise sometimes walked the distance between the two. He had not fenced since leaving school (his free time at UCT had been too filled with activities to consider fencing in addition), and he was pleased to rediscover the pleasure he took in fencing sabre. He had lost none of his speed, and within a few months, his tactical skills had returned. Through the Tuks Fencing Club too he made two or three non-seminarian friends; Protestants, or even agnostics. His cultural outlook was broadened in this fashion, but nonetheless, Blaise was obliged to practice the constraints and disciplines of a resident seminarian, and so was unable to participate fully in the social life that these "Tukkies" (as University of Pretoria students were known) would otherwise have offered him.

Blaise missed the mountains and the wild places more than he would have thought possible. The University of Pretoria's hiking club met on Sundays, and Blaise of course was unable to participate in these hikes in the nearby Magaliesberg, for he could not possibly have skipped the Sunday Mass at the Seminary – which was, anyway, obligatory. And yet, even with daily attendance at Mass, there was something missing. Blaise only very rarely experienced that intense consciousness of the real and actual presence of Christ Jesus in the Mass that in the past had seen him enter a state of euphoric ecstasy, and had on one occasion at least even caused him to levitate. It took Blaise a while to understand that this absence of easily and frequently attained spiritual ecstasy was a necessary part of his Jesuit formation: the Jesuits did not wish for otherworldly mystics; they required sound, down to earth, practical members. Fortunately, Blaise had already shown that he possessed these qualities alongside his streak of mysticism. Had he shown only the attributes of a mystic, the Jesuits would have begun to question his suitability for membership of the Society.

The possessor of a Bachelor of Theology degree from Saint John Vianney (the seminary did not offer postgraduate studies), Blaise, with the blessing of his superiors in the Society, registered for a Philosophy Honours course at the University of the Witwatersrand for 1986. But he spent the end of year vacation in Cape Town. January 1986 saw him make only his first visit back home in three years, where he stayed at the Rosebank community, and visited with his family and renewed old acquaintanceships (the most enjoyable of these reunions being that with Roderick).

With little difficulty, Blaise obtained his Philosophy Honours degree at WITS (as the University of the Witwatersrand was known) at the end of 1986, having become during the course of that year an established member of the Saint Ignatius Jesuit community in Auckland Park. After a holiday in Cape Town, he spent the year 1987 studying for his Masters of Philosophy at WITS. Only in January 1988, having obtained his Philosophy Masters, did he commence what was termed, within the Jesuit formations process, his Regency, with a full-time posting to Saint Xavier's in Rivonia in Johannesburg's northern suburbs, to assist the priest in charge, Father Stephen Gresham, in pastoral and youth club duties. Father Stephen was an urbane, sophisticated, theatre-going, dinner party throwing Jesuit in his early fifties, and he regarded Blaise as something of a useful ornament to the parish. Certainly, the congregation at Mass on a Sunday quickly expanded in size following Blaise's arrival, the increase largely down to the number of women, particularly matrons of a certain age and teenage girls, who now began attending Mass regularly, eager for the chance of a chat with Blaise over coffee and cakes after Mass.

Blaise found a particular opening for one of his talents in both singing in and leading the church choir. With only two men present in it – a tenor and a bass – when he arrived, he was able to encourage two more men – another tenor, and, happily, a baritone – to join the choir. With his trained and rich tenor leading, he encouraged the members of the choir to aim for perfection. He had not sung in a choir since leaving school, and doing so again brought him enormous pleasure. Blaise was sometimes a hard taskmaster; he would not accept second best from the members of the choir. But the choristers knew that when he made them repeat a phrase, over and over, he did so for sheer love of the music.

'I think our choir is probably among the best in the Diocese, thanks to you, Blaise,' Father Stephen told him. 'People have told me how much they enjoy the choir at Saint Xavier's.'

Sharing a similar social background, Blaise got on easily enough with Father Stephen, but for a more meaningful friendship, Blaise relied on occasional visits to and from Father James Maclean, whom he had first met as a Scholastic at the start of 1983 at the Auckland Park community, and who was now an assistant priest at another of Johannesburg's northern suburbs parishes. But when Blaise wished to open his heart fully, he wrote to Roderick Boyd in Cape Town.

A year passed, and in January 1989, the Regional Superior in Cape Town discussed Blaise with Father Edmund Bartlet and with Father Gerald Daniels, the then Formations Director. 'Blaise seems to have quietened down, don't you think?' the Regional Superior asked the two priests. 'I would like to see him ordained a deacon shortly.'

Father Edmund Bartlet, with whom Blaise had been maintaining an occasional correspondence, said, 'I do not know whether to be sad or glad for Blaise that there have been no more reports of inexplicable phenomena or miracle working. I agree with you, Father Superior. Blaise is ready for the Diaconate.'

Father Gerald Daniels, who did not know Blaise personally, concurred with the opinions of his colleagues.

Blaise's father and both his brothers, along with Roderick, were present for his ordination as deacon at the Cathedral of Christ the King in Johannesburg in March 1989. And in December that same year, he was at last ordained a priest. He celebrated his first Mass during Advent, not long before Christmas. This was a joyful season, awaiting with eagerness the birth of Jesus, and as Blaise brought Christ down in the form of the bread and wine he had consecrated, he felt, if not the actual presence, then the nearness of the Lord. In terms of the Jesuit formations process, his progression to the Priesthood had been a comparatively speedy one. Blaise was thirty-four years old, still remarkably youthful in appearance, even if he had lost something of that spirit-filled glow that had given him the name of *"Ubuso Ukhanyayo"* at Saint Raphael's in Gugulethu.

'I'm very proud of you, son,' Guy Cressingham told his first born. Guy was there for the ordination, together with Blaise's Aunt, Fiona Denholm, and Lawrence and Hugh. But Blaise's beloved grandparents, Ambrose and Teresa, were both too old to make the journey from Cape Town. Blaise's grandfather was now eighty-seven years old, and frail; his grandmother was eighty-three. Both however were still in full command of their mental faculties. Blaise came from sound stock.

Roderick had travelled up to Johannesburg again, and Nicolette, née Dillon, now Mrs. Fitzpatrick, whose husband owned two antiques shops, one in Cape Town city centre and one in Claremont, near Bishopscourt, had also made the journey.

'Your mother would have been immensely proud of you, a priest for a son!' Guy continued, beaming at his eldest son.

And Blaise believed that his father was probably correct; his mother would have been proud of him: a priest and a Jesuit. He realised suddenly that he would now be able to say private Masses for his mother's soul. He could call down God for his mother!

Nicolette had introduced Blaise to her husband for the first time, a pleasant enough fellow much the same age as Blaise. 'I've heard a lot about you, Father,' he said to Blaise. 'Nikki tells me you were her first love.' He smiled, for with his potential rival for his new wife's affections now firmly out of the running, he did not feel threatened by Blaise.

Blaise laughed. 'We were childhood friends, that is true. Nikki's brother, Gregory, was my best friend at school.' He turned to Nicolette. 'How is Gregory?' he asked her. Gregory was working for a nation-wide firm of civil engineers at their Cape Town office.

'He's doing fine, Father,' she replied. 'He's engaged now.'

'That's great! Give him my best wishes.'

Roderick and Blaise embraced, and Roderick experienced heartfelt joy for his friend. Roderick was of course still single, and would likely remain that way all his life. By the time same-sex relationships were permitted in South Africa, Roderick would be forty years old, and so deeply shaped by the homophobic society within which he had spent the first four decades of his life, that any chance of his experiencing an intimate relationship with another man would remain slight to non-existent. And anyway, Roderick, the friend to whom Blaise could open his heart, had only ever been in love once, and he had remained so right up to the present time, and the object of that love was, of course, Blaise himself. How could he ever fall in love with anyone else? Roderick alone, among all the people that Blaise knew, was aware that Blaise mourned the loss of that intense consciousness of the presence of Jesus Christ that had once seen him experience sublime joy during the celebration of the Mass. Blaise had had to sacrifice a fundamental element of his own spirituality, in order for his superiors in the Society of Jesus to have considered him suitable at last for ordination to the priesthood, and only Roderick knew what this had cost him.

Was this what the acquisition of maturity felt like, Blaise wondered? Was growing up more about loss, than gain?

Following his ordination to the priesthood, Blaise was appointed assistant priest at Saint Xavier's in Rivonia, and Father Stephen was grateful: he could take things a little easier now, and devote more time to his rich social life. But no one who truly knew Blaise could imagine that he would derive complete fulfilment from such a post: ministering to the pastoral needs of wealthy white Johannesburgers was not how Blaise as a young man had imagined his future within the Order. In addition, while Blaise was still able to rehearse the church choir, he was rarely able to sing in it anymore, as he would invariably be co-celebrating the Sunday morning Mass with Father Stephen.

Chapter Twenty-Two

In June 1990, Ambrose Cressingham, Blaise's grandfather, died. He was eighty-nine years old. Blaise flew to Cape Town for the funeral. It was a bitter-sweet homecoming, and he experienced mixed emotions as the aeroplane landed at D.F. Malan Airport. He had loved his grandfather. In the eulogy he gave as Ambrose Cressingham's eldest grandchild, Blaise gave thanks to God for his grandfather; for his firm Catholic faith, for a long life well lived, a life full of achievement and contentment, strong both in the love he gave, and in the love he received from friends and family.

The farm, and of course Ambrose Cressingham's business interests, were left to his son, Guy. Guy's mother was to have the right to full enjoyment and occupation of the farm as long as she lived, as was Blaise's paternal aunt, Fiona Denholm, with her family. Ambrose Cressingham had in effect ensured that his son could not sell the farm out of the family – not for as long as either Teresa Cressingham or Fiona Denholm and her family wished to continue living there, and this made Blaise happy: he would have felt devastated had the farm been lost to the family.

Ambrose had bequeathed his immensely valuable 1938 Rolls-Royce Phantom III to his mechanically gifted grandson, Hugh. This legacy thrilled Hugh, who had admired the car since his childhood, and had often helped his grandfather work on it.

'Whether I can afford to maintain it, is another question,' Hugh said to his older brother. 'But I'd hate to have to sell it.'

'You will need a workshop now, wont you?' asked Blaise.

'You're right. I'm going to have to buy a house now, and build or convert a workshop,' answered Hugh, who up to that time had been living in an apartment above Clifton Beach.

During this visit, Blaise ascended the Jan Smuts Track with Roderick one Sunday afternoon. It was winter time, and the days were short, so they did not hike further than the Hely-Hutchinson Reservoir, but even this comparatively short hike brought joy to Blaise. He felt as if the years had been stripped away, and they were both in their early twenties again. And to be sure, each was still a young man; both were still fit, Roderick because he had continued to hike in the mountains once Blaise had left for Johannesburg, and Blaise remained fit because occasionally he was granted leave by Father Stephen to absent himself from the Sunday Mass (he would have celebrated the Saturday Vigil Mass the evening before, at which he was, anyway, almost always the sole celebrant), and go hiking in the Magaliesberg range with the Wits University Mountain Club, of which he was now an alumnus member.

Tremendous things had been happening on the South African political front since the late 1980s. By early 1990, a few months after Blaise's ordination as a priest, Nelson

Mandela (who had been imprisoned since 1964, and was already internationally famous) became a free man. The notorious Pass Laws had been repealed as early as April 1986, and in June 1991, that foundation stone of Apartheid, the Group Areas Act, was to be repealed. (The Group Areas Act had forbidden the various races from living in any but their designated areas). It was clear to Blaise and to many others that the Apartheid system was in a state of terminal collapse. For people like Blaise, whose sympathies had always been with the oppressed, and generally poverty stricken, black majority, these were hugely exciting times.

In March 1992 (Blaise was now thirty-seven years old), the somewhat dull tempo of his life was upset, as he commenced what the Jesuits termed his Tertianship. This was a period of reflection, of revisiting the essentials of Jesuit life, of pondering on what one had learned since ordination, of refreshing one's memory of the history and Constitution of the Society. Blaise made the Spiritual Exercises laid down by the founder of the Jesuits, Ignatius Loyola, and he was expected to work for a while with the sick, the terminally ill, and the poor. Following his Tertianship, which might last anything up to a year, Blaise would make his Final Vows.

The question of where to send Father Blaise Cressingham during his Tertianship exercised the minds both of the Regional Superior and (to a lesser extent), the current Formations Director, Father Gerald Murphy (who had had little part to play in matters affecting Blaise's formation, this because the Regional Superior regarded Blaise as a special case, and had wished to keep decisions on his formation in his own hands). The Regional Superior was afraid that if Father Blaise were once again sent to work among poor black people, his inclination to work miracles might once again manifest itself. The Regional Superior spoke with Father Gerald Murphy, and also with Father Edmund Bartlet – who had known Blaise so well in Cape Town. It was decided that work among the poor could not, in terms of the Jesuit Constitution, be evaded. Father Blaise had shown no inclination for many years to work what some might see as miracles; Father Michael Schmidt, the Regional Superior, hoped that such an inclination might not, after all this time, be resurrected.

More to the point, Father Peter O'Leary of Saint Raphael's in Gugulethu had recently become seriously ill, and he would require surgery and many months – perhaps up to a year – off work. All other considerations aside, Blaise – who knew Saint Raphael's, who was at home in Gugulethu, and who spoke Xhosa – was the perfect choice for sending to Saint Raphael's in Father Peter's place. And so it was decided to take a chance, and send Blaise to Gugulethu.

Blaise was delighted. Now some real work lay ahead of him at last! But first, he would have to spend three months at the Jesuit community of Saint Ignatius in Auckland Park, as he explored the intellectual and philosophical aspects of his Tertianship, and grounded himself anew in the fundamentals of Jesuit thought and community. An assistant priest from a parish in Transkei would fill in for him at Saint Raphael's in Gugulethu during that time, but he was a stopgap only; he could stay no longer than three months at the most.

In late June 1992, spiritually refreshed after his three

months at Auckland Park, Father Blaise Cressingham arrived at Saint Raphael's in Gugulethu beneath a grey, lowering sky, with rain threatening. He said hullo and goodbye over coffee to the priest from Transkei who had been filling in for him, and it was with joy that he celebrated the Mass in Xhosa that first Sunday. And indeed, it was a joyful Mass, for the congregation remembered *Ubuso Ukhanyayo* with affection, and the miracle he had performed when he had healed Elizabeth Sandile's little girl of blindness, had not been forgotten. News had got around, and the church was packed for that Sunday Mass, and many of those among the congregation were sick or crippled, and were hoping for a cure. And although there were no miracle cures that Sunday morning, even the sick went away afterwards with their spirits uplifted.

That winter, when he could find the time amidst his many duties, Blaise began writing a choral Mass for the Xhosa language. Blaise had been taught to read and write music by his choirmaster at school, Brother Luke Carter. This creative pursuit brought Blaise much pleasure, and Catherine Mxenge, his housekeeper, grew accustomed to hearing snatches of liturgical song in her native language arising from Father Blaise's study as he worked on the Sung Mass. He intended this composition to exploit the wonderful capacity for harmony of the African voice. It was an ambitious work, particularly as Blaise had never composed before, and he was not sure that he would succeed in it, but he persevered. In this he was assisted by the church choir, with whom he would practice his most recent composition (and often amend it as a consequence), and the choristers were as eager to celebrate the completion of this work as Blaise was.

The Sung Mass in Xhosa was completed by early December, and having rehearsed it over and over, he celebrated it with the Christmas Day Mass. Roderick was there for Christmas Day (he would be spending the night at the priest's house, so that he did not have to leave in the dark at the end of the day), as were a reporter and a photographer from the *Cape Times*, which respected daily Blaise had contacted. This proved to have been a mistake, for the reporter had chanced upon the story of the miracle cure of January 1983, and he had mentioned it in his article, which was published on the Tuesday after Christmas.

There was by now a new Regional Superior, Father Robert McDowell, and when he read this report, he was not happy. However, Father Edmund Bartlet (who was now the Formations Director), was still based at the Rosebank community, and the Regional Superior spoke to him, aware that he had known Father Blaise Cressingham a long time.

'How would you advise I respond to this?' the Regional Superior asked Father Edmund, who had just been reading the report in the *Cape Times*.

'I think the wisest course of action would be not to respond at all,' Father Edmund replied. 'The excitement will die down in time.'

'I have been reading Father Blaise Cressingham's file,' the Regional Superior continued. 'He has quite a history of mysticism, of – how to put it? – of engaging in inexplicable religious phenomena. But it has been almost ten years now in which nothing of that nature has occurred. I'm inclined to agree with you, Father Edmund. But should Father Blaise perform another so-called miracle, we will have to think of sending him somewhere far from Cape Town.'

'I believe that Father Blaise's miracle working days are over,' Father Edmund responded. 'I do not think it will come to that.'

'Let us hope you are right,' the Regional Superior said. 'You know that Father Peter O' Leary is going to require frequent and regular medical treatment in Johannesburg for at least another year? He will be remaining with the community in Auckland Park. I am appointing Father Blaise Cressingham as priest in charge at Saint Raphael's. We have no one near as qualified for the post as Father Blaise. I shall give him John Ellington as a pastoral assistant.'

John Ellington was a Scholastic in his late twenties who was beginning his Regency in January. He had grown up in the Eastern Cape, and he spoke Xhosa.

'I am delighted to hear that, Father Superior!' exclaimed Father Edmund. He was pleased also with the choice of John Ellington as pastoral assistant for Father Blaise. He was a down-to-earth, practical young man, and perhaps he would act as a counterweight to Father Blaise's inclination to mysticism. 'I know that Father Blaise will be very happy.'

'And I have decided to ask Father Blaise Cressingham to take his Final Vows,' the Regional Superior continued. 'I cannot help feeling that I may be taking a chance on him, but against that, I feel that the Society is obligated to Father Blaise. He came close to suffering a martyr's death while serving with us in Rhodesia in 1979, where he suffered the same agonies that Our Lord suffered.'

'I am glad, Father Superior,' agreed Father Edmund. 'I agree with you: we owe Father Blaise. I cannot think of a member of the Society for many years who has actually suffered crucifixion. I believe that God would be angry with us if we did not welcome Father Blaise fully into the Society.'

And so, in early January 1993, in the chapel of the Rosebank community, Blaise pronounced the Perpetual Solemn Vows of poverty, chastity, and obedience, and in addition he took that fourth vow unique to the Jesuits, of special obedience to the Pope with regard to the undertaking of mission anywhere the Holy Father might send him. Furthermore, as one of the Professed of the Four Vows, Blaise took five additional Simple Vows. These were: not to actively seek any prelacies (ecclesiastical offices) outside the Society; not to actively seek any offices within the Society; a commitment to report any Jesuit who displayed such an ambition; and, should a Jesuit become a bishop, to permit the Superior General to continue to provide advice to that bishop. And the fifth of these Simple Vows saw Blaise promise not to "campaign," or even to offer his name for appointment or election to any office, and if chosen for one, he must remind the appointing authority (right up to the Pope himself) of these vows he had taken.

What a long road it had been for Blaise. He had been in effective Formation since at least early 1978, when he had begun living in the Jesuit community in Rosebank; he had become a Scholastic, commencing a more structured Formations programme, in early 1980. Blaise felt a great burden – a burden he had welcomed, to be sure – lifted from his shoulders. Now he was free to do God's work without being constrained by the Formations process.

During the first two or three months of 1993, Saint Raphael's was packed with worshippers every Sunday, indeed, they were spilling out of the church into the open ground in front of it. Although few township dwellers read the *Cape Times*, the recollection that Father Blaise of Saint Raphael's had once worked a miracle in Gugulethu, had spread by word of mouth following the story in that newspaper. Many of these people were from outside the parish. A sizable number were not even Catholics. Many of them were sick or crippled, some being pushed to the Mass in barrows, a few in wheelchairs, others arriving on crutches. But no explicit miracles took place, although many among the sick spoke of a general improvement in their wellbeing, and over time, although the church remained packed, the size of the crowd coming to Sunday Mass diminished to the extent that worshippers were no longer assembling outside as well.

But until now, the story of the miracle that Blaise had worked in 1983 had been almost unknown outside Gugulethu, unknown to any outsiders but the then Regional Superior, Father Michael Schmidt, and one or two Jesuit priests. And it had happened anyway a long time ago. Following the article in the *Cape Times*, however, this story now became more widely known, and many in the broader white community who had never heard it before, including Blaise's own family and friends, now read about it for the first time. Many wondered when Father Blaise Cressingham would work his next miracle?

Chapter Twenty-Three

On Good Friday, the 9th April 1993, in a packed church, Father Blaise Cressingham was conducting the Passion service. Blaise felt particularly filled with the Holy Spirit, and, as probably no other priest then alive, anywhere in the world, could hope to match, he identified (as he did every Good Friday) on an intensely personal level with Jesus Christ, crucified and suffering on the cross. And with the reading in Xhosa of verse thirty-three from Luke 23,[*] Blaise began to perspire heavily beneath his cassock and surplice. It seemed that his whole body was rapidly drenched in sweat. Feeling faint, his eyes closed, a dull roaring commencing in his ears, he pushed with his hands on the wooden lectern which was serving him as a pulpit, and he was unaware that thin streams of blood had begun to run from his wrists, and from his feet also, in their open sandals. But those sitting in the front of the congregation could see what was happening, and they stared, dumbstruck, as did both the altar servers,

---

[*] "When they reached the place called The Skull, there they crucified him and the two criminals, one on his right, the other on his left." Luke 23:33

one of whom was John Ellington. Then the two readers, one to either side of the Sanctuary, who had been reading turn and turn about from the Passion story in Luke, saw what was happening, and they too became silent. Then those further away also realised what was happening, and a woman shrieked. Suddenly the church was full of women's high anguished shrieks, and many in the congregation threw themselves to their knees, shouting *'Nkosi! Nkosi Yesu!'* ('Lord! Lord Jesus!') And before the horrified gaze of the congregation, *Baba Blez* collapsed in a heap of black and white cloth in a pool of his own blood, and the lectern was knocked over and crashed to the floor.

John Ellington kept his wits. He rushed forward to Father Blaise, and tore several strips from the fine cotton of the priest's surplice, and using them as bandages, wrapped the material around the priest's wrists and feet. He saw that Father Blaise's face had gone almost chalk white, and was running with perspiration. He snapped a command in Xhosa at one of the two readers.

'Nathaniel, go to Father Blaise's study in the priest's house and use his telephone to call for an ambulance!'

The man hurried to do his bidding, but as John sat there, cradling Father Blaise's head, and watching the cloth wrapped around his wounds turning red, the minutes passed, and all the while women were shrieking, and most of the congregation were on their knees, calling out to the Lord. It was more than five minutes before the man returned, and told John that ambulances would not come to Gugulethu.

'Help me carry *Baba Blez* to his car outside,' he asked the two readers, still speaking in Xhosa. Where, he wondered, would Father Blaise keep his car keys? 'No – I must find his car keys!' he exclaimed. 'Wait here for me! Look after *Baba Blez*!'

The young man hurried through the vestry, which connected with the priest's house, and in Father Blaise's study, after a hurried search, he found the car keys in a desk drawer. He ran back into the church, and the two readers took hold of a shoulder and arm each, while John Ellington, a well-built young man, took Father Blaise's ankles, and they managed to get the priest to the garage where he kept the car, a large crowd from the congregation, crying out and praying loudly, following them. Fortunately, the priest at Saint Raphael's had been given the use of a large car by the Society, a Volvo station wagon, which he kept in a locked garage. The young Jesuit found the key to the padlock on the key ring and opened the garage. Next he unlocked the car, and the three men managed to arrange Father Blaise on the car's back seat. John Ellington doubted that the Gugulethu Community Healthcare Centre would be the best place to take Father Blaise, especially today, when it would probably be severely undermanned, so, taking one of the men with him, he set off for Groote Schuur Hospital.

The two men remained at the hospital until they had been assured that Father Blaise, who had had a blood transfusion, was in no danger. They then returned to Saint Raphael's, where John Ellington telephoned the Jesuit community in Rosebank and left a message with one of the Scholastics. Once the Regional Superior (who had been conducting the Passion service in a parish further down the Peninsula, and had stayed for lunch afterwards), had returned, he was made aware that Father Blaise Cressingham had displayed the stigmata during Saint Raphael's Good Friday service, and in the most dramatic fashion imaginable. The Regional Superior's worst fears were realised.

He and Father Edmund Bartlet visited Father Blaise at Groote Schuur early that evening. John Ellington was already there. He had returned with pyjamas, toiletries, and a change of clothing for Father Blaise. Blaise looked more than ever like a tortured saint rendered by El Greco: his cheeks were fallen in, his eyes glittered, his face was the colour of parchment. He had been given a blood transfusion, and made comfortable. The two visiting priests prayed by his bedside. On their way back to Rosebank afterwards, Father Edmund remarked, 'Thank God for John Ellington and his quick wits.'

'What in Heaven's name are we to do with Father Blaise Cressingham?' the Regional Superior asked.

'Perhaps we should see this extraordinary event as a powerful act of witness,' replied Father Edmund. 'I believe it will bring many more people in Gugulethu and further afield into the Faith.'

The Regional Superior, who was not a very imaginative man, had not considered this possibility.

'My advice, Father Superior, would be to leave Father Blaise Cressingham at Saint Raphael's. He has an excellent rapport with the people, and I think he will be needed to instruct those who will now be commencing initiation in the Faith. Xhosa-speaking priests, as you know, are comparatively rare in the Society.'

'But the publicity, Father Edmund! We cannot hope to keep this under wraps!'

'And is that such a bad thing, Father Superior? Such a phenomenon as this will bring many more people into the Church.'

The Regional Superior was a deeply conventional, deeply cautious man, but as he pondered Father Edmund's words, he found himself beginning to come around to his way of thinking. The occasional miracle, after all, never did the Church any harm.

But the news of the dramatic events of the Good Friday service at Saint Raphael's spread quickly, and before a fortnight had passed, Father Blaise Cressingham, physically recovered and back at his post at Saint Raphael's, had received telephone calls from both the *Cape Times* and the *Cape Argus*, asking if they might interview him. He declined. So each newspaper went ahead anyway, and published a short piece about the Gugulethu Good Friday Miracle (as they named the phenomenon); and suddenly, the extraordinary event was known across South Africa, and then the international news syndicates picked up the story, and within three weeks it was known across the world. And in Rome, the Superior General of the Society of Jesus turned his thoughts to Father Blaise Cressingham in Cape Town, and wondered what action – if any – he should take. After a while he telephoned the Regional Superior in Cape Town, and after discussing the extraordinary event, the Superior General told Father Robert McDowell that he would leave the matter in his hands.

Hugh and his father discussed Blaise over Easter Sunday lunch in Bishopscourt. Guy Cressingham had of course been contacted and informed that his son was in hospital, with wounds to his wrists and feet which appeared to resemble stigmata, and he had taken Hugh with him to visit Blaise on Easter Saturday.

'What sort of a man did your mother and I bring up?' Guy asked Hugh. 'The general consensus seems to be that Blaise is a saint. What I don't understand, is why us? Why our family?'

'I don't understand it either, Dad,' Hugh answered. 'But he's still our Blaise, and although I never really understood what made him tick, we watched him grow up, and we know him, and we must not feel so much in awe of him that we become nervous of him. He is family!'

Guy Cressingham wondered when his second son had become so wise.

After much thought and prayer, and further discussion with Father Edmund Bartlet (who had known Blaise better, and for longer, than any other Jesuit priest had), the Regional Superior decided that Father Blaise was to remain as priest in charge at Saint Raphael's. When the following year, South Africa's first nationwide multiracial elections were held, and later that year, with Apartheid's final collapse, Nelson Mandela became South Africa's first black President, Father Blaise shared something of the spirit of victory and joy that his black parishioners felt. But Blaise knew that the struggle for justice was not yet over: it would continue to be waged, he thought, on the economic front. Until the vast chasm between rich and poor (and most of the latter were black) was bridged, there could be no true justice in South Africa. But Father Blaise was increasingly occupied in spiritual reflection: as time went by, the things of this world meant less and less to him.

During the years 1993 - 1996, two Scholastics serving their Regencies were sent in turn to assist him, and learn from him. The presence of these young men, and in particular, the appointment of the parish's first assistant priest in late 1996, was to allow Father Blaise more time to spend in prayerful contemplation. In addition, he wrote a spiritual treatise in English, and several devotional guides in Xhosa.

The Society came in time to accept that a man who had undergone what Father Blaise Cressingham had undergone – a man who had suffered the same agonies on the cross that Our Lord had suffered – could not be expected to be quite like other men. As time went by, Blaise withdrew more and more from worldly affairs. He acquired a reputation as an ascetic and a mystic, and he continued to bring about conversions to the Faith.

Reports of Father Blaise Cressingham levitating during the Mass continued to reach the Regional Superior, and over time, his successors, and Father Blaise was to display the stigmata again on several occasions, almost always on a Good Friday. He became, despite his wishes, well known not only in South Africa, and in eastern Zimbabwe (where he continued to be venerated by the local people, who claimed further miracles in his name), but around the world. Father Blaise was happiest among the poor black people of Gugulethu, far happier than he would have been had he been attached to a plump white parish. And this suited the Society, for they felt that Father Blaise could do little harm in Gugulethu, and much good, whereas his brand of extreme piety and spirituality might not be as much appreciated in a white parish.

Father Blaise was not lonely. From 2002 onwards, the assistant priest at Saint Raphael's was a black Xhosa speaker from the Eastern Cape. Some of the young men serving their Regencies at Saint Raphael's continued to visit him even after they had moved on. As long as he lived, Father Edmund Bartlet remained close to Father Blaise, and they met several times a year. So too did Blaise's brother Hugh, and his lifelong friend, Roderick Boyd, remain in close contact. Once Saint Raphael's had acquired an assistant priest, Blaise was able more frequently to visit his family, and he never ceased to love the mountain: at least twice a year he would ascend Table Mountain with his friend Roderick – who was of course also Blaise's first convert. Blaise, along with his brothers, was at his father's bedside, when Guy Cressingham, aged seventy-nine, died in late 2005.

In 2023, the Society granted Father Blaise Cressingham retirement from active parish duties. He was sixty-eight years old, and had been responsible for the entry of many souls to the Catholic faith. By this time, Father Blaise had withdrawn so far from the concerns of this world that he no longer attended with any great diligence or energy to his pastoral duties. But, although no longer the priest in charge, he continued to live at Saint Raphael's in Gugulethu, and the young Scholastics who came to know him (many of them by now from the Cape Coloured and black communities), invariably felt great affection for him. The purity and sanctity of his spirit was, despite his advancing years, reflected in his appearance: he was as beautiful in old age (his features more ascetic than ever, and his flaxen hair having turned pure white) as he had been as a young man.

Saint Blaise

Father Blaise spent hours on his knees in prayer every day. His spirituality could safely be exercised within the confines of Saint Raphael's and remain for the most part shielded from the unhealthy interest of the greater world. Once in a while, he would be seen to rise several inches from the floor as he knelt at the Elevation of the Host during the Mass; on two or three occasions, invariably on a Good Friday, the wounds of Christ on his wrists and feet would begin to bleed again.

Father Blaise Cressingham SJ was considered by many, especially among the black communities amidst which he had lived (most recently in Gugulethu, but he was still remembered and his name invoked in Manicaland), to be a living saint, and he would without doubt one day be canonised. Father Blaise was an intimate of God, with whom he spoke every day, and he knew Our Lord as most people would know their best friend.

Robert Dewar, Lochaber, July 2024.

This book is printed on paper from sustainable sources managed under the Forest Stewardship Council (FSC) scheme.

It has been printed in the UK to reduce transportation miles and their impact upon the environment.

For every new title that Troubador publishes, we plant a tree to offset CO_2, partnering with the More Trees scheme.

MORE TREES
LET'S PLANT A BILLION TREES

For more about how Troubador offsets its environmental impact, see www.troubador.co.uk/sustainability-and-community